Ola Awonubi was born in London to Nigerian parents. She grew up and attended school in Brighton and lived in Nigeria before returning to England in 1992. An avid reader, she enrolled in writing classes and went on obtain an MA in Creative Writing at the University of East London.

Her short stories have first prize in both the National Words of Colour competition and the Wasafiri New Writing Prize 2009.

 instagram.com/olaawonubi

W0071772

Also by Ola Awonubi

A Nurse's Tale

THE MARRIAGE MONITORING AUNTIES' ASSOCIATION

OLA AWONUBI

One More Chapter
a division of HarperCollins*Publishers* Ltd
1 London Bridge Street
London SE1 9GF
www.harpercollins.co.uk
HarperCollins*Publishers*
Macken House, 39/40 Mayor Street Upper,
Dublin 1, D01 C9W8, Ireland

This paperback edition 2025
1
First published in Great Britain in ebook format
by HarperCollins*Publishers* 2025

Copyright © Ola Awonubi 2025
Ola Awonubi asserts the moral right to be identified
as the author of this work

A catalogue record of this book is available from the British Library

ISBN: 978-0-00-870330-1

This novel is entirely a work of fiction. The names, characters and
incidents portrayed in it are the work of the author's imagination. Any
resemblance to actual persons, living or dead, events or localities is
entirely coincidental.
Printed and bound in the UK using 100% Renewable Electricity
by CPI Group (UK) Ltd
All rights reserved. No part of this publication may be reproduced, stored
in a retrieval system, or transmitted, in any form or by any means,
electronic, mechanical, photocopying, recording or otherwise, without the
prior permission of the publishers.
Without limiting the exclusive rights of any author, contributor or the
publisher of this publication, any unauthorised use of this publication to
train generative artificial intelligence (AI) technologies is expressly
prohibited. HarperCollins also exercise their rights under Article 4(3) of
the Digital Single Market Directive 2019/790 and expressly reserve this
publication from the text and data mining exception.

But they who wait for the LORD shall renew their strength; they shall mount up with wings like eagles; they shall run and not be weary; they shall walk and not faint.

Isaiah 40:31

To my late Mum
Deborah Iyabode Awonubi
Thanks for all your sacrifices and love.
"Sun re, Iya Ijebu."

Dedicated to all those that wait for life and love.

Chapter One

I love Christmas. There is something in the air, a bubbling optimism full of renewed hope that in the days leading to Christmas Day, something magical and special will happen to make all the other 364 days meaningful. I like the shops with the warm smells of cinnamon, ginger, chocolate, chestnuts, and candy-cane peppermint intermingling with pine, as Donny Hathaway reminisces in "This Christmas."

Church is always packed on Christmas Day. I am surrounded by a sea of bright headwraps and hats, tinsel and good cheer, as we sing carols without really thinking about the meaning of words, because we have recited them by heart since we were kids. "Joy to the world – the Lord has come. Let Earth receive her King" – that is my favourite. I soak up the festive mood in the air. I will need it when I go to my mother's after the service.

Jesus was born as part of God's divine family. Thinking of families, I know I am not the only one who is looking longingly at all the cosy family units around me right now. Today I am seriously struggling to feel joyful and that does not make sense because it is Christmas and everyone is supposed to feel happy at Christmas – even more so if you are a Christian.

The problem is that the holidays are when we singletons feel the single bug even more acutely. Holidays spell sharing and caring, and when you have no one special to share that time with, surely God will not begrudge you feeling a little hard done by. I know I could get a cat and I have my family, but it is not the same. I have my best friends Vicky and Sam, but it is always dinner with the girls, pictures with the girls, holiday with the girls... Is it too much to ask for a bit of sensible, decent-looking male company as well?

My sister, Kike, and her hubby, Ayo, invited me over for Christmas dinner. I guess they don't want me to stay at home watching slushy old films that remind me of love lost for ever and love-that-I-would-rather-stay-lost, like Simon – who is still wandering around in my head like the ghost of Christmas past.

After a lovely dinner with all the trimmings, we open the pressies and settle down to watch *Sleepless in Seattle*. But my brother-in-law cannot bear to watch it for the "hundredth time" so he goes upstairs with their twin boys to watch something more manly, like *Madagascar*.

Kike and I watch transfixed as Tom Hanks finds Meg Ryan on the top of the Empire State Building, and a song comes to mind – I must have been a kid when I first heard it. I can now think of my own version:

> *Where have all the nice men gone?*
> *Married off to young uns every one*
> *Oh, when will they ever learn?*
> *When will they ever learn?*

I mean, I'm not expecting a chap to fall for me like Jude Law did for Cameron Diaz in *The Holiday*, but what is it about Christmas that makes me long for my own love story?

Why can't I get over Simon and get on with my life? It was five years ago, when I was forty-five. Plus, Simon is no Tom Hanks, but when we had dated it had been great – until his mum… No, I won't go there today.

It's just that ever since then, every Christmas I have the same conversation with my mum. It goes like this: "Eh? Every Christmas you are at your sister's with her husband and the children. Eh? When are you going to invite them to your own house for Christmas with your family?" This is then accompanied by a long sigh, or sometimes even tears.

Mum, I have my own house. Isn't that enough?

———

I wake up with a massive headache and every part of me aching. My abdomen feels as if it hosted an overnight rave. I run my hands over it and feel the lumps under my skin.

Fibroids. Could be ten or twenty, I realise. My belly seems to be even bigger and now resembles a small, snug kangaroo pouch, which is probably why that fool Daphne came to my desk the other day at work with a stupid smile and gave me a hug.

Awkward. Daphne and I had not spoken to each other ever since the day she came into the canteen while I was reheating my lunch, which was just yam pottage and fresh fish, and said, *It smells as if something has bloody died in here.* This was followed by a Clint Eastwood barge-into-saloon silence, while colleagues watched to see what I was going to do next. You could even hear their brains ticking over while they awaited an Angry Black Woman moment.

I stared her down, brought out my lunch, and ate it silently, until everybody started talking again. I could swear the disappointment in the air was palpable. Her hug and congratulations were a tad random.

"Such a cute bump. Do you know what it is?"

"It?"

Daphne flung back her long brunette hair and giggled. "I didn't even know you could have kids in your fifties."

My lips twisted. Daphne was still young so she could make jokes about things that hung in someone's heart and emotions – like the unrelenting pain of knowing that the chances of ever having your own children were extremely slim. That was something that I hoped Daphne would never have to experience, no matter her behaviour.

The last time I sat in front of a doctor he asked me what I was keeping the fibroids for. I do not know. Maybe I plan to raffle them off for all the single women that the *Daily Mail* says are going to grow up alone with a cat if they don't return to traditional ways of being feminine.

Maybe, Dr Hoity Toity, I wanted to reply, *I cannot be*

bothered with pre-menopausal women angst — I just do not want to lose my womb.

"Maybe it's the last connection with my maternal hopes," I said aloud from the depths of my irritation with the medical profession and my sore back and my general fed-upness about everything.

He'd snorted and looked at me as if was a precocious child. "You must be joking." Then he demanded, yes, demanded, that I go for a hysterectomy. Instead of wasting precious NHS resources. He did not say the last bit, but I heard it in my head.

I could imagine him scribbling it down on my notes.

Female. Pre-menopausal. Career woman. Deluded. Prescribe immediate evacuation of uterus.

I then told him I needed to get a second opinion.

He shrugged. "That is your prerogative."

So, I am fifty, in pain from debilitating invaders of my uterus, overwhelmed, battling with the odd depressed moment, and pissed off by a hoity-toity, patronising doctor.

Right now, there is nothing more to do but to hobble downstairs for breakfast.

God has much more important things on His busy agenda than my problems. If the whole world was a spreadsheet, would not the column for young homeless people sitting on filthy sleeping bags outside my train station feature higher on His task list than the column with my issues?

To medicate I decide to help myself to a full English breakfast.

I arrive at my mum's house for dinner in the dark, greeting her by dipping my knee slightly and handing her the Christmas gifts.

"I hope you didn't spend a lot of money."

I smile at the hint of criticism as she collects the gifts. "I wanted to get you something nice."

Mum shakes her head as she tears open the first gift and holds up the fancy bottle of perfume I'd wrapped. "This bottle is worth more than the perfume!"

"Mum, don't start."

She is still staring at it. "Thank you, my daughter. It is just that these shops like to deceive you young people with packaging."

"It is a designer perfume, Mum. Packaging is part of the brand. Open the next one."

"Ah... This looks like..." She tears open the wrapping paper to reveal a box with a ribbon. "A hat for church?" Her face brightens up as she opens it and brings out the hat. "Turquoise. Just the colour for my new dress. It is beautiful."

"Perfect for church or any occasion."

Mum looks pointedly at me. "Perfect for a registry wedding. You know, before the traditional and white wedding. I pray that this new year will be your year."

"Mum – I don't even have a boyfriend."

She nods sadly. "I know."

Ever since I refused to go out with the son of one of her friends at church, who didn't even live in the same country, Mum has been like this.

This kind of manipulation represents everything I hate. People telling me what to do and their attempts to guilt-trip me into an across-the-sea romance that I do not want. I knew how this went. I'd heard all the stories. Man, desperate to come to Blighty for better life, decides to swear undying love to woman with British passport with the hope of getting a free pass to live and work abroad.

Mum gives me the hard sell. "I have been told that he is a very nice man. All he needs is someone to give him a chance. Someone to assist him."

I could really care less. "He is almost fifty years old. If he has not decided what he wants to do with his life by now, he needs resuscitation and not someone to 'assist' him. Besides I do not want to have to prop any guy up at this age."

Mum is defensive. "You should give him a chance. That is the problem with you people of nowadays. You want a ready-made man. If I had waited for your dad to have everything in place, I would never have married him. We worked together and saved until we bought this house."

"Mum, you were both in your twenties at the time. I am fifty and this guy is about that, too. It is not the same, is it?"

My mother's voice is full of indignation and disappointment. "Sometimes it is like you just don't want to marry."

"I would like to get married someday, Mum. I just do not want to be married just to be married, if you get what I mean."

Mum gives me a look and twists her lips as if I have made her swallow something bitter. "It is well."

But I wonder when it will ever be well between us.

The man issue is constantly brought into our interactions. And each time, I take a step back from her, from this madness that is Nigerian culture and from all her expectations of what a good Nigerian first daughter should be doing.

The temperature between us is dropping and my tolerance levels ebbing, yet my voice is steady as I ask her, "Shall I go and put the tea on, Mum?"

She sighs deeply as if she is exhaling my singleness. "Okay. Remember to add some lemon."

I go into the kitchen and hear the opening tune to *Emmerdale* blare out from the TV. Mum loves her soaps. I remember, as a young person, playing with my sister in the living room while Mum sat in the chair as soon as she got back from work, without taking off her coat. She would stare at the screen until the soaps had finished and we had tea. Then it was bedtime, and we would fall asleep to the sound of her prayers that we would get top marks in class and not disgrace her in front of her enemies.

I sigh and pour water into a glass, remembering to add some drops of lemon. Just like my singleness: sometimes they can infuse a bitterness into the most joyous of moments. I never get respite.

Not even at Christmas.

Chapter Two

The New Year's Eve concert at church – a gospel rap group and our gospel choir – is great.

What is my prayer for the year?

Dear God, give me my own man to show up Simon and his Pretty Young Thing. Let him live with the regret of listening to his mother and breaking up with me.

As the clock strikes midnight it brings me back to reality. Everyone goes round wishing each other Happy New Year. I greet a few friends and then hear a familiar voice call my name. I turn round and it is Simon.

He mumbles something under his breath and turns away, swallowed up by the New Year merriment. Pretty Young Thing is not in earshot. He never greets me when she is around. Sometimes I wish he wouldn't bother.

Then out of the corner of my eye I see one of the church mothers making a bee-line for me. Remembering the last time I saw her, I urge my feet in the opposite direction, but it is too late. I am enveloped into a bear hug.

"This is your year, Sade! God has told me that this is your year!"

I smile wryly with a sense of déjà vu because she greets me like this every year. And she will carry on until I find a significant other. "Happy New Year, Aunty Susan."

Then my friend Vicky interrupts us and gives me a hug as well. For us there is no need for yearly platitudes.

Karl, Vicky's fiancé, hugs me and wishes me a happy New Year. I like Karl. Solid, dependable, an all-round nice guy. A bit thin on the ground nowadays, these nice guys.

———————

Today I make a pledge to myself. I will enjoy my life this coming year.

Totally stupid, I know, because it's pointless making New Year promises to yourself that just dissolve into the air as the year progresses, submerged under work deadlines, family stress and life – so why do I even bother?

Maybe I just need something to make me feel inspired again after seeing young Sonia Thompson, whom I taught in Sunday school when she was a teen, walk into church hand in hand with a nice-looking chap. She spotted me trying to make myself perpendicular behind a pillar and said, "Hi, Aunty Sade."

Over the past twenty years I have spent in this church I have gone from being Sade to Sister Sade to Aunty Sade. And before they start calling me Mummy Sade, it would really be nice to be married.

To a nice bloke. Not a millionaire or a rock star. Just a

great bloke with GSOH and a dream that he is already working towards.

I mean, am I really that unlovable that thirty-five-odd years from my first teenage kiss with some guy at a school disco, with the sound of Shalamar's "A Night to Remember" pounding in our ears, I am still single?

I am definitely pre-menopausal.

Or maybe I have impostor syndrome?

Most of the time I am confident, focused, and just get on with it. That is the me I allow most people to see; but sometimes I crave a husband, a home, and children – desperately – even more than the career I have. Then I go back to reality and my alter ego takes over for the rest of the week.

Chaka and Whitney. I am not every woman. I am two women.

A few days later and I hear a message drop on the mobile and see it is from my new gynaecologist. By 2 p.m. I'm sitting in the doctor's waiting room. Watching the excited faces of the mothers-to-be around me. One brunette, with blue eyes and a big smile and sitting with her mum, notices me and takes a quick glance at my midriff.

"Early days ay…" She pats her considerable bulge. "I'm ready to go, me."

I nod silently. My spirit heavy.

I need help, Lord…

A needle-like sensation hits me in the lower abdomen

and threads itself through into the muscles of my back. The pain is indescribable.

Doctor Bassey just stares at me, waiting for me to give the answers, as silence stretches between us.

I shift in my seat.

"So, how can we help you?" He is looking at the pink referral sheet from my GP.

"I thought you could advise me on my options?"

He shrugs. "You don't have that many options."

"But what about..." I mention all the procedures I have heard of from my internet research, snippets of advice from friends who had the same medical condition.

One by one, the consultant shakes his head. Too far gone, the fibroids in my abdomen are just too large for keyhole embolization, etc., etc.

"Your only option is the myomectomy – it's a surgery to remove the tumours whilst maintaining your option to have children – but you need an MRI first to make sure that they are still benign."

I swallow. At least this procedure sounds better than the hysterectomy.

He checks his schedule and suggests April for the surgery if the MRI comes back clean. And just like that, I have a date for the myomectomy.

Goodbye, fibroids. I look forward to having every one of you excised from my overburdened body.

Later that day, Vicky and Sam come round to watch an episode of *The Bachelor*.

It's reality TV of the worst variety, but it is a weekend, and after a long week, our brains are programmed for some junk TV.

"If only it was like that in real life," Vicky sighs as I dish out the Chinese takeaway.

I reflect on this. "We live in the real world. I'm not too sure I would want any guy going to that length to get my attention."

"Chance would be a fine thing." Vicky is flicking through *Enrich*, my Christian magazine.

"She would actually have to leave her house first for that, innit." Samantha snatches the largest piece of chicken from one of the plates I am laying out and I smack her hand away before going back to the kitchen to get some glasses.

"Oh, please don't start. The whole dating scene is tiring."

"But you want to meet someone, and how will you do that if you don't step out of the work-church-home triangle you're stuck in?" Vicky observes and passes Sam the magazine. "You got to do something different."

I look up as Sam waves it in front of me. "Come and have a look at this. XtianKonnect is starting a new website for singles."

I let out a long sigh. "Sam, for goodness' sake … internet dating … really … it's crazy out there. Besides, the men on there are mainly looking for one-night stands, or they're divorced with baggage, or they're scammers and criminals."

Vicky wades in. "Whoa, that is a bit of a generalisation. I

don't think she meant that at all, but you were lamenting how you never go out."

Samantha continues. "Who just said this last week, 'Sometimes I wish I could get out there and make more friends of the opposite sex because I am fed up of women's company all the time'?"

"I was just making a comment," I say. I am on the defensive now.

"No, you were whingeing and I'm tired of hearing you whinge if you are not going to do anything about it." Vicky is relentless. "Make your love life your priority just as you do your work!"

"You're just nagging me now because you've both found a man!" I shake my head in mock dismay.

Vicky looks down at her hands. "You know I didn't mean it like that."

Sam sighs. "I have seen the way Karl looks at you, Vicky. We practically had to beg him to let you spend the evening here. He said he had something planned, and all that. You guys are older than me and I want to see you both settled before I jump on the matrimony bandwagon. So now the only person I must worry about is you, Sade."

"Me?" I try to laugh, but it gets stuck in my throat.

Samantha waves me away and continues. "Sade, hold on, do *not* turn the whole thing into a joke. This is a new year – why not start going out more and having some fun? Apart from weddings, naming ceremonies, and birthdays, when was the last time you went out and did something different? You are either at work or you are vegetating at home, binge-watching sentimental rubbish and reality TV."

"Don't hold back now!" I quip, but she's hit a nerve. She's right.

Sam opens the magazine to show me the page and all the glowing testimonials from the fresh-faced couples that met using the site.

My lips curve as I read aloud. "Look at this from Becky from London. 'We are so happy we found each other. Thank you, God, for using XtianKonnect to bring us together' ... and there's Colin and Anneka from Cambridge: 'I had used other websites for years and never met anyone I liked until I logged on to XtianKonnect. I met lots of like-minded single professionals like me and decided that Anneka – a nurse – was the one for me. We are getting married this summer and we are so happeeeeee...'" I fling the magazine back at Sam. "You can't be serious."

She nods. "Go on – what do you have to lose? You never know, there might be some lovely Christian guy out there sitting in front of a computer waiting for you to click."

"Okay, just for the record." I wag my finger at them. "It is not going to happen, let me tell you that. First, I have got my mum giving my number to random men who want to live in the UK, and now I have my supposed best friends telling me to throw away my pride and self-respect and advertise myself on the World Wide Web for a husband."

Sam sighs. "You want something different – you do something different. Enough of 'waiting around waiting for Mr Right now' or 'Mr Right ten months down the line.' It is up to you."

I just mutter something under my breath and change the channel.

Chapter Three

Sometimes I reflect on the different people my mum, my uncle, various church aunties, and other well- or ill-wishers have set me up with in the past.

Sam and Vicky do not understand that my aversion to online dating has a history. I have had some harrowing experiences.

One of them was this guy ... luckily, I cannot remember his name. My brain cannot deal with the trauma of the memory. I mean, on the site he seemed perfect. He met all the attributes on my mother's list.

He was in the medical field. Pharmacist. One tick.

He was tall and fair-skinned. Two ticks.

A confident and intelligent speaker. Ten ticks.

Yoruba. Fifty ticks in my mum's book.

So, he took me out for dinner to this swanky restaurant one fateful evening. I was excited, until he ordered for me.

"You will like this. Trust me," he said, grinning.

Charming.

Then he proceeded to talk about himself. His education. His esteemed university. "Redbrick," you know. He said this twice. His awards. His job.

I just sat there out of breath, not bothering to try and get a word in edgeways. Then he moved on to talking about his ex, which was when it got dark. He told me how she was a feminist who had tried to emasculate him by studying for her PhD and buying a house. How she would make decisions about important things, like deciding to change her hairstyle, without telling him first. After all, they were going to be married.

The main course arrived, and he told me that he needed to get married within six months, max, as he was in his late forties and had no time to waste. He wanted two boys and they were going to go to Eton, because he hadn't made the cut and it had always irked him. He did not want any girls because they would never carry the family name.

I just sat there and blinked.

Help. I am a single woman, get me out of here!

While he talked, I toyed with my lasagne, but my appetite had walked away into the cold night and left its coat behind. I had not spoken a word for an hour, although it felt longer, just listening to him rabbiting on.

He then informed me that if we started dating and he decided to marry me, I would have to give up my job because there would be no point, as he earned more than me three times over and I would need to be at home with the kids. I was in my late thirties at the time and thought he was having a laugh, but the more I stared at his handsome, pompous face I realised that he was dead serious and I started feeling claustrophobic. I just wanted to disappear.

Then came the dessert. That was the pièce de résistance. The waiter, a nice enough young chap, brought over the ice-cream and this guy started yelling at him that he had ordered some other Italian delicacy.

"I'm sorry, Sir. I will go back and check the order."

"Are you calling me a liar! Get me your manager!" my date roared.

The waiter disappeared, leaving me staring at my plate and wondering whether Basil Fawlty was going to appear in a minute. The whole evening felt like an episode of that famous show.

The manager, a big burly chap, came over and calmed my date's flustered feathers. He apologised that there had been a mistake with the order and offered to take a percentage off the meal for any inconvenience caused.

At this, my date changed and became all friendly and conciliatory.

"Don't worry about it, mate, these things happen."

The manager's expression was impassive as he moved off with the hapless waiter and I faced my date.

"Why did you do that?"

"Do what?"

"Shout at the waiter like that? You embarrassed him and you embarrassed me!"

His brows disappeared into his hairline. "He made a mistake. Mistakes cost lives in my profession."

Perfectionist, too. Zero ticks in my book.

"We were ordering desserts – not writing out prescriptions."

His voice changed. "So, you think that's all I do – write out poxy prescriptions?"

"That's not what I meant."

His eyes narrowed. "I do not think I like your tone. I bring you here to this expensive restaurant, fine dining and all, and you just sit there like Mona Lisa while I talk. I like a woman with a bit of banter. I tend to go for the curvier type, too, but I liked your face on the site so I thought I would give it a try."

I blinked. "Since you are disappointed, I think we had better call it a night. I can find my own way home." I rummaged in my purse and brought out my card.

"Oh, don't be silly!"

But I got up and went in search of the waiter to find out how much my share of the bill was.

He did not come after me, and, as I left the restaurant, I made sure I blocked his number.

Then there was Steve.

Steve was six foot, blue-eyed and worked in finance. I don't know whether he had a trust fund, and I really didn't care. He was also looking for a bit of exotica.

He thought it was a compliment to compare me to food.

On our first date, as we sat drinking before the meal, he blurted out, "I think Kanye's really cool."

"Yeah? I don't listen to Kanye."

"Oh. I thought you might like him. Er, what about Craig David? Or maybe Billy Ocean is more your thing? We're both getting on, innit." He gave me a nudge and I spilt my drink.

I finished what was left, wishing I could finish the date now, too.

Steve pressed on. "I am so glad you came. I like Black women."

I blinked. "Really. Wow, I am so honoured."

Steve was divorced from his Jamaican wife. He told me with a shrug, "That should have taught me – but I still fancy Black women."

"Oh. You make it sound like a dirty secret."

Steve blushed. "No. I did not mean it like that. I am not racist or anything. What I meant is that I like my women dark and sweet."

No, he did not.

The waitress brought our food, but my hands hovered over my plate.

Steve started eating. "You know, like chocolate," he said, his mouth full.

I hate it when people equate non-white people with food – vanilla, chocolate, spice. I do not know how I got through that date but managed somehow, mumbling replies as he cheerily ploughed through his meal, intermittently talking about his work, his project, his salary, and how it was doing his head in.

I tried again. "So what do you like about the job?"

He stared at me, his face flushed. "Who said I like the job? It's about paying the bills, innit?"

The End.

Blocked as soon as I got on the bus home. The fact that this guy didn't seem to be passionate about anything other than food was the final nail in the coffin.

There was also Kole, who met me at my sister's and stayed glued to his mobile phone throughout the visit. Followed by Pelumi – he was introduced to me by a friend at church, and only uttered a few words while the friend was there and then shuffled off immediately. Every time I saw him in church, he behaved like a rabbit caught in the headlights. We still attend the same church, where we pretend not to see each other every Sunday.

Then there was John. John was in love with his ex-girlfriend. He kept talking about her and what she had done to him. He could not seem to get past it so I gave him the "it's not you, it's me" spiel.

"Let us not do this anymore," I said. "Who knows, maybe you guys can still get back together?"

He looked at me with so much hope in his eyes and said, "You really think so?" – and, God forgive me, I lied. I told him that I really thought he should keep on praying and she would come back. So, he did, but then he came back a month later and said his ex had got married and he was sure that I was now The One. I said, "I beg to disagree," and avoided him, which was not difficult in a big church – until the day he bumped into me as I was leaving the building.

"I don't see you around anymore," he whined.

I know, mate. It's a hundred per cent intentional. I make jolly well sure of it.

After Steve, there was Mark, alias Mt Vesuvius or The Hulk. The nickname had nothing to do with his size. You had to be a fan of Marvel superheroes to work it out. Mark was an accountant. After a few dates, he started calling me while I was at work and then would fly off the handle if I didn't pick up. One day he was pressurising me to take off on a weekend away with him – I said no. The next thing I knew, he was professing his undying love and bombarding me with gifts. It was giving me major red-flag vibes so I broke up with him. Only for him to follow that up with some online stalking. I had to come off LinkedIn for about a year to throw him off the scent.

Unfortunately, Aunty Gbemi bumped into us at Westfield one day when we were still dating and swore to everyone in our family that God had told her that Mark was my husband. She kept on with it until she got Mum involved as well. The small details of the stalking and the incessant phone calls after we broke up were all brushed away as the actions of a man who was in "love."

Aunty Gbemi had to add in her tuppence-worth. She hissed at me, "A man with a job is pursuing you in your forties! You do not ask questions. You just grab him. Lucky girl that you are."

Aunty Gbemi is a member of what I like to call the Marriage Monitoring Aunties' Association – MMAA. They lie in wait at birthdays, christenings, and weddings to spring out from corners on unsuspecting single women and quiz them about their single status, ask them the kind of uncomfortable questions they do not ask their single sons, and ridicule them for not being married.

Sigh.

A few years after Mark, I met Timi. Timi was very outspoken and ebullient. On our first date, his form of small talk was to ask me whether I could speak Yoruba. During the first course he asked whether I knew how to make Moi Moi.

I just stared at him.

"Sorry?"

Timi smiled as if he was explaining something to a child. "Moi Moi. Bean cake is my favourite. I need the woman I marry to be able to cook, and cook well. From your accent, you sound British. I need a wife that can speak my language well."

I shook my head because I knew that this was not going to work out. My Yoruba is rudimentary, though I can cook Moi Moi and am happy to celebrate my British and Yoruba selves. To me they complement each other, and I do not need any man asking me to redesign myself like something out of *Changing Rooms* to find me more appealing.

I am too old for that.

"Can't you cook?" I challenged.

He laughed. "I see it – you are one of those people?"

"Which people?"

"Those feminists."

I gave him a killer stare. "The fact that I said it wouldn't be bad if a guy knows his way around the kitchen doesn't make me a feminist." *Mate.*

Then he cleared his throat, as if trying to get this part of the date over and done with. "I hope you don't mind, but how old are you?"

"Forty-one."

"Wow," he said, his eyes rolling out of his head. "*Omo.* You are very well-preserved. Innit?"

The End.

We never saw each other again after that. It was not just

because he said I was "well preserved", like an ancient fossil, or that he felt cooking was a special gene embedded into all women's DNA from birth, it was how he added "innit" at the end of every sentence. It was so unnecessary, especially as he said he prided himself on his Nigerianness. As an avowed custodian of the Yoruba language, he was supposed to know that you never added "innit" after a word in your mother tongue. Very tacky.

I met Simon soon after that and thought that I had finally met The One.

Yeah, right.

Simon was the only chap I had been serious about, the one who never tried to pressure me into sex before marriage. The one I was supposed to marry. I thought, anyway. According to my family, we were as good as married. He was everything a mother would want in a son-in-law – well-mannered, came from a good family, had a good job as an accountant – and he was good-looking, too. Then he took me to meet his mum.

The first thing Mrs Okorie did was to welcome me with a tight-lipped smile. "Welcome, Madam."

Why is she calling me Madam?

I curtsied as I had been trained to as a well-brought-up Yoruba daughter. "Good afternoon, Ma."

I had just about taken off my coat and Simon had got me a drink and said hello to his brother, when his mum suggested that we go into the kitchen, so we could have a talk to get to know each other better.

I gave Simon a quick glance, but he was engrossed in the footie on TV with his brother.

She whispered, "Leave the men with their football. Let us have a little chat."

She sat down on one of the highbacked stools and patted the one in front of her. "So how old did you say you were again? Fifty?"

I was about forty-seven at the time. I was silent because I could see the writing looming large on the walls of my mind: ABORT MISSION. NOW.

She viewed me as if I was an insect she wanted to squash. "Madam. I want my son to have children. Do you want to tell me you do not have children you are hiding somewhere? At your age?"

"I wouldn't lie about something like that, Ma."

She shook her head. "Eh? Look, let us not waste each other's time. I like you. You seem like an intelligent woman. Simon says you are a project manager at some firm in Canary Wharf."

"Yes."

"Your mother must be proud. I am proud of my son, too. He is my first-born. I know he has dragged his leg about getting married – but at forty-five I need him to find a nice young girl that can have children – my grandchildren – like his brothers have. At forty-seven, you and I both know that is not very likely."

"But surely Simon should know what he wants."

Mrs Okolie's eyes flashed at me. "Look here, missy. You want to play psychologist with me? I am his mother. I brought him into this world. I know better what my sons want. You cannot be coming into my house presuming to know what is best for my son. If you had all the answers, you would not be standing in front of me – with your forty-seven-year-old tired eggs! You would have found yourself a husband by now!"

I sat there, speechless.

Mrs Okorie looked relieved. "So, we understand ourselves? I would suggest that you go away and break up with him. If you do not, I can make life very difficult for you. Remember you cannot try and break the bond between mother and son. I would not expect you to know – after all, you are not a mother."

She then stood up, picked up a tray of drinks, shoved it at me, and motioned with her hands in the direction of the sitting room as if she was shooing me away.

"Take the drinks into the sitting room. I will bring the food."

To think that I sat there after that and picked at my chicken and rice, making small talk with Simon and his mum as if we had just been discussing the weather.

No wonder Simon was still single at forty-five. His mum was the gatekeeper to his prospects and she did not take prisoners.

I told him what she had said as he walked me to the train station, and he laughed it off with a shrug.

"Do not worry about Mum. She is a bit protective of me. That is all."

"Simon, you are forty-five years old. What is she protecting you from?"

"Can we just drop this? Mum has been there for us since Dad passed. She is my queen."

Your mum is your queen, at your age. Touché.

I did not have the desire to push her off her throne. All I wanted to do was love the prince.

Then Simon's mum decided to add reinforcements.

She had opened the wound with the first stab and after that she would continually add fresh jabs here and there. Can you still have children? What have you been doing for all these years that you could not find a man? Are you sure there is nothing wrong with you? You Yoruba people do not know how to cook proper soups except Ewedu and Egusi, so what makes you feel you could cook for my son? And by the way, where is your dad?

By the time the last jab came, the relationship was on its last legs; tottering around and ready to collapse face-down in the ring. All it took was for his mum to introduce him to pretty Nneka, a thirty-year-old pharmacist, and it received its death blow. It limped along for a few weeks until Simon put it out of its misery with a sucker punch via a text beginning:

> Sorry Sade … I do not think this is working between us.

Sade Nil. Simon's Mum 2.

Chapter Four

I now work for Ryder & Hamilton, a consultancy on the tenth floor of a gleaming office block in Canary Wharf, as a project manager.

I had studied Business Management, but decided that I wanted to get into project management. It was when I got tired of being filed under "Admin" in my former place of work.

Life Work Life Work Life Work and Work.

I have always believed that when it comes to work – the office is like a bee colony. You have the queen bee, then, way down the pecking order, you have the admin people. For those who think they are above such mundane people, "admin" can be defined as those put-upon frowning-faced minions whose names are hard to remember or who are referred to as "thingy from admin" and who spend most of their time photocopying hundreds of papers that do not need photocopying, updating figures and bits of information that are too important not to capture but too trivial for you to bother yourself with. The nameless blob of humanity who get blamed when deadlines get missed. They do not figure greatly in the grand scheme of things, so if you are in a meeting discussing why certain papers got sent out late to members of a panel, just blame it on "admin."

There was this day one of the partners came into the office with some VIPs, introduced the directors and managers and then casually gestured at us – "They are *just* admin" – and walked past us.

That was when it dawned on me that I could do more for myself; the day I decided that I was going to pay to start a project management course. PRINCE2, the project management method certification programme, basically saved me from a life of relentless and low-paid admin.

Though there were days I thought I couldn't do my job and the course at the same time, I knew it would be worth it in the end and stuck to my study at night. And once I got my qualifications, I started attending interviews and landed a much better-paying job, in a much better working environment at Ryder & Hamilton, Churchill Square, Canary Wharf.

I splurged on classic pieces such as tailored shirts, skirts, and jackets, and a couple of leather flats and high heels for meetings with clients, and practised my newly focused, high-level professional walk.

This morning, I file the final paperwork on last week's project – managing the launch of a new library in the City –

before turning to this week's task, a presentation to the Chief Executive and management team of a bank.

I glance up from my screen and see that Bridget, my work pal, is looking a bit fed up. Perfectly made up as ever, but not engaging with her job as usual. Most of the time she's pretty efficient, working on deliverables, charts, and Power-Point presentations, but not today. I make a note to chat with her after our meeting today.

If Bridget is in a bad mood it could be a few things: her mother-in-law has flown in from Lagos, or her sisters-in-law have landed in London. Or IVF woes.

Sade, yet you want to be married.

Yes. Minus mother-in-law and sisters-in-law from hell. Marriage, my pastor says, can be heaven or hell on earth.

My parents' marriage, especially when my father returned to Nigeria, had been like a stormy British day: brief with bouts of occasional thunder. Many of my mother's contemporaries had horrible marriages, and those that were married had husbands that perpetually lived abroad and, like my father, acquired younger wives and had more children who grew up hating their siblings born overseas.

Except for Uncle Peter.

He was Aunty Remi's late husband. My memory of spending time around them was always seeing him give her a quick kiss when he thought we weren't watching. He was constantly praising her and giving her gifts of shoes and lace materials from Liverpool Street market. He said that when his wife looked good, it made him happy. Then he became ill and the house, once full of the noise of children, became a house of whispers until he passed.

My MD, Gary Ryder, is one of those guys you love to hate. In his late forties, he is the quintessential guy on *Location, Location, Location*, with the blonde wife who still looks like a model after two children, who's looking for a country house that costs millions. While you wonder how a guy of that age has that kind of money, Kirsty's voiceover explains that he set up a tech/IT company in the early 2000s and the successful business went global and was recently bought by a company in Silicon Valley.

Gary has five companies and this consultancy is just one of them. We specialise in helping public-sector bodies and not-for-profit, art, education, and STEM initiatives, with particular interest in youth entrepreneurship.

Unlike my previous jobs, I like this one and it brightens me knowing that my contributions are recognised and celebrated.

I like to hold our weekly project meeting on a Tuesday morning, not just because it is one of the free spaces in my diary, but because on a Monday most people's brains are still in weekend mode and I cannot afford any mistakes in my team. But I also feel that early in the week is the best time to get information and communicate with the project team and stakeholders.

After the meeting I catch up with Bridget.

"I'm thinking of taking some time off on Thursday and Friday this week," she says, barely breaking her stride.

I smile. "That's fine. You can ask Julie to cover the project meeting with the building client."

"Thanks."

"Hope you got something great planned?" I ask innocently.

Bridget sighs and it seems to come from the bottom of her belly. "My mother-in-law is here again from Naija and has packed enough entitlement and passive aggressiveness in her suitcases to last for a century."

"I'm so sorry."

Bridget shakes her head. "Sometimes I do not even want to go home. She just sits there watching my every move. *The soup is not tasty enough, the TV programmes are not funny enough, the bed is too hard.* This woman has already demanded my husband buy her a new bed. Last night she asked for money to go shopping up in London, and when hubby was trying to explain that things are a bit tight, she says, *It is not as if you are spending any money on children.*"

Bridget's light brown eyes fill with tears, and I can see the stress and pain etched into her pretty features. "That is low."

"I am sure she still has more tricks up her sleeve. My husband likes to stay oblivious to everything. He tells me that his mum deserves the best because she is the one that sacrificed so much to keep them in school, with a roof over their heads, after their dad lost his job."

I mutter something sympathetic. The idea of the Nigerian mother-in-law with a bone to pick is enough to freeze the bravest heart. "I hope things sort themselves out."

She manages a smile and goes in search of coffee.

It's early April, and noon. I walk as fast as I can along the Canary Walk colonnade, noting the gleam of the tentative spring sun as it bounces off the skyscrapers reflected in the water, watching as smartly dressed people bustle around me. Everyone rushing around to get lunch, get to business meetings or back to the office. Oh, to be as lucky as the groups of tourists standing by the quay watching the boats go by.

I trudge into the nearby Metro supermarket to pick up a sarnie and a drink for lunch, feeling a bit weary after the meeting, which was useful, but too long as usual.

I pick up my meal deal of tuna salad, cheese and onion crisps, and squeezed orange juice. The last item makes me feel slightly more virtuous. I stare at the tuna salad and crisps and ponder my choice for a second. It wasn't as if I intended kissing anyone in the office. No more client-facing meetings today either.

Then I hear a slight cough behind me and I turn to see a tall ebony-skinned man with a grey designer beard. There is a hint of a smile as he nods towards my lunch.

"Great choice."

I blink. "Sorry?"

He smiles again and holds up his shopping. Identical to mine except for a bottle of water instead of orange juice.

I guess he isn't kissing anyone this afternoon either.

The woman on the till is running my stuff through and gives me a smile. "Nice hair, love. Is all that yours?"

Any other time, the question about my braids would have irritated me, but the nice-looking guy is standing behind me and I am acutely aware of his all-encompassing gaze.

33

"Thanks, but they're extensions," I murmur, packing my stuff into a bag.

"It's lovely. I have always wanted to have my hair done like that," she continues.

"I agree," the man behind me says. "The style is lovely, everything about you is just on point. Smart, corporate ... what can I say?" He laughs, and a silly smile threatens to tug at the corners of my lips and then I let my usual bland mask slide back into place.

The woman on the till grins, her pale green eyes full of mischief as she starts putting his stuff through. "You're a right charmer, you are."

Mr Charming shrugs. "Well, if I see a well-dressed lady, I can't let her go without complimenting her, can I?"

I fidget with my bag, part of me wanting to take off and part stubbornly resolved to see where this will end. Whoever knew that my silk avocado blouse teamed with a black flared skirt and boots would get so many effusive compliments.

The woman on the till winks at me. "Aww, ain't he lovely, ay? If I was a few years younger. Always wanted a toy boy."

My admirer – who I can't help noticing has a bit of Idris Elba in his confident swagger – gives her a cheeky smile, then he joins me at the other side of the till.

"I am sorry. I did not mean to embarrass you."

"Not at all." I shrug, but I also can't help but notice how broad his shoulders are under the classic fit of the suit. He works out.

"Do you work around here?" he asks casually.

"Yes."

He shakes his head. "I work across the city. I just dressed up for the part." He looks a bit self-conscious. "I don't usually make this much effort. I had a meeting with funders today. You know, they do say the suit makes the man." He glances at me again. "Look, I am so sorry eating up your lunch break like this ... pardon the pun." He stretches out his hand. "My name is Jimi Taylor and yours is…"

"Sade." I was not saying more than that for now.

"Sade. My favourite singer," he murmurs. "I love old school music."

"'Smooth Operator' is my favourite," I volunteer.

He smiles. "And what do you do?"

"I'm a project manager."

"Projects – that is interesting. We might need your services soon. Well, it's been nice meeting you. I must let you have your lunch. Do you have a card or something?"

"I don't usually carry cards around on me."

"Of course. Cards are so old-fashioned anyway." He reaches into his jacket pocket and retrieves his phone. "I will give you my number. It would be great if we could have a chat. I have this project that needs a lot of help to get off the ground." He smiles, looking me straight in the eyes, "I do hope that's okay."

"Yeah, of course." Fumbling in my bag, my fingers moving past my keys and my notepad and the bottle of tablets needed to reduce the size of my fibroids, to find my phone.

We exchange numbers, and he still gives me his card.

It dawns on me that I only have a few minutes until my

next meeting and that in less than ten minutes of knowing him, I have told a total stranger about my tastes in music and given him my number.

He smiles again, and an inexplicable kind of warmth spreads through me. "Well, got to get back to work," I say awkwardly, "but I look forward to being in touch."

"Me too," he says. His head dips slightly and he raises a hand in salute. "Goodbye, Sade."

I turn and keep walking until the crowds on the colonnade thicken, so if he is still checking me out, he will not be able to see me moving as fast as I can back to the office.

Later, at my desk, I get his card out of my bag. It has embossed brown lettering.

Jimi Taylor. Founder, NuChance.

With the strapline *Enhancing life through sports and exercise.*

I take a deep breath and try to focus on my work. I spent my lunchbreak being chatted up by a handsome stranger. No. I spent my lunchbreak networking with a potential client.

Oh, whatever.

Throughout the afternoon, I keep seeing his smile in my head so I break and Google the details of his charity, which takes me to a very modest website.

NuChance was set up by former Aldery FC footballer Jimi Taylor and former Chelton Town midfielder Cyril Peters. Plans are underway to work with schools and PRUs to ensure that wellbeing, mental health, and job opportunities are the focus. More details to follow shortly.

Former footballer, ay. Good job my knowledge of football is on the elementary level so that I am not too starstruck.

I decide to save him on my phone as METRO MAN.

Chapter Five

S am has not been responding to our calls. We call her boyfriend, and he is not responding either. So we are here banging on her door energetically.

No response, I observe, as Vicky peers through the front window.

I bang on the door again, harder this time, in frustration, until after two minutes Sam appears at the door. Her eyes look bloodshot, her dark brown hair tousled, and she has a wary, weary expression.

"What is it with you guys and the noise?" she says crossly. "I still have to live here, you know. Don't disturb the neighbours!"

We push past her and shut the door firmly.

"What's going on, Sam?"

She smooths her hair away from her face. "I had a colossal row with Martin."

"What about?"

"I just felt… Well, he's been really off, lately, behaving as if I am getting in his space."

"Has he said that?" I ask.

"No, don't be silly." She flung herself onto her settee. "It's just a build-up of little things. Answering in grunts. Awkward silences. Not hungry. Not even interested in…" She lowers her voice. "You know."

I sigh. "Maybe he's tired – work stuff?"

Sam runs her hand through hair that looks as if it has been dragged through a hedge backwards and throws me a guarded glance. "Yeah, like you would know."

My lips tighten. "What's that supposed to mean?" *Et tu Sam?*

Vicky makes a hissing noise. "Sam – that was mean!"

"Forget it." Sam shrugs. "Anyway, I've been lying low so I wouldn't have to inflict myself on you two. You can both—" she seems to gather herself "—take your leave." She gestures towards the door, like an eighteenth-century hostess showing us the way out.

I ignore her. "Shall I make some tea? Does wonders for self-pity," I say, as I move past her to her small kitchen.

As I make the tea, they gather around the kitchen door.

Sam shakes her head. "So, on Tuesday I asked him about our holiday – we were meant to be going to Barcelona."

"Yes. The trip you have been looking forward to for ages," Vicky prompts.

"Yeah. So he said he doesn't really feel he is up for going now. Since when is anyone not 'up for' a holiday! I was furious and said so."

"What did he say?"

"He just shrugged and turned on the TV. He said nothing for the rest of the night. It was horrible. So, on the second night of not talking to me I asked him if he wanted me to go back to mine – to get a reaction – and he said it was up to me!"

"For real?"

"Then he said, 'This is not working.' I just stood there like a lemon and he said we should go our separate ways."

"Oh, Sam. Do you think there's someone else?"

"I asked him that, and he said no, he just needs some space to think about where we go from here. So here I am in my flat, thinking about where we go from here."

I ponder this. Martin lives in one of those yuppie flats that overlook the Thames in Canada Water that are extremely expensive.

"I guess he needs the space – for his ego and the rest for his head," I say, and Vicky laughs.

Sam doesn't find it funny. She glares at me. "What do you know about relationships, Sade? Have you even had a successful one since Y2K?"

My eyes widen. "Seriously, Sam? *You* are going to try and single shame me right now, because I am not in a relationship? I could have told you for free that living with a guy is the fastest way to make him commitment phobic."

Silence. Both Vicky's and Sam's eyes bore into me.

I put my hands up. "Okay. Look, I was just trying—"

"Just go." Sam's face is red, like she's about to cry.

"I'm sorry," I begin, but Vicky shakes her head at me and I pick up my bag. I make for the door.

"Y2K is me being generous, by the way. You have not had a successful relationship since your crush on George

Michael when he was in WHAM!" Sam has a bitter edge to her tongue.

"That's enough, Sam," I hear Vicky say in a tired voice as I slam the door.

At home, I mull over the events of the past few hours, with my mum's words haunting me – *Words are like water. Once loosed from your mouth you cannot collect them again.*

I should not have been so brutal, so tactless to Sam. I have been told many times that I can be cold, sarcastic, cynical, and, yes, insensitive sometimes, but for Sam to start comparing my relationship history to the past forty years of British pop music is uncalled for. Besides I was not that much of a WHAM! fan even as a teenager.

A month later, and today on the tube I had an episode. It was not hot – I mean, how hot could it be at this time of the year? – and yes, I had on a jumper and a pair of trousers under my winter coat, but this kind of heat started from the inside and seemed to permeate my very pores. I almost fainted – not that anyone stood up for me to sit down. The guy in front of me thought I was plastered because I kind of swayed in his direction before I could steady myself.

Either I am iron-deficient, or it is one of the many pre-menopausal symptoms I have been researching online. From haphazard sleeping patterns, sore gums, and hot flushes I know deep down inside that menopause and the rest of my life are waiting for me on the other side of my last period.

About twelve years ago, my mum came round to my flat for a chat. This was nothing new, except that she announced that there was going to be a chat, and me not wanting to have that chat would not stop the chat from taking place. Anyway, Mum showed up armed with fertility pamphlets and another one about egg freezing.

She laid them on the table and looked at me as you do when you are about to start a card game. It was like *Oya. Which one are you picking?*

"Mum, what is this?"

She looked at me as if I was stupid. "What does it say? You are now thirty-eight and I just cannot be looking at you. Have you thought of freezing your eggs so that when your husband comes at least you could then have children?"

I just stared at her. So many people had so much to say about my life, even though it was none of their business to gossip about in the first place. It just seemed to trigger my mum, who would then trigger me. "Because those gossips from the Marriage Monitoring Aunties' Association have suggested this to you as my last hope."

"Are you okay? Who is this Monitoring Association of Marriage?"

I sighed. "Mum, I don't feel this is for me right now."

"So when is the right time then? Is it when your eggs have gone into retirement? Sade, this is something you should really consider if you want to be a mother."

I got up and left her sitting there holding the pamphlets and went to my room to lie down. Anything for a quiet life back then.

Now I can't even contemplate the stress of IVF.

Chapter Six

I call Mum after work today in response to her text.

CALL ME.

"Eh. You remember me today, ay?"

"It is not like that, Mum. I've just been busy. You know, work and everything."

"So, because of work you don't know you suppose to call the person who born you for four whole bloody weeks?"

Mum never swore so I guessed I was in her bad books again. I am silent, going through probabilities in my head.

"Folasade," she says, using my full name. "I told you that we are having Thanksgiving in church next month and you suppose to call me to get the dress and there was no call from you. Do you even love your mother at all? You know all my friends and Mrs Shobowale are going to be there and I cannot afford disgrace."

"Mum. You and this Mrs Shobowale, are you still having this rivalry? It is like *Game of Thrones* with you two."

"Game of what?"

"No worries, Mum. I will put thirty pounds in your account for the material."

"Thirty pounds? What about money for the tailor? Do you want me to use my own money to pay for your dress again? Or what kind of nonsense are you telling me?" I hear her long-drawn-out sigh of disgust, as if to say, *Lord. What do I do with this kind of daughter?*

"Well, how much is the money for the tailor?"

"How much do you think tailors are charging nowadays? Stop asking me questions. At least a hundred pounds for skirt and blouse nowadays, and you need Gele as well."

"Mum! It is just a Thanksgiving. I do not need a head tie. It is not as if it is a wedding."

"No, it is not a wedding. There is only one reason why God has spared my life, and it is to witness your wedding!"

Walked straight into that, girl. Fair and square. I have disturbed trouble today. "Mum…"

My mother sobs. "My first daughter. FIFTY and not even the smell of a boyfriend let alone husband, and you do not want me to cry. *Olorun kini mo se? Kini mo se Olorun?* What did I do? God, do not allow my enemies to rejoice over me. Mrs Shobowale's youngest daughter is now pregnant. A girl that was born when you were in secondary school. See my life, oh, Ebunola, see your life!"

I take a deep breath as I hear Mum referring to herself in

the third person. "Mum, I don't know what you want me to say."

"Look. I am tired. I need to sleep. Put one hundred pounds in my account for the tailor and this time sew a better style. Do not disgrace me. You know my whole church will be there looking at me. It is bad enough that they will be looking at you and thinking why you are not there with your husband and children like your junior sister Kike – so do not show up looking like a ruffian."

I am tired, too. Tired of having the same conversation with my mother, my maternal aunts and all the church mummies that have this special knack of catching me at odd moments at unavoidable family gatherings. Tired of being compared with Kike, of not having attained respectability or made my mother proud, as she sees it. "Okay, Mum. I had better go. Just wanted to see how you are."

"You want to see how I am? What do you bloody think? I am happy *abi*? Of course, who will not be happy when her first daughter is still single at fifty? People are looking at me that I did not train you to be a responsible somebody. If I had, maybe somebody's son would have put you in his house."

The storm clouds circle around my head. Words like *responsible*, *somebody's son* and *in his house* tend to do that. "Mum, I have my own house. I do not need somebody to take me to their house as if I am homeless."

Mistake One. My mum starts to clap. When a Nigerian mother claps on your head it is like – *Well done! You are being congratulated for being the stupidest of the stupid.*

"You see yourself?" she says. "Why do you like to be allowing nonsense to be leaking from your mouth like this?

Maybe it was your mouth that chased Simon away. Even though he was not Yoruba, he was a good man. Did I not tell you not to get a mortgage? I told you that women with mortgage chase men away. I also told you about going for an MA. I want you to get married and settle down – what is hard in that? You are a woman. Woman must marry and have children, that is all. It is in the Bible."

Then my second mobile rings. "Mum, I got to go. I have an important phone call." Sorry, Lord, I know Christians are not supposed to lie but the call from Vicky provides a welcome reprieve.

"It's okay. I have work to do. I will keep praying for you sha. I am your mother. What can I do?"

"Mum." I toy with the idea of telling her about what is on my mind, what kept me up into the early hours, and my fears about what might be going on in my body, and then I stop myself. I just can't find the words.

"Yes?"

"No, it is nothing. I will call you later this week. I must go now."

"Okay. Have a nice week."

"Bye, Mum—"

I realise she has already hung up and so I answer the call waiting from Vicky.

"Vicky, you're a lifesaver."

"We aim to please. What am I saving you from?"

"My mum."

"Oh. Mandem issue again?"

"You're a mind reader."

"Your mum is Nigerian. I know it goes with the territory. She will nag you up the aisle."

"I need a break. I'm looking forward to spending time with people who can discuss other things than Aso Oke, weddings, and what a disappointment I am as a daughter."

"Of course your mum doesn't mean that."

"Let me tell you something. This is how it goes. When you are at uni, they do not want you to have boyfriends, but as soon as you leave uni, they are asking for a fiancé. When you are at uni, they are proud of you – shaming all the people in the yard that did not go to uni until they hate your guts – but when you do not get married at the time they think is best, they start single-shaming you."

"And yet you still want to marry inna that culture? No sah."

Vicky is from Jamaica, and I envy her because her mother favours a laidback approach towards marriage. Of course, her mother wants her to get married, and now she is dating Karl in her mid-forties, but the difference is that her mother just wants her to be happy.

And there is the elephant in the room between me and Mum. She cannot be happy unless I find a man and get married. While I would love to be married, I do not feel it should be a prerequisite for happiness – so it looks like we are going to continue with our stalemate with neither of us being happy with the other.

———————

That night I lie on my king-size bed staring at the space next to me, wondering what it would be like if there was a living, breathing, human being lying there.

What would life be without a man? Life is either being

in love with one or loving life – or trying to convince the world that you are loving life – without one.

Surely I could write a book about that.

Am I a loner? No. Do I get lonely sometimes? Yes. I have gone on girls' trips and holidays, but one by one, most of my friends either have married or are in relationships and now spend their free time with their husbands or significant others.

The sense of being the Last Single Standing in my group of friends and colleagues feels like a sweater that was once comfortable but is now too tight. Sitting there while they talk about romantic evenings, pregnancies, swapping pictures of their children's first day at school or, as time goes on, their children's engagements and weddings. It's excruciating how quickly you start to feel like the odd one out.

When I am not working, there is the occasional temptation to dwell on what did not work, what could have been, and what I wish could be.

Sometimes you do not know how lonely you are until it is the end of the day and you have a bunch of things to talk about, but there's no one there to listen except your reflection in the mirror.

Okay, I confess.

On the outside I am this career-driven woman who seems to have it all together, but brimming under the surface is this crippling fear that one day my long-suffering period will just decide to leg it and never come back. Just up and flounce off into oblivion. Like a spoiled teenager.

I have not prepared my mind for this life-changing event. You see, when that happens – according to my mum – it will mark the end of my chances of snagging The Perfect Naija Husband, because how can I expect him to marry me if I cannot have children? Marked-down goods, you know, like an expired product, ten years past the sell-by date.

Sometimes it is lonely being single. It is hard and it hurts but sometimes being single can also be very liberating, freeing, and empowering.

Sometimes I cannot decide.

But look at the advantages. I do not need to rush home to cook like my colleague Bridget, or put up with a nasty mother-in-law from hell, and their offspring, as she must.

I can roll from one side of my bed to the other.

As I live my life free of men and their shenanigans, I look much younger than my friends and relatives with men filling up their lives with their issues.

Nobody tells me what to do.

Nobody tells me what to do with my money.

Right now, singlehood looks okay.

I reach for my Bible and look for my favourite verse this month. Isaiah 62, verse 14:

Thou shalt no more be termed Forsaken, neither shall thy land anymore be termed Desolate; but thou shalt be called Hephzibah and thy land Beulah: for the LORD delighted in thee, and thy land shall be married.

Then I remember Jimi Taylor, the smooth operator. The faint lines around his eyes crinkling when he'd smiled at me, a kind of mischievous glint hidden in their depths.

Of course, I am not going to call him.

He'll have to call me first. He was the one who wanted my number.

Jimi's card is on my table at work under a pile of letters and files. I can just see Sam and Vicky shaking their heads about that.

That is right, burying your life and dating opportunities under the camouflage of work again, are we?

Whether it is business or social, my boss would say I am passing up a potential client, a corporate opportunity. But I know myself, and not being proactive with Jimi is the right decision for my emotions.

I am old-fashioned that way.

Besides, he's probably just another player anyway.

Chapter Seven

I wake up in pain again. Another month. Another five days of body-wracking agony await.

Cannot wait for the op.

February fourteenth is just a day. February fourteenth is just a day. February fourteenth is just a day.

If I keep repeating this to myself slowly, it will sink into my head.

Work is the same as usual today, oh, except that massive bouquets arrive for several members of staff. So what if I half hoped that a mystery admirer would send one for me? It didn't happen, and I am glad, because it would have meant a lot of explaining to some of my team members.

Valentine's Day is for lovers. Eat your heart out, you singletons out there. The paper today has a Valentine's Day page, framed by lurid red hearts.

"There are 15 million Britons living the single life. It may be a day singles dread and some might spend it watching a weepy movie and eating a TV dinner, but cheer up – there are many reasons to enjoy your single status!"

Apparently, I can:

1. Make the best of my freedom and go out on the town and pull anyone I fancy. *I already fancy someone and where that is headed is anyone's guess, if I never call him.*
2. Go out with my girlfriends and get totally plastered – *but then I don't drink.*
3. According to life coach Veronica Dayton, pamper myself. Cook myself a nice meal, and down a giant bottle of soft drink and eat chocolate. *Done that.*
4. Go to Paris/Venice/Rome with my mates. Who knows who I might meet in these cities of lurve? *Too expensive around this time of year. Besides, I'm sick of bumping into loved-up couples.*
5. Have a girls' night in and watch a movie and have a good girlie chat. *Just done that.*
6. Is my ex still single? He might still be pining after me. Call him and ask him to come round "for a deep and meaningful chat." *No. Simon has well and truly moved on.*

A few days later. On Saturday morning, mind you. The phone on my bedside table is insistent.

I close my eyes and hope it will just stop but it is relentless and I glare at it. No, I have not made a mistake. It really is 8 a.m. The last time someone rang me this early it was Mum's brother, Uncle David, alias Uncle D. Full of advice and sermons that he does not use on his own life or family. Had about two girlfriends on the go, last time I heard, yet thinks nothing of lecturing me about family values because I am "still" single.

"Your mother is not getting any younger," he said, last time I spoke to him. "She wants to see your grandchildren while she can still play with them."

My stomach tightens as I pick up the phone.

"Hello, Sade." A crisp British accent awakens all kinds of possibilities in me.

"Who is this?"

"It's Jimi Taylor. Remember, we met at Canary Wharf a couple of weeks ago. During lunch…"

"Oh, yes … Jimi." I am trying to sound breezily vague as if he had not been flitting in and out of my thoughts in the last fortnight.

His voice is friendly and warm. "Hope you're well?"

"I am very well. And you?"

"Very well. I was wondering when we could get together." His voice lowers and trails off as if he is waiting for me to respond.

"Um…" I am searching my brain for context. Get together? Get together for what?

He seems to read my thoughts. "We were going to talk about work, about this project of mine. We can talk about ourselves later."

"Ourselves?"

"Sorry. I am not explaining myself well. I just mean that I would like to know more about who I am working with." His voice is perfectly modulated as if he is speaking to his funders or something.

"Of course," I say, matching his businesslike tone. "And it's good to manage expectations … with clients."

His laugh is husky and does all kinds of things to my insides. "Expectations … yes, absolutely."

For some reason, a bead of sweat is making its way down my back. "That's something we can discuss when we meet," I say.

"Speaking of which, would next Saturday be okay?" he says smoothly.

"Saturday?"

"I just want to take things forward as soon as possible," he says, but I hear a hint of nerves.

"Sure." I try and infuse as much professionalism into my voice as possible. "I have a few appointments – let me check my schedule and get back to you. I want to ensure that I can provide the most well-costed and evaluated response to your proposal."

"Great."

"I need to prep. The way we do things is that I send you some forms and you tell me about what your needs are, then we look at resources so we can maximise the time in our consultation meeting."

He chuckles. "I understand. But when you get to know me better, you'll see that I like to think out of the box. Besides," he adds, "the client is always right, yes?"

"We haven't signed anything yet."

"I know, but I just have a hunch we are going to get along. I knew it the first time I saw you."

"Really? You saw me in the supermarket and thought to yourself – I just have to work with her."

He laughs. "It crossed my mind along with some other things…"

This is flirting. Unmistakable and exhilaratingly exciting flirting and it's deliciously unprofessional. Which is why it has to stop.

"Fine. Send me the details for Saturday and we can discuss your project," I say, injecting some formality into what is happening. "I'll email over some information, and some stuff for you to fill in first."

"Cool. Look forward to it. And to Saturday," he says. "Very much."

"Okay. See you then." I fight against the warm feeling running through my system.

We end the call and my thoughts continue their own separate journey of what-ifs and what-if-nots.

At work a day later, I decide to call my cousin Dolapo, who at thirty fits into the millennial bracket and who's probably the only person in my family who gets the non-traditional way I like to live my life. She is practically a professional when it comes to dating, though she's in a relationship now. I need her advice.

First, I mull over what I want to ask her, in between responding to emails, attending project meetings, and writing briefings for clients.

Hiya. I need you to give me some dating advice, like what to do on a first date, because I seldom get invited for a second or third or fourth?

That sounds pathetic.

Hiya. I have got a work meeting with a guy I really like. I want to keep it professional but at the same time let him know I'm interested in him. You never had a problem pulling guys when you were single. Tell me, what am I doing wrong?

That sounds even worse.

Okay, what about this? *Hiya. What keeps men interested on a date? Any tips?*

Yes, this will do.

The women I see getting married these days are young. It's too simplistic to say it is because they are pretty and have youth on their side. It's also about attitude. They have good energy, they're not jaded and cynical, and they seem more resilient about all the frogs they have to kiss before they find their prince. They're hopeful, not bitter. I am not too proud to ask advice from Dolapo – she's got a lot to teach me. One must be practical.

After work, I call Dolapo and tell her what I need.

She gives an excited pretty-young-thing squeal. "Aunty! Have you got a date?"

"No, I am just doing some research about dating when you are not a millennial. You know, when you're around my age. It is for a project I am doing for an online-dating firm."

Father, Lord, forgive me for lying.

"Okay, Aunty. So, don't take this the wrong way, but older women are too serious. They need to let their hair down and be more open, less judgey. Men don't want to think they're on a date with their mum, if you see what I mean."

"Sure." I have a wry smile as I jot that down.

Do not be too serious. Be open.

"And maybe, be more feminine, not so feminist."

I raise an eyebrow. "Go on."

"It's like dating is when you get a chance to be softer, more playful. No politics. No talking shop. No impatience or sarcasm. When a guy thinks about you, he needs to think kindness, warmth, gentleness. It is the way you look at him, a look from under your eyelashes, the curve of your lips, a hint of cleavage…"

I am about to write "cleavage" but my hand hovers over the pad. "A hint of…"

Dolapo continues. "A push-up bra. Wear that crimson passion lipstick that looks so good on you. Aunty, you are stunning, you should flaunt it. Ditch the trousers and wear a dress. A nice figure-hugging dress. It just does things for the average male. Be mysterious—"

"Dolapo," I intervene. "I am doing research, as I said. This isn't about me."

Dolapo squeals again. "Okay, I got you." She giggles. "Our little secret!"

I don't reply. It doesn't take a genius to work out I was asking for myself, but I still feel too embarrassed to come clean to my cousin.

"Aunty, I have to go," Dolapo says. "Bae needs me. But I hope I've been helpful with your … research."

"Yes, very helpful, thanks," I say innocently. "This is all really useful info."

We end the call, and I'm left wondering if I really need to transform into a completely different person. Because clearly who I am is not going to cut it.

Chapter Eight

Wednesday, mid-week service, and I'm in church for the evening.

Living Waters is my home church. Has been for the past nineteen years. I like Pastor Keith there, and his wife Sandra. Lovely couple. When I first started attending, Living Waters was a small, family church of about fifty people – mostly couples with children and a few singles, of whom I was one.

Almost twenty years later Living Waters church is now 1,000 people strong. The children I first met there have grown up, gone to university, and started working, dating, even got married and had kids of their own.

I am still one of the singles. Not a child, nor a young person, not responsibly married but not old enough to be in the elderly people's fellowship.

Just before service starts, I glance around, feeling like the outsider looking in at the perfect picture of all the families, husbands and wives and children – people smiling and laughing. The buzz of conversation as one of the church mothers walks past and congratulates another dewy-eyed young couple.

Immediately after I turned thirty-five, the dates started drying up – from a handful a year to one every couple or three years. I was getting the dregs, the leftovers, the weirdos, the ones no one else liked. In fact, some of them did not even like themselves.

Under that calm cool exterior we wear under our Sunday best, our hearts long to beat with passion again. Souls that crave a hug, intimacy, and the companionship of the opposite sex. Our bodies have not forgotten that we are women – even if the church has.

Sometimes I get scared.

Scared that one day I might do something stupid. I feel like a pressure cooker because, like most mature singles in church, under my quiet, poised facade my pain and insecurities have been obscured by artfully applied makeup, designer clothes, and a little bit of bravado. Sometimes all it takes is the wrong time of the month, a tactless comment, another question from someone asking why I am not married yet, to drive me into the pit of self-pity, regret, and introspection.

I also realise that many of the female friends I made at church have fallen by the wayside. Once they got married, they could hardly wait to forget about their lives before, happy to move on, to walk off and leave long-time single friends and confidantes in the past. Some of them even told me that they feel I, and others like me, have been too choosy and it's no surprise that we're still "on the shelf", whatever that means. They're smug, as if marriage is like graduating to a higher place in life, and we singles have all flunked the exam.

When it first started happening, I was hurt and quietly accepted the judgement that came my way, but I have learned to stand up for myself and become more assertive. I am no longer going to allow people to categorise me and mark me down because I did not fit into their neat little box of married with 2.5 children and a mortgage by thirty or thirty-five.

It's a culture thing. In my culture, you are prepared for marriage and not for life if there is no marriage or if it happens later than expected.

Later this evening I get an excited phone call from Sam, who is now over her annoyance with me, it seems. Martin has called her to apologise and they are now back in love again. All is right with the world.

I have my questions, because I care, but decide to keep them to myself. In the past year they have broken up at least twice and, honestly, I do not like Martin. The guy really believes his own hype – with his blond hair and blue eyes, his rugby playing and his public-school education – and sees himself as the gift and Sam as the lucky girl that got him.

Once, Vicky and I went for a drink with Sam and Martin, and he looked at us and said – and I am not making this up – "I am my own role model."

Wow.

Every single sentence from Martin is like a TEDx

sermon. I mean, he is so nineties. He reminds me of most of my ex-bosses. If they could have all come together and written an anthology it would be full of buzzwords and vague management clichés thrown around in team meetings and catch-ups.

It is a win-win situation.

We need some out-of-the-box thinking people in this department.

We operate a non-blame quota here.

It is hardly brain surgery, my dear, are we all on the same page here – and the killer – *we pride ourselves on our diversity.*

Look, at the end of the day (pardon the vague management cliché) I felt like slitting my wrists during that drink, and I could tell Vicky felt the same way. Martin probably told his friends, *I like Black people. I let my girlfriend have them as friends, don't I?*

Martin once described one of his Black female co-workers to us as *Too Big and Too Loud.*

While I believe Sam deserves better, Vicky – well, she is still hopeful that Martin will magically change into a top bloke. I have long gone past the frog-turning-into-a-prince stage. Never believed that story even as a kid, because my mum had told me that it was scientifically impossible for an animal to turn into a human being.

But I am in no position to judge Sam, as she pointed out to me recently. I hate when others force their opinions on me, after all. I'll just have to keep my mouth shut.

On Thursday at noon, I sit in the sterile waiting room once again observing the people around me.

There is a lovely West Indian lady with her granddaughter. The granddaughter is dabbing at her eyes and the older woman is comforting her. Their two heads are almost touching, one black and the other peppercorn-grey. There is also a middle-aged woman who has her head in a book – and an elderly couple, her head on his shoulder while his hand is linked with hers. I stare at them and the woman turns her head and gives me a smile.

For the next few minutes to an hour, we all have something in common. An MRI that will determine our lives.

I pick up my phone by instinct and glance through it idly. Social Media. I should stay away from it, but it will keep luring me into its depths and I find myself commenting on things I should just ignore and get on with my nice quiet life. But, I mean, look at these posts berating single women on Facebook.

Do not mind these career women. They turn men down in their 20s and 30s playing hard to get and hit a brick wall when they find themselves 40 and lonely with a cat to keep them company.

Charming.

See, these "educated ones" they do not know that by the time you are 30 – all your eggs are pretty much not viable. The clever ones got married early, had their family and then went back to their studies. I mean you have the next 40 years to work but you have a short window in which to have children – which they ignore – it is the main reason why women are born, and all that reproductive equipment is just a waste sitting inside you, dying away!

Interesting deduction.

At 30 a woman is an Expired Product good for nothing but the scrap heap. Let her just invest in wine and cats!

I give up.

No one wants a used car with a million miles and quite a few previous owners!

For goodness' sake!

You can't be here on these streets dating at the same age as your younger relatives. That's so ewww…

No words.

I pity those stubborn over 40 spinsters that have made book their priority over marriage. Your best bet by this time is to find the next man – maybe your friend or colleague and beg him to make you pregnant so that at least you will have one child to look after you in your old age. A word is enough for the wise.

Welp!

Waaaay … past expiry. No guy in his right mind will give you a second glance…

Says this one, who looks like he has been dragged through the hedge backwards. Several times. Him and his bald self. No man. You are not Samuel L Jackson. You are just bald.

I feel like screaming back at these keyboard defenders of the Right Way to Live: *We have heard you and we do not want to replicate the dysfunction we grew up into. Marriages just for sleeping and waking up, eating food, and having pointless arguments whilst raising kids interspersed with weddings and funerals – while you age until death comes.*

Nah. I cannot be having that.

The MRI is like a tunnel to another world, and as I lie on the table, I am given headphones to shut out the noise.

I close my eyes and think about my life. My plans, my desires, and my mistakes. I think about my friends. I think about my mum and my family. I wonder if she would feel hurt that I'm facing this health scare without her knowing. Kike wanted to tell Mum, but I told her I could not deal with her drama and stress on top of everything else. I will tell her in my own good time.

As the scanner takes detailed pictures of the inside of my body so the doctor can identify the location, shape, and number of the alien beings that plague me, another detailed picture floats into my head.

Jimi Taylor, standing there like some kind of angel in the spotlight holding a big bunch of flowers.

For goodness' sake, girl. Only you can daydream at a time like this.

After thirty to forty minutes the test is over and the technician informs me that the images will be reviewed by the radiologist, who will send a report to my consultant.

I sit there staring at the technician's impassive face, trying to decipher whether he can give me any more information about what he has seen in my body. If he looks sad, then it could be bad news. On the other hand, if he looks happy – could it mean I am in the clear? His face reveals nothing but professional kindness as he wishes me goodbye.

I frame the question in my head as I put my coat on, pick up my bag, and leave to get the bus. All the way home, I torture myself with different permutations of what might happen to me.

Then I get a text from Jimi.

> Looking forward to our catch-up on Saturday!

The next day, Friday, I ask Vicky what to wear on Saturday. She's more pragmatic than Sam and will not bash me if nothing comes of it with Jimi.

"Okay, so it could be business and it could be a date," I begin.

She says nothing.

"Say something, man. What should I wear?"

Vicky frowns. "I'm trying to understand whether there is some kind of conflict of interest here."

I close my eyes. "Vicky, please turn off the Terms and Conditions manual in your head and help a girl out here. He could be a potential client but ... he is also quite cute and we were having a bit of flirtatious banter and it was quite nice."

"I don't know whether to be happy that you got a date or worried that you don't know whether it's a date or not."

"Vicky! Oh, just forget I asked."

"Okay. Okay. Let's say it is a date. Wear that navy blue dress with the white collar that you wore for Penny's party."

I breathe a sigh of relief. "Cool – that sounds nice. Formal enough for a work event and smart-casual enough for a date that might not be a date."

"Be careful, Sis."

"He is a nice guy. I kind of feel safe around him."

"I am not worried about him. I am worried about your heart and emotions."

"I am as tough as old boots, me."

"Hmm." She doesn't believe me either.

Later that evening I am working on a presentation for Friday morning when my mobile rings. It's Kike. She sounds muffled, as if she has been crying. "Hi, Sade."

"What's up?" I look at the time. My sister rarely rings

this late. A busy job and boisterous twins mean she goes to bed as early as she can.

"It's Mum."

I feel my world shatter into a million little pieces. "What's wrong?"

"She collapsed on the street on the way from evening prayer meeting."

I jump up and throw my coat on, my head pounding and my head racing with a thousand random negative possibilities.

———————

According to Google:

HYPOTENSION
If untreated, hypotension may lead to complications, such as:

- Frequent falls due to postural hypotension
- Dangerously low blood pressure that can reduce blood flow to the brain, heart and other organs, resulting in stroke, heart attack, kidney failure or even shock

———————

I sit in the waiting room and realise that this is the second time I have been in a hospital in two days. My nose is beginning to get used to the sickly disinfectant smell and the suffocating sense of anxiety and sadness; but into every rainy day a little light must come, and it is in the shape of Mum's doctor.

He is young and Nigerian. I would put him at late thirties to early forties. He is quite fit.

Dr Adelaja.

A whole doctor.

Tall, dark, and with designer stubble. In the nineties he could have been in one of those R&B bad-boy bands, like Jodeci or Boyz II Men.

This one is culturally appropriate too. Knowing exactly how to appease the toughest Nigerian elder with the right terms to affirm their elder statesperson status by calling them Ma, Pa, Mummy, or Daddy.

According to him, Mum has low blood pressure.

Apparently, when the blood-pressure reading is below the specified limit of 90/60mm Hg it can cause symptoms such as dizziness, tiredness, and blurred vision due to the reduced blood pressure restricting the flow of blood to the brain and other organs, which caused the fainting.

The doctor says that this is common with people of her age and that he will work with her and the GP to develop a care plan that will include some lifestyle and diet changes.

Anyway, my mum is in love.

It is written all over her face as she stares at him while he speaks. Her eyes are soft and attentive and she is smiling, something that is as seasonal as the British sun.

Mum is sitting up in bed all spruced up in her new M&S nightie and her dressing gown with a big bow at the neck. Her grey plaited hair is packed up into a turban scarf.

I know she is not listening to a word the doctor is saying, she is too busy checking out his left hand for a wedding band and thinking to herself, *Is this not a nice young man? Why can't my daughter bring this kind of somebody to my house for marriage?*

Sadly, for her, there is a ring; it flashes as he picks up his iPad and updates it. I look outside at the car park and see the sky, serene and opaque, so different from the chaos and pain in the corridors. The fact that Mum managed to get a private room at such short notice is like winning the lottery.

"Mrs Sodipo. We just need you to get more rest and stop worrying, Ma."

I look at Kike. We both know what's going to happen next.

My mother sighs. "Hmm. My heart is not at ease at all. How can I stop worrying?"

The doctor smiles gently. "Mama. What is there to worry about again? You have a lovely family and, from what I hear, grandchildren and everything. You have been blessed with a great family."

"Doctor, *ma gbo mi*. Listen to me. This is my eldest here." Mum gestures at me. "Not married at fifty years of age. My heart is in pains. My enemies are rejoicing." She points to me as I will the grey tiled floor to open and swallow my mortification and silent, frustrated rage.

Kike sees my face and interjects. "Doctor, don't mind my mum. We are all proud of Sade. Marriage is not that big a deal that a person should put their career aspirations on hold. As long as she is happy that's the most important thing really."

I see my mother give Kike a look and then purse her lips. "You see, doctor. The young people of today, they do not understand our ways. The importance of family values.

I can see that you are married. Is that not what any responsible mother would want for their daughter?"

The doctor looks contemplative.

A nurse pops her head around the door. "Dr Adelaja, you are needed in Room Ten."

The relief on his face is palpable as he hurries to the door. "I must go, Ma. I will check on you later today to see how you are progressing."

"*Pele. Omo Dada.* Please, if you have any nice doctor friends, Dr Adelaja – from a good home – please let me know. Even if they are divorced or widowed. I do not mind."

The doctor disappears and as the door closes behind him, we all fall silent. I look at my phone and Kike does the same, mumbling about picking up her children from football practice.

I am torn. I have been humiliated, but my heart aches for my mother's stolen dreams.

"I will come back later tonight, Mum," I say, bending down to kiss her cheek.

She nods and stares ahead. Kike does the same and bolts. But I hesitate when I notice the glimmer of unshed tears in my mother's eyes. My mum never cries.

I never cry.

No one in our family ever cries.

"Mum." I reach out for her, but she has turned on her side, facing the bare wall that is as unyielding as herself.

"I am going to sleep now. Thanks for coming to see me." Her voice is quiet. I can hardly hear it.

I nod and leave the room, and this time I wipe away a tear.

Chapter Nine

A few days later, and Mum is back at home. Snappy, fussing around, and difficult – but, thank God, on the mend.

Doctor Adelaja has advised that there is no actual treatment for low blood pressure but with some lifestyle changes Mum should be fine. Getting up slowly from sitting down or standing up; drinking more water; eating small, frequent meals. He also suggests support stockings to improve circulation and increase blood pressure, but Mum's face tells him exactly what she thinks of that idea.

"While we're at it," says Kike, "you could do with some adjustments to your diet, Mum. You eat too much processed food."

Mum groans as Kike goes into Mum's cupboards and gets out the white flour, white sugar, white rice, and pasta, and a whole crate of malt drinks. Then she goes into the freezer and takes out a lot of stuff. So now the freezer is almost empty.

Mum almost screams, "Hey! Do you want me to starve?"

Kike does not even look up. "Calm down, Mum. You can't eat this stuff anymore. Apart from anything else, it's packed with sugar. You want diabetes on top of low blood pressure?" Mum looks down at her hands, like she's a child who's just been told off. "I will take all this away and go to the supermarket and get you healthy stuff with more vegetables, salads, wholemeal bread, fish, white chicken. The doctor said you need food that digests slowly like pulses and wholegrain, you know. Clean and lean."

Mum snorts in derision. "Which one is clean and lean? What of good decent Nigerian food? Obe Ata with fried meat. Beef, goat, or bushmeat."

I shake my head. "No, Mum. You need to cut down on that kind of meat."

"Just a little meat." She is almost begging.

"Yes. Chicken," Kike responds.

"Chicken is not meat!"

I hear my mobile go and have a quick check. It's Jimi wanting to know how Mum is.

"Where is my milk? What is this soya stuff? Are you people sane?" Mum shouts from the kitchen.

I sigh. "She's definitely back to normal, in one way," I tell him. "Thanks, Jimi."

"That's good to hear." He laughs that smoky laugh. "Shall we reschedule our catch-up for another time?"

"Yes, of course," I tell him. "I'll text you later."

Kike drives to the supermarket while I text Jimi. I'm half listening to her both complaining and worrying about our mother.

"I just hope she takes it easy after this. She has to slow down with all her gallivanting around town at Naija parties and church events."

"Gallivanting? You sound more and more like her every day," I say, focusing on my phone screen and typing.

Kike manages a laugh. "Funnily enough, my kids say the same thing." She glances at me. "Who are you texting?"

I stop typing immediately. "Just a friend."

Kike's ears prick up like our old dog Tiger's used to when it was time for us to take him for walks. "Who is this friend? If it was Vicky or Sam, you'd say. Why are you being secretive? I smell Man."

"Kike! Give me a break. So what if it is a man? Could it not just be a colleague?" I shake my head. "Like I said, you are getting more and more like Mum by the day, and it's worrying."

"I also smell a touch of defensiveness. Tell me more about 'Metro Man.' Yes, I sneaked a peek just now."

I blink and hold the phone to myself instinctively.

Her voice lowers. "Wow, you must really like this chap."

I look out the window at the road in front of me. Yeah, I really do. After one conversation and a couple of texts. I like him, but at the same time I am happy for him to remain in that fluffy, make-believe part of my mind, where he can live as 100 per cent perfection, untainted by reality or the complexity of normal relationships.

A few days later I go to the doctor to discuss the results of the MRI.

"The MRI showed about ten large masses that were pedunculated," he tells me.

"Pedunculated? What does that mean?"

"It means they are attached to your uterus by a stalk. The operation will evacuate them. Then we will evaluate them."

"Evaluate?"

His expression is calm. "We will have to rule out whether they are cancerous," he says, adding, "but most of the time they aren't. So let's hope for the best."

On the way home, I pray for myself and try to drown out the noise of my fear along with the loud chatter of the schoolkids on the bus home.

———————

Today is Mother's Day. All my life I have wanted to be a mother.

Kike and I grew up playing house with our dolls. We had Sindy and Paul. Sindy was blonde and blue-eyed, body measurements roughly 38–24–36.

Back in those days women were just seen through the prism of their looks, their vital statistics, and their ability to be a homemaker and have children.

How things have changed. Not.

Anyway, Paul was tall, tanned, and looked like one of the Beach Boys or the handsome one in *Scooby Doo*. For those millennials out there: like a Californian surfer. Like a young Zac Efron.

I also had a baby doll. I called her Susan. She was white, too. There were hardly any Black dolls then, so I had to make do. I would rock Susan in my arms and pour water into her closed mouth and watch it dribble onto the carpet, to the irritation of my parents.

Then, when Kike was born, I watched in awe as Mum nursed her, as well.

I just assumed that everything would fall into place after university and I would find a nice chap, settle down, and have cute babies.

It hasn't happened yet, and I am one operation away from the chances of it being very slight indeed.

Sometimes I daydream. I look at women with their kids in their prams, yummy mummies, harassed mums on their way to day-care or teenage mums, and I feel jealous.

I have these moments where I alternate between being angry with God and all those men out there that have played Eeny Meeny Miny Moe with my life and my time, only to throw me back in the dating pool, to float around looking for a prize salmon out there amongst the toads, tadpoles, and minnows.

Why am I equating a good husband with salmon? I must be hungry again.

Anyway, Mother's Day has this way of bringing out all my angst and pain because it is a day you are made acutely aware of your otherness. You are a woman with a womb that has been lying there useless for the past thirty years and every second that ticks away takes you closer to menopause and there is nothing you can do to stop this happening.

We childless singles who are part of the church family

are constantly reminded that we are not living up to our purpose as mothers, because no man has picked us. Everything in me has always rebelled against this, because it ties my destiny and my achievements to childrearing. If I was a man, I would be allowed to just be me.

Yet I am not without blame, I guess. I had bought into the ideal of waiting and praying for a good church guy to see how wonderful I was and ask me to marry him. I must confess, dating and being social were not priorities for me when I was young. My career came first and finding Bae second. Was I wrong? I used to sing in the choir, and would fervently pray that a husband would find me – faithfully singing away in my alto.

My husband's satnav must be seriously damaged, I guess.

———————

Mum does not do flowers but she likes a nice cake, so I asked Aunty Remi to bake one and asked Kike to drop it over after church. I will join Mum later and we'll probably watch a film and try and talk about everything but my marital status and the fact that, at seventy-one, Mum is still waiting to hold my children in her arms while she can remember who I am.

I do pray that she will live to see my sixtieth birthday, even though she might be sad on the great occasion – her mind fixed on my marital status and not that I managed to dodge childbirth, teenage angst, terrible in-laws, and my husband's occasional or habitual infidelities.

I will never be a Great Nigerian Wife.

After Sunday service I arrive at Mum's.

Somewhere in the middle of talking about her health and finishing my plate of rice and fish I finally tell her about my operation.

Everything is arranged for the surgery. Vicky and Sam have offered to take it in turns to help me, as the doctor has advised that I will need help to get around my house, as well as bathing and cooking, for the first couple of weeks while I heal.

"What kind of operation?" Mum asks as she stirs her hot tea with a slice of lemon.

"To remove fibroids."

"Fi— what?"

"Fibroids, Mum. They are benign growths in the womb. That is what has been causing the two-week periods and the pain."

It has been difficult sleeping because of the ache in my back and I am having problems walking as well. I feel like Ripley in *Alien*, as if I am incubating some strange being that demands total domination of my body.

"I know what bloody fibroids are." My mother shakes her head. "God, what is all this? Why are all these things happening to my daughter? I pray for you all the time…"

"Mum, things happen to people that pray." I shrug. "That's life, unfortunately."

"It is well. Thank God you can still go for IVF."

I am fifty. I am not exactly at the right age to be popping out children.

I look away from her to the wall because I might as well be talking to one. There is no point in telling her that the doctor warned me that though having the myomectomy can preserve my chances of having kids, it can also be a quick step into the menopause. In fact, the way my life is now, I don't even know how I could fit kids in anyway.

We sit there and look at each other. I see disappointment and pain in her eyes. The silent criticism.

Why can't you just be like your sister and get married at the right time and have children like normal people?

I wish I could ask her: can you not just love me just as I am? Fifty. Greying. Occasionally sarcastic and a bit worse for wear but a bad-ass project manager.

She sighs. "So when is this operation taking place?"

"In May."

"You will need to stay with someone. Have you told your sister? So you can stay with her?" My mother does not do sick children after childhood.

"Vicky and Sam are going to stay in the flat with me," I tell her. "So I will have some help for the first few weeks. After that, I should be okay."

"It is well." Mum sighs again. She gives me the cup. The tea untouched. "Please make me another tea. This one is cold."

Just before I go to bed, I realise that despite texting with Jimi, we still haven't set another date for our "meeting." I know the ball is in my court, and I also know I am a procrastinator if things are left too open. Ah well. I have bigger things on my plate right now, things that make everything else relatively insignificant.

Chapter Ten

Life has become hectic. Simultaneous deadlines at work. Prep for Mum's Thanksgiving at church – made more important now because of her recent health scare. She wants to thank God in the presence of friends and family, especially now that she feels more assured that her feet are still firmly planted in the land of the living.

I spent last night at Kike's, so we could leave early today for church, and this morning she pops into my room as I am getting dressed and glances at my belly. I see the fear in her eyes. The bulge just sits there stubbornly and I put my hands over it.

"I am not pregnant. Honest."

Kike reaches out and hugs me. "Come on, Sis. Don't joke. I am so glad you're going for the op."

"I am glad too. You know I have been struggling with the discomfort of this, the pain, since we were teens – it's time for them to come out so I can get a life. I've been so anaemic from multiple fibroids – who knows how many are percolating away in there? No wonder I've been feeling like death warmed up every month."

"Oh, Sis…"

"It's fine. Once they are out, I will be back to my sunny happy-go-lucky self."

Kike laughs. "Glad to see your sarcasm is still intact." She sits down on the bed.

"Gets me through the day, Kike."

"Well, take it easy on Mum. She is worried about you." Kike eyes me pointedly. "What is that you are wearing? Man, you are brave – wearing that to Mum's church with all her friends and church mummies there."

I look in the mirror. My crisp white shirt has a high neck and seventies-styled flap sleeves and I tuck it into my wide culotte-style trousers newly made of Ankara material. Anything else would have emphasised the bulge in my abdomen. My plaits are packed into a small headwrap, made of the same material, and I've added my new buy: gold hooped earrings. I apply my favourite muted red lipstick and love the way it gives my lips this matte nineteen-forties look.

"I think I look quite nice – if I may say so myself."

"You look fab, but you aren't auditioning for the part of an extra for a seventies reunion party, Sis."

"Well, thank you kindly, ma'am, but you don't get to tell me what to wear."

Kike looks at herself in the mirror in her smart tailored skirt and matching blouse and her Aso Oke head tie. "Mum is not going to like this."

I pick up my lipstick and run it across my lips again. "Look, I cannot spend that amount of money in making something I won't wear again. My wardrobe is full of these kinds of elaborate outfits. They aren't even my style."

"This is not about you, Sis. This is about Mum. Can't we just all meet up without any drama, Bwoy?"

"Woah, let me get this right. If my being at family events always causes drama, I can happily stay away. I hate this Nigerian party rubbish anyway!"

Kike sighs. "Look, Sis. I didn't mean it like that. It will be fine." She gets up and goes to the door. "I'll get the boys ready."

As soon as we walk into church, a sea of faces turn to look at us. I spot Aunty Gbemi's head tie first. It covers the face of Dolapo, who, like me, has decided to opt for something different with her material: a long, strappy dress which exposes a generous portion of cleavage. Her fiancé, a doctor whose name I can't remember, is wearing a white Buba, Sokoto, and a satisfied expression.

Mum is at the front of the church, elegant in navy blue and silver lace with a matching head tie in silver and a silver-grey Iborun on her right shoulder. Her best friend, Aunty Remi, is next to her on her left. Her arch enemy, Mrs Shobowale, sits in the other corner of the church wearing green Aso Oke with a matching hat that looks like a wilting flower pot. The woman looks as if she has eaten something that hasn't agreed with her.

I can see my mother's lips tighten slightly as she gives me a quick once-over from head to toe but she maintains her composure and nods as we greet her and take our seats beside her.

We have the sermon on the five loaves and two fishes, and the pastor talks about Jesus and faith. His voice is deep and rich and brings stories alive, keeping you interested and not dropping off, which I have been known to do occasionally at my church.

The sermon ends and while the choir sings, the pastor makes several calls for offerings, including one for different women's clubs and outreaches. For each offering, Kike and I, as long-suffering family members, must accompany Mum to the altar, dancing and singing, with sizeable amounts in envelopes for the clergy. The rest of the congregation sit and watch us politely.

It's on our sixth trip back to our seats when I see this guy at the back of the church. He is tall and dark with a greying beard and dressed in a smart suit. No tie today, though.

Jimi Taylor. My admirer from Metro supermarket.

Blood rushes to my head and I almost stop, then Kike glares at me and I take a deep breath and return to our seats feeling his gaze at the back of my head.

He doesn't look like part of the congregation. More like someone who is an observer or guest for the day.

But my attention is taken by my sister asking me to keep an eye on my nephews while she pops to the ladies.

After the service everyone gathers around my mother as she makes small talk with the associate pastors. I look around the crowd for Jimi, but he seems to have vanished.

Chapter Eleven

Aunty Gbemi looms in front of me in her skirt and blouse. "You always have to be different, Sha," she says, looking pointedly at my culottes.

I put my hands into my pockets and clamp my lips together. Glad that my hands have something to do apart from clenching themselves.

"I think you look stunning, Aunty!" Dolapo enthuses.

I must have done something right to get a millennial's approval of my wardrobe. "Thanks, Dolapo."

Aunty Remi Adekoya is here in a long dress made from the same material I am wearing, and she gives me a big hug. "I like it. Makes me remember when me and your mum used to go to parties in the seventies. I had the same outfit with a matching hat."

Mrs Shobowale suddenly appears and rests a hand on my shoulder. I feel as if I have been apprehended. "Hello, Sade. I have been asking of you from your mum."

I nod. "Good afternoon, Aunty." I can see her opening

her mouth and know what is coming next. I know the script.

"So ... when are you bringing your husband to come and greet me?"

Kike carefully intercepts the conversation. "Aunty..." She curtseys and introduces her boys to the older woman and soon Mrs Shobowale's eyes flick over me to Kike and the twins, her lips widening into a big smile. "*Pele*. My children! How are you doing? Come and give Aunty a hug."

I see my mother approaching and her voice is sharp enough to cut the air. "What are you people all waiting for? You should be heading for home to oversee the food! I need to see some of my friends here and will meet you at home. I have booked an Uber."

We all trudge off in the direction of Ayo's car and get in with the kids. But when Ayo tries to start the engine, the car lets out a protesting splutter.

"That doesn't sound good." Kike shakes her head as she tries to quieten the twins, who are arguing about who gets to play computer games on her phone.

"I just had this serviced," Ayo grumbles.

He tries the engine again and the same splutter happens, so he jumps out and goes round to the bonnet to check.

Kike looks worried. "Mum is going to do one if we don't get home before she does. We are meant to be serving the refreshments for the guests."

I hear voices outside and turn to peer out of the window, seeing Ayo only up to waist height. He is talking to a man who is taller than him and opening the bonnet.

A minute later, Ayo rushes round to the driver's seat of the car and gets inside.

"I'm running the engine," he calls.

"Okay. Try the ignition again."

I recognise the voice. It's Mr Metro himself. Jimi strolls round, wiping his grimy hands on a handkerchief. His eyes settle on me and he grins – a flash of white teeth.

"Looks like the engine has overheated. If you can manage it home and get the mechanic to have it serviced," Jimi addresses my brother-in-law but his eyes are fixed on me.

"Thanks so much," Ayo mumbles. "This car gives me so many problems. I don't know why it's overheating."

Our rescuer nods. "Could be anything from a damaged or broken thermostat, non-functioning cooling fan, defective radiator cap... I am sure your mechanic will advise."

"Pity he didn't notice when he serviced it." Ayo rolls his eyes before breaking out a grateful smile. "Thanks so much," he tells Jimi. "I hope your suit didn't get dirty."

Jimi smiles again and I feel something flip in my stomach.

"No worries. Nothing that a good dry cleaning can't sort." He glances at me again and his smile deepens. "I am just glad I could help."

Kike tries again. "We came for our mum's thanksgiving. You know – Mrs Sodipo. We are having a little get-together at her place. It would be nice if you could pop in. There will loads of food." Her voice sounds hopeful and then she sneaks a look at him again. "You can invite your, eh, wife as well?"

I blink in irritated embarrassment.

"Thanks for the invite but I really must go. And no," Jimi smiles again, "there is no wife. On any other occasion I would have taken you up on your kind offer but I'm due on a shift at work so … got to go."

"That's a shame," I hear myself say and regret it immediately as he gives me another look and our eyes lock. His lips have this kind of twist to them and I'm sure he just winked. I sense Kike and Ayo exchange glances.

"Have you guys met before?" Kike asks.

We both nod.

"Through work stuff," I add airily, my eyes on his, begging him not to say anything else.

"Interesting." Kike's eyes narrow.

"We really should have that meeting, Sade." His voice is firm and businesslike. "About the project."

The words tumble out of my mouth like a torrent. "Of course. I will send over a new date."

"Great." He nods as Ayo starts the car.

"Thank you." Kike waves while I make a half-hearted attempt at a smile in the back seat.

He waves and I whip out my phone, not to search for anything but to avoid Kike's interrogation. My mind is turbulent.

Ayo drives off.

I sense Kike turning around to look at me, but I do not look up.

"He likes you."

I feel giddy inside. A kind of foolish, teenage, thumping joy is leaping inside me that I have not felt since Lewis Johnson asked me out in Year Ten and took me to the school disco. *Jimi is just a potential client*, I reassure myself.

"Is that Mr Metro?"

"Yes."

Kike shakes her head. "Wow. You have been keeping such a fine distinguished gentleman like this a secret. Catching up to discuss a project ay? Okay, now. Bring it on!"

Ayo laughs. "I think Sade is the project."

His wife is still talking to herself. "I'm going to ask Mum about him. Do a bit of undercover work. He did say he was not married."

I close my eyes. "Don't ask Mum, she will start matchmaking again. Besides, he is a potential client right now, nothing more, so don't get your hopes up. If we do a CSI on him, we will probably find out that he is a Millwall FC fan or supports the Tory party, something like that."

Kike throws me another glance. "I don't understand you sometimes. Do you just like to sabotage your happy ending?"

"Please, you can't just pick a guy and start seeing us married in a couple of seconds."

"Sis. You have to start somewhere. He was pleasant. You seem to be getting on well. He spoke like a perfect gentleman and he winked at you."

"No, he didn't."

"Yes, he did, Aunty. I saw him," says my nine-year-old nephew Toju. His brother Tade lets out a laugh and covers his mouth when his mum frowns at him.

I fall silent.

Kike and Ayo fill the car with their laughter and teasing.

"He did seem nice though. You run into the guy you've

been chatting to – in an Anglican church. Love is all around us."

"Hang on, I just said he was nice. I didn't say I'm that keen. I mean, he could be an axe murderer by night for all I know."

"See what I mean, Ayo. How are we ever going to get her married off?" Kike shakes her head again.

I fall silent and comfort myself with the knowledge that a fit guy winked at me.

The last time I got a wink was from one of the old men who frequent the bookies not too far from my mum's house.

"Caribbean Queen..." he had sung tunelessly as he gyrated his hips and puffed on his cigarette and licked his lips at me. I'd stepped up my walk and shuddered. Okay, I was fifty, but technically wasn't fifty the new forty?

When I get home after the Thanksgiving meal, I decide to practise a confident man-killer walk, with hands on hips, and pouting at my reflection in the mirror. I wonder whether I need to get those artificial eyelashes Dolapo wears all the time.

I look down at my chest and for once wish I was a bigger cup size. I squint at my distended abdomen and wish I had a waist I could actually see.

In the mirror I speak to my reflection with all the oestrogen flaring up in me. *You really have got it bad. If this does not work out, how on earth are you going to pack all these emotions you have taken out of storage back into place?*

I'm getting ready for bed when I receive a text from Jimi.

> **Hey, great seeing you again.**

I smile and type a reply.

> **Hi, surprising to see you at my mum's church. Small world. Didn't know you attended St Thomas's?**

> **I don't. Okay, I pop in every now and then to make my old man happy, but that's about it. I'm not really a church person.**

> **Oh … okay.**

> **Good to see that your mum is much better.**

> **Yes, thank God, she's doing much better. We've been trying to get her to take life much easier. Finally, she is beginning to listen to her doctor's advice. Sometimes, she forgets she isn't twenty anymore.**

> **My dad is the same. Look, when can we catch up? Shall we say next weekend?**

> **Sure, let me check and get back to you.**

> **That's fine. You take care. Looking forward to hearing from you.**

> **Thanks. Goodnight, Jimi.**

> **Sweet dreams, Sade.**

Imagine that, ay? Going to bed after someone telling me to have sweet dreams. See me living a Hallmark Channel fantasy for five minutes, lol!

Chapter Twelve

Saturday afternoon and I pack my bags and head for Lewisham.

The text said The Naija Tapas Club for 5 p.m.

According to the menu The Naija Tapas club does Nigerian non-alcoholic drinks and platters of hot Nigerian food, but in small bites. Black bean cake, barbecued groundnut chicken on skewers, coconut, and vanilla doughnuts with Hibiscus cordial. Slightly pretentious of the menu to describe Moi Moi, Suya, and Puff-Puff alongside Zobbo drink for a European palate – but it has great reviews.

I am wearing my green and orange Ankara top over my jeans. I have added my tan leather boots and coat and piled my braids into an updo.

I am going to project-manage this.

Gloss. Nude.

Expectations. Zero.

I'd googled "lunch date with member of the opposite

sex" and seen it defined as a casual, low-fuss meeting between two individuals who might be interested in pursuing a romantic relationship. It might involve getting together over a cup of coffee or any drink and some snacks. The key word was "might." Advantages:

1.Low stakes – this way you can both discern whether there are any sparks or interest or whether you bore each other silly and want to call it a day instead of having to sit through a formal two- or three-course dinner.

2.Coffee shops provide an intimate setting where you can get to know each other and have meaningful discussion without being distracted.

3.As you are drinking coffee and nothing stronger, both parties avoid getting drunk and have a better chance of meaningful deep conversation and possibly form the basis for friendship that might lead to something more lasting.

4.Public and convenient. It is safe and conveniently situated around high streets so you can leg it to the tube if either of you cannot stand the thought of spending another minute together.

I walk from Lewisham Station and enjoy the crisp air. The railway hub is bustling and the station's architecture a mixture of modern and historical charm. The rhythmic clatter of trains echoes around me.

Exiting the station, I turn into Loampit Vale, a busy street lined with shops, cafés, and bright murals, the scent of blooming flowers blending with the aroma of freshly brewed coffee. I pass by local markets, street vendors, and shoppers, and arrive at the restaurant, which is exactly as described online, a contemporary West African eatery.

The aroma of Nigerian spices and the buzz of voices greet me as I step inside. The interior is a black-and-white themed palette, interspersed with bold African prints on the tables and low sofas. It is not too busy, which is good. Fela Kuti's "Water No Get Enemy" is playing in the background, which I remember listening to growing up at home. Mum likes to pretend she only likes Christian music, but could be heard blaring Fela's back catalogue from her bedroom on Saturday mornings and Jim Reeves on Sunday.

I spot him sitting at a table next to the window, reading a book, and I savour the chance to observe him while he is at ease. His broad shoulders visible under his brown corduroy jacket. His long legs stretched out in casual jeans and sneakers. I squint at the book and as I get closer, I see it is Colson Whitehead's *The Nickel Boys*.

He seems to sense my approach and puts the book down and gives me a welcoming smile.

"Great to see you."

I nod and say nothing, my well-rehearsed greeting drowned by my nerves. I offer my hand, but he bends to give me a side hug.

"So glad you made it. Hope you got here okay."

I nod again and sit down, taking in the atmosphere around me, then smile at his book.

Jimi explains. "I decided to get a head start with this. It was a gift from a friend and I've been hearing great things about the writer."

"I've got a few books I haven't started yet," I tell him. "If

I said that the last one I read was *Americana*, you will know how bad I am at finishing up my TBR list."

"Hey, don't be so hard on yourself. Life gets in the way. You just got to take each day as it comes. That is what I have learned to do."

I find myself relaxing and I smile.

He looks at the menu as a server approaches and asks if we're ready to order.

"Shall we get some drinks and then we can choose what we want on our platter – or shall I call it our calabash?"

I look around at the trays with wooden calabashes of the most tempting food. All bite-sized. "I will go for Calabash One." Yam and plantain balls, catfish sticks, chicken drums, and coconut Puff-Puffs. "And I will have the Zobbo drink. Thank you."

"Sounds good." He smiles at the waiter. "Calabash Two for me, please." This is the same as One, plus the bean cake and fish fritters. "I'll take the Zobbo drink as well."

The server takes our orders and comes back with our drinks and the dark red coolness quenches my thirst.

"Thanks again for helping us out with the car at the Thanksgiving."

He shrugs, as if it is normal to just attend to people's car problems while dressed in an expensive suit. "*Ko tope*. It's nothing. I just happened to be there."

I nod. "I've been told you work as a physiotherapist." I decide to keep my deep-dive Googling to myself. Softly, softly. I don't want to jump in too fast and ask about his charity or being an ex-footballer. Although I know nothing about it, it probably makes him more interesting than most of the men I've dated before.

Jimi explains. "Yes. I'm a locum so I work at different hospitals. I hope to settle down soon and get a permanent position but right now…"

"Sounds interesting."

"So, Sade. Tell me more about you. Apart from your work as a project manager and the fact that your mum goes to my dad's church, I don't know a lot about you. Do you enjoy what you do?"

"Yes. I like troubleshooting and dealing with challenging projects. I find it pretty fulfilling. What about you? What drew you to physiotherapy?"

"I like helping people. It's not just about their physical health, recovering after an op or sports accident, it's about increasing their self-confidence, their mental health. I'm all for helping people make decisions that help them turn their lives around. With what I do, I have the opportunity to inspire people to live a healthier life."

A man that wants more from life than nine-to-five. A man with a cause. That's a new one. "That's very commendable," I say. "Inspiring in itself."

"Thank you." He beams as the waiter arrives with our food. Two huge platters of hot, tantalising food.

"Those are large portions." I think of my usual meal-deal lunches and repress a smile.

"Tuck in. There are doggie bags available if you can't finish everything." He smiles at me.

I sample some Puff-Puff, which melts in my mouth. I can taste the coconut and immediately want more. I hear him chuckle.

"Criminally delicious, isn't it?"

I nod and wonder whether I have food around my mouth. "So, tell me more about the project."

He shakes his head. "First, tell me more about your job – your motivations. Why project management? What's your dream?"

"My dream." This is an easy one. "Well, I like my work at Ryder and Hamilton, but really I want to run my own consultancy business one day – ideally work from a sunny island with my laptop." We both smile, before I go on. "Why project management? Well, because I like to think I can control things." I see his shoulders shake with wry laughter. "You get my drift…"

"Sometimes we make our own plans – sometimes life makes them for us." He takes a sip of his drink. "A sunny island sounds good. Which one?"

"Anywhere in the Caribbean or Hawaii. Or South America. And I've always wanted to go to Brazil."

I see a light come alive in him and he leans forward. "Brazil ay…"

"Yeah. There's something about the place. My friend Vicky went there last year and talked about the beaches, the sheer natural beauty, the architecture, culture, and the food."

Jimi nods. "And the best footballers come from Brazil. Pele and Neymar."

"So, you've been there?"

"I have."

"Holiday?"

"Work," he says, then gestures at my meal. "How is the food?"

"Fantastic."

"And your mum, is she better now?" he asks.

"Much better, she has already started bossing us around again. I'm sure your mum does the same."

He smiles, but I note it has a sadness about it. Maybe his relationship with his mum is like mine. Sometimes it is more bitter than sweet.

The waiters are hovering, asking if we need anything.

Jimi turns to me. "Would you like more food, drink?"

I shake my head. "I'm wondering how I will get myself out of here, with all I've eaten!"

He smiles. "We can walk it off on the way to the station."

The beat of my heart quickens. Then I remember why I am here. "So, tell me about NuChance – why that name? Is that part of the branding?

"I worked in Brazil for some time. Did some volunteering in a small school in one of their favelas, and when I saw what those kids had to face in terms of lack of opportunities, education, and health outcomes I decided to set up a football club. One of the businessmen that sponsored what I was doing was an ex-footballer, like me, and we got talking and I told him about my dream of having a football academy for young people who had been dumped after getting injured. I wanted it to be a place where kids can get emotional, mental, and physical support in getting themselves back together. So, that's how I came up with the name NuChance."

"Ah, that's interesting. It's all about new beginnings."

He leans back and looks at me. "Yeah. Everyone deserves a new start. I mean – all this came about because I had a second chance myself."

I fall silent because he looks reflective, and I don't want to push it. "It's … good to know these things about a client – you know, for the brief."

He laughs and it's warm and deep and makes his eyes fill with an intensity that leaves me feeling like a teenager. "Ah yes … the brief!" He leans forward. "Well. We're looking to put on a special event."

I bring out my notepad. "Okay, when would you like the event to take place? What are we looking at – summer, autumn, or winter?"

"My business partner was thinking about autumn. I must introduce you to Cyril. He is the ops person. Deals with the financial side and day-to-day running of the charity. We have a consultant that helps us with events, but the few we have done have been basic. We need someone who knows what they're doing and your company has got a pretty good reputation for project managing the kind of events that make an impact. I checked out your bio – the kind of companies you've worked with … made me know I – I mean we – would be in good hands."

"Thank you. My team and I will make sure that your event is one to remember."

———

Jimi insists on paying and we are walking back towards the station when he suggests we take the same path we came through the park. The late afternoon shadows hover but the park is still quite busy with picnickers, cyclists, and teenagers loitering around.

"Do you live nearby?" I ask.

"Greenwich, but a friend told me about the restaurant, so I checked it out and liked the food."

"Great choice. Amazing food."

It's lovely and serene in the park. We are surrounded by blossoms like soft candy-floss over our heads as we walk.

"Cherry Tree Walk – perfect for couples," says Jimi.

I don't know what to say to this as the petals flutter down like confetti over us.

"It's a great springtime walk – a symphony of colours, scents, and sounds," he continues.

I smile to myself and sigh. "It's peaceful here."

He turns to me. "Are you okay? You seem a bit … down?"

I put my hands in my pockets. "I'm fine. Just getting ready for the new week. You know how it is. Work deadlines. Life."

A serious operation in a few days' time.

He falls silent. "Work will always be there. We won't. That's why my motto is *Carpe Diem*."

"Seize the day."

"Exactly."

I turn and look at him. "I'm getting a good idea of what you want for your event. Bold. Straight to the point and packs a punch."

"Is that how I come across?"

"A little."

"Don't go all diplomatic on me. I like the 'say it how it is' side of you."

"Side of me? You hardly know me."

"I'm trying to … get to know you, I mean."

My laugh is nervous. "Of course, a client should get to

know their project manager, that makes perfect sense." I peer into the distance. "I can see Lewisham Station looming."

"So, what are you doing next week? So we can discuss the event further." His eyes are asking a question. "We need to explore it in more depth."

I nod. "Sure. Marketing. Merchandise. Digital products."

He laughs. "I see I am in perfect hands. Every time I get sidetracked, you have this way of bringing me back to focus on the matter at hand."

"You probably have a lot on your mind."

He shrugs. "Not really. Just a couple of things. Maybe just one thing."

"I'm sure it will sort itself out," I say briskly, because I'm scared of the pull between me and this man.

His voice is matter-of-fact. "No, it's something I need to sort out myself. You know, get straight to the point and go for it." He eyes capture mine again and the traffic, the noise, and the bustle of the high street seem to stop – waiting for me to say something.

My mouth is dry. "Sounds like something you really want."

He is still standing there as if I am some mystery he is trying to crack.

"I think it is." His eyes flash. "I'm just hoping my investment is going to pay off."

I am trying to keep the tone of my voice businesslike. "I suppose that depends on the terms and conditions of the contract."

"I wasn't talking about a contract," he says simply.

I feel that heat engulf me again as it dawns on me where we are going with this.

He smiles. "So where do we … I mean *you* … go from here?"

I hesitate. "Home."

He smiles again and leans slightly forward and I wonder if he can hear my heart thudding faster than my brain can process.

My eyes widen and he chuckles as he touches my hair and shows me some pink petals in the centre of his palm.

"You got some blossom in your hair."

"Thanks." I laugh, then riffle around in my bag for my travel card. "And thank you for a great lunch meeting. I've got some vital information to put into the brief."

He puts his hands in his pockets and observes me. "You've certainly got me hooked in anticipation of what you are going to come up with. I am expecting you to blow my mind."

"No pressure, then," I say and laugh, then check my watch. "I'm going to try and get the ten past five train – I need to get home for six."

Jimi's eyes narrow. "Is that when your carriage turns into a pumpkin?"

"I see you like fairytales."

"I like your humour, Sade," he says. "Dry, like mine." He pauses. "So, what are you doing next week?"

"I'm off work," I tell him. "For a while, actually."

"Holiday? Lucky you."

"Not really."

He looks a bit puzzled.

"Sick leave."

"Oh." He blinks and squares his shoulders as if preparing himself for what I'm about to say. "Nothing serious, I hope?"

I shake my head. "Just a routine op … and some recuperation time."

"Sorry to hear that. I know it is not really my business but I work in healthcare. Might be able to get you some resources on your recovery and return to work … depending on what the op is. I understand if you don't want to discuss it with me." His voice lowers with respect. "We have just met…"

"It's a myectomy," I interject. "I'm having some fibroids removed."

I didn't need to tell him that but it's actually a relief to tell someone other than my family and friends. And he seems like a good someone. You know, sometimes most people hear you but very few listen. He has listened more to me in the past two hours than all the men in my lifetime put together.

He nods and then reaches out and squeezes my hand. "You will be okay, Sade. I'm sure you're in very good hands. Are you going private or NHS?"

"NHS, but my consultant is great. Really put my mind at rest."

Jimi's eyes are warm as he looks at me. "If you had told me that you had an op coming up, I wouldn't have pushed meeting up today – even though I really wanted to."

I smile. "No worries. I wanted to come. Apart from anything else, to take my mind off things—"

"Charming." He laughs, and I do, too.

"Okay, that came out wrong."

"Come on," he says. "I'll walk you to the platform."

As we stand and wait for the DLR to Stratford, Jimi checks something on his phone.

"What day is your op?" he asks.

"Thursday."

"I will tell my dad to pray for you."

I would have loved to hear him say that he would pray for me. I sneak a look at him. He is about to say something ... but the train arrives and he waves as I get on board.

"Bye, Sade. Good luck. I will call you."

I wave back and manage to find somewhere to sit, staring at him as he stands there on the platform, smiling.

It's hardly *Brief Encounter* and allowing myself to indulge these emotions flitting around in my head is probably asking for trouble. But I do. Just a little.

Chapter Thirteen

Vicky begs me to attend our yearly singles conference at church on Sunday afternoon, even though my op is just around the corner. She says it'll be a distraction. I'm not so sure.

Even though Vicky is engaged to Karl, she still insists on taking me, like a mother hen. Not everyone who comes to the conference is single, which is another oxymoronic scenario, but I guess until a marriage has taken place you're technically still a singleton.

The singles arm of the church is called Successful Singles and after twenty years I have developed a strong sense that the branding sucks. Singles do not want to identify with being single and the church does not treat singles as if they are successful, so it is a bit of an oxymoron. After attending twenty of these conferences, I deserve a medal. Or a plaque, at least, on one of the chairs saying: *Sade Sat Here, 2000–2018.*

I have given up on the singles ministry a long time ago, finding it little more than a women's fellowship anyway.

I know that Vicky feels that this might be an opportunity for me to catch the eye of another single guy, but being veteran singles-conference attendees, we both know that the event does not draw in loads of men. One guy I know at church compared it to a kind of Christian meat market or *Bridgerton*-like Regency drawing room where hapless bachelors are paraded in front of desperate maidens.

The auditorium fills up fast. There are loads of women in the aisles, on the bleachers, on the chairs, with a few men scattered in.

Vicky keeps on walking, scouring the aisles for empty seats. She spots spaces for me, her, and Karl and we all sit down.

"This is the first time I have come for this conference," Karl announces, pulling at his collar as if he feels suffocated.

"And the last..." Vicky grins up at him, squeezing his hand.

I glance around me and spot a familiar face.

It is Simon sitting behind me with his PYT, Nneka. She sees me first and makes a grab at his arm and whispers in his ear. His head shoots up as he gives me a nod.

I nod too, and turn back to my friends. I'm reluctantly sat at a conference that will probably be full of things I have heard before, propped up in front of the man I once loved and his fiancée who hates my guts for some reason I cannot really explain. Every time we pass in the church corridor, she ignores me. Once I was in the ladies and she walked in with some of her friends and they stared me down. I left without drying my hands.

I wasn't scared of them. I was scared of what I might say to them.

Vicky saw it differently. Her words came back to me.

Sade. How can you lose a man that was never ever yours? If he loved you, he would never have let his mum set him up with her friend's daughter. You are not the loser. In fact, you probably dodged a bullet there.

I realise she was probably right and sit now, with their eyes boring into the back of my head, feeling rather ambivalent.

"I want to start the conference by giving you a nugget of truth that I feel you all need to understand. Some of you here will never get married," says Pastor Keith, casual in his white shirt and faded Dad jeans, as he perches his glasses on his nose and stares at the auditorium for signs of life.

We know that Jesus was the most influential person who ever lived and He was never married.

The days are evil and let every man live as if he is single. Learn to be single, content, and whole. In fact, this desire means that you are still carnal and need to mature in the things of God.

I am definitely still carnal.

Pastor Keith reiterates. "Did you hear me? Aim to be a successful single like Jesus. Celebrate your gift of singleness. Have you considered that many of you have been given that gift?"

I look around to see if this has registered, but the assembled faces are expressionless, which means they are either too polite to say what they think about the Gift and want to know more about the return policy, or they believe that nothing else awaits them but a lifetime of singleness and they have to grin and bear it because Jesus was single and He is our example.

Pastor Keith continues. "Singleness is a time for serving God. Apostle Paul says he wishes that you all have the gift like him so you will be free to serve God without the responsibilities that having a family would bring. Not being married gives you the opportunity to serve God with your full mind, heart, and spirit, without distractions." He pauses and looks around for this to settle in.

Okay. For "distractions" spell S-E-X.

I think about Jimi Taylor walking with me to the train station and how much I had enjoyed our conversation. Yep, that was one distraction and a very nice-looking one, at that.

The woman in front of me mutters something under her breath.

Pastor Keith leans against the lectern, his eyes fixed on his audience. "I know some of you might feel – it's all right for him to say, he gets to go home to his wife and family while you are all alone in your one-bed semi somewhere but ... I have to tell you that the fact that you are not married now is God's way of telling some of you that it's not yet time. He is still processing you."

The lady in front of me gets up and says clearly so that everyone can hear her: "Mi sixty years old, and yu a tell mi seh God a process mi? Cha. Mi gon. Mi cyah listen to dis nonsense no more. No sah."

Karl smothers a chuckle and Vicky gives him a stern look as we watch the woman leave.

Pastor Keith is still going for it. "Yes, I know some of you have been waiting for years. Pastor, I want children. Pastor, what about sex? God understands that but what He needs you to know is that when you serve Him with all your heart and soul, the desire for Him will eliminate all those desires."

The hall is stone-cold silent. You could have heard an eyelash drop.

Pastor announces a short break and asks the music team to play some music to fill the silence.

———

The next session after the break is a Q and A between two young ladies both under thirty-five. Two Pretty Young Things.

I watch them sitting there, full of bubbly effervescence, the arrogant glow of youth and ignorance of what the future holds. Lord, was I that young once?

Pastor is asking the questions.

"What kind of advice can you give those singles out there that are still praying to find Mr or Ms Right?"

"Oh," says PYT Number One, who has been married all of a few months. I cannot remember her name. "Just trust God. You see, the minute I took my mind off men and started volunteering in the church, Bae showed up."

"You see." Pastor smiles. "Ladies out there, take note. Just keep serving and waiting. This is what our young lady here did and see, she got the ring... Show the audience the ring."

PYT Number One flicks her long weave to one side and

shows us a sizeable bauble on her hand. A collective sigh runs through the audience.

She is practically purring now. "You see, I always tell the singles that I mentor in the team, age is just a number. Even if you are worried about having children – just remember Sarah in the Bible. She had Isaac at ninety years old."

I close my eyes and shake my head. Vicky winces.

Then it is the turn of PYT Number Two.

Pastor asks, "What do you have to say to members of the church that are out there that will make them want to be proud members of the Successful Singles ministry?"

"Thank you, Pastor, for the privilege of being able to minister to the people. I feel that women should stop searching for men and let the men find them."

Somebody in the audience says something and laughter ripples through the place.

"Where are the men?" she adds.

The pastor repeats the question thrown at him. "Where are the men?" He is trying not to smile. "To my sisters out there. This is where you come in. Go out there and be fishers of men. Maybe your husband is still out there on the streets, chasing women, smoking weed, or in the bookies… We need to be more intentional about bringing them to church."

The lady in the audience stands up. The pastor nods and the usher goes over and hands her the mic. She looks angry, or maybe just passionate about what she has to say.

"Pastor, men are the best people to talk to men. We can't keep passing the buck to single women."

The pastor nods again. "A good point. We are taking all this into consideration and would really appreciate if you fill in our feedback form. We are trying to make this ministry one where the singles feel appreciated. After all, our Lord and Saviour was single into his early thirties."

I look at Vicky and she shrugs.

That was when I decided that I was going to write in and give leadership my ideas about what needed to be done to the singles ministry. I would hate any young person to constantly feel like tearing their hair out in frustration.

It's Sunday after church.

I have just found out that my cousin is getting married next month. Aunty Gbemi mentioned it casually, the way you do when you need to pop down to the shops: *I'm just going down to the shops to get a loaf of bread and while I mention it – your niece is getting married in a couple of months' time and I need you and your daughters to shell out on expensive bridal material for Aso Ebi and not be pissed off.*

I was in the hallway when she told Mum in her small sitting room. I almost burned my mouth as the tea I was drinking went down the wrong way.

My mother's alarm increased the volume of her voice. "Are you okay, Gbemi? You are just telling me this now? A couple of months' time. I need time to play my part in this wedding – at least help you out a bit – at least give me some time to get some stuff together."

Aunty Gbemi rubbed her hands together in entreaty as if she was begging for her life. "Anti Mi. It is my bad memory … I have been running around organising this here and there. You know how it is. You had so much to do yourself when it was Kike's wedding. I thought I had told you, Sis. *Ejo. Egbon mi.* Forgive me because of Jesus," she said, kneeling down and hugging my mother's unresponsive knees.

Jesus, indeed. Even Jesus would not be impressed by lies, Aunty Gbemi, I thought as I sipped the tea and looked at her with one eye.

I can bet that Aunt Gbemi doesn't want me or Mum, but especially me, to know about the wedding date. I guess the idea was to hold off for as long as they could before we knew – just in case we used bad energy to jinx the wedding. Obviously, all unmarried women in their fifties are jealous of their younger relatives.

Mrs Sodipo sighs. *"Ki ni mo fe se?* What can I do eh? Your child is my child. I share in your happiness too eh. It is well."

"Yes, Anti Mi." Aunty Gbemi gets up from the carpet and fluffs up the sleek tortoiseshell-coloured weave on her head. She looks feline, if you ask me. Like her spirit: ready to pounce at any moment. Her lips are arranged into a contented smile until she sees me looking at her, like – *Yeah. I see you, Aunty.*

"Sade. Is that you?" One eyebrow is raised as if she wants to ask me another question. She is always asking pointless questions.

My expression falls back into the usual blank canvas it assumes whenever I am around fakery; which, when it comes to some members of my extended family, is often. "I'm fine, Aunty, and you?"

Aunty Gbemi makes sure that I have very little contact with her daughter. Especially since she left college. I am aware that she believes that my singlehood at fifty is contagious. I don't have the energy to reassure her that it is not something I can infect young single women with when they get too close to me. Singlehood is not contagious. Every time she sees me, I can hear her mind whirling away.

YOU ARE A FAILURE. DON'T COME ANYWHERE NEAR MY DAUGHTER AND TEACH HER ALL THAT FEMINIST STUFF THAT KEEPS YOU SINGLE THIS LONG.

I see her lips twist in my direction, as if she is trying to forget the smell of something bad.

"How is your job going?"

"It's fine."

"Eh. Have you heard our great news? Your little aburo Dolapo is getting married to a good man o." She is looking at me intently while she said this.

"Praise da Lord!! That's wonderful, Aunty." I ham it up to the max.

"I was just telling your mother about it."

"Wonderful. God is so good."

"We are selling the Aso Oke for the family. It's two hundred pounds for six yards and twenty pounds for the Gele. It's baby pink and silver."

I catch the worried look on Mum's face. Another set of Aso Oke and she is a pensioner. Her whole cupboard is stacked with a rainbow of outfits for different events for friends and family over the years. Most of these things have hardly ever got a second wear and are out of date – and sometimes out of size – in months, but one has to keep buying them in order to be seen as loyal and supportive. Everybody knows that the price of the fabric is inflated in order for the bride's mum, or whoever who is organising, to recoup a bit of money for event expenses.

"It is well." Mrs Sodipo sighs.

"I know you will help my big sis out with her material." Aunty Gbemi smiles. "God will bless you. I know God will hear your own cry one day and send you a good husband like Kunle."

Amin o Loruko Jesu. My mother looks at me accusingly. "Won't you say Amen with me?"

"Amen," I repeat and reach for another biscuit.

My mother looks at me as if to say, *How can you be eating biscuits while children younger than you are marrying?* then shakes her head, picks up her phone, and starts scrolling.

My aunt has this kind of pretend sickly-sweet smile on her face. "Why did you allow your hair to revert to its natural state under those braids? I saw you with an Afro the other day."

Of course, an Afro is feminist, too. God forbid.

"The hair didn't want to be pulled, preened, or subjected to chemicals. It is an organ and I did not want it damaged any further." My voice is matter-of-fact.

Hers, however, has that familiar scornful edge. "Most of our men like women with long hair."

African aunties and their obsession with long hair. Even if it is untidy and straggly and has mutated into something unrecognisable, if it is long, it is superior to the natural hair God gave us.

"Most of our men?" Obviously, that doesn't include Jimi, who seems to like me even though my hair wasn't in long artificial waves down to my waist when we met.

Mum interjects. "Gbemi, come and see something on

115

this Facebook. Is this not your daughter Dolapo with one young man in Dubai? She is half naked."

Aunty Gbemi smiles self-indulgently. "Anti Mi. That is a bikini. She and her fiancé are on a short holiday in Dubai... You know our young people. They are not like us."

"Hmm." My mum adjusts her glasses so she can see the picture further. "Can they not do all this stuff in a couple of months' time on the honeymoon?" She blinks as if she has seen something she wants to unsee. "Is Dolapo not in the church choir? Does her pastor know about this?"

"Anti Mi. It is now 2024. They are adults," says Aunty Gbemi smoothly.

Mum sips from her cup of hot water with a slice of lemon. She says it clears her system. She points at a picture on the phone. "This is one where he is kissing her like this. It is well o. I wonder whether there will be any honey left for the honeymoon."

"Kunle is a doctor, Anti Mi. He is a sensible boy. His mother loves Dolapo. She is coming over from the States for the wedding. She is so excited."

My mother purses her lips and resumes looking at the TV. "*Olorun a m'ojo ro*. It will be a glorious day."

Aunty Gbemi doesn't ask me about my hair after that. She changes the subject to the dress she is making as Mother of the Bride. Silver and pink with a train of its own. Her daughter is getting married to a doctor and it is going to be her day.

After Aunty Gbemi leaves, we watch *EastEnders* and then I do the dinner. Yam pottage and fresh fish. When we sit down to eat, I can see Mum's mind is far away and that her hand is shaking slightly as she pours some water into her glass.

I see my mum's fragility and mortality, and her hair, uncovered from her usual wig or head tie, is snowy white. It comes with being seventy-one, I suppose.

I have friends whose mums are no longer here. My heart is tied up and something sticks in my throat.

Mum sighs. "God will not fail me. God will honour you, *akobi mi*. I will dance down the aisle with you one day sha."

I smile. "Amin Mum." Then I do something I rarely do, I go to hug her.

Alarm flashes in my mother's eyes at the unexpected affection. "Are you okay?"

"Yes, Mum. I just wanted to hug you."

"Oh." She frowns. "Make sure you get your dress sorted out for the wedding. This time I want you to dress properly. You never know who you might meet there." She sniffs.

"At least the Thanksgiving was a great success, Mum. I really enjoyed the service." *Father, forgive my lies.*

"Really? I thought you had no time for my church. You said it was for old people that like singing hymns. Our church is not funky enough for you innit?"

I help myself to some food. "We had a bit of a problem getting back home. Ayo's car had a problem. If it wasn't for this nice chap from your church that helped us look at the engine, we would have been stranded."

"Our churchgoers are very helpful."

"Yes, he was. He sat at the back. Tall dark man with a beard. Smartly dressed. Going grey."

My mother shrugs. "There were so many people in church. How would I bloody know?"

"No worries."

I'd been hoping she could give me some info on Jimi.

"Hmm. Change the channel. It's time for *Emmerdale*."

After watching the first half, I pick up my bag and say my goodbyes.

My mother does not even look away from the TV. "I know who you are talking about now. The man in the suit with the pink tie."

"Yes."

"That is Jimi. Jimi Taylor. That boy is trouble."

"What do you mean? How do you know that?"

My mother's voice is equivocal. "Did he not grow up in our church? He is our Bishop's son and has given his parents – his father – so much worry and concern. Now he is back from his travels, we all hope he is going to settle down and be a responsible son."

I try to laugh it off. "Mum, how do you know he isn't responsible?"

She gestures at the TV. "I want to watch the rest of this episode without disturbance. You should start going home. I don't like you being out late."

On the bus home I sit staring out of the window, anxious about what Mum said. But still, I can't seem to get Jimi's smile out of my head.

Chapter Fourteen

A few days later, I decide to pop in to see Mum again. I'm just through the front door when I hear heated voices coming from the sitting room. It seems as if Mum and Aunty Gbemi are having an argument about wedding-preparation plans.

I stand transfixed in the hall, listening to their shrill voices. Aunty Gbemi's comes to the fore.

"You think you know it all eh. You look down at me because I'm a single parent, but look at me now! My daughter is getting married, and you cannot even be happy for me!"

Mum's voice is even and matter-of-fact. "I am not looking down on you, Gbemi. You know that your happiness is my happiness, and this is a great day for our family. I celebrate with you."

"My happiness is your happiness, eh? You did not think of that when we were young. You were the one that our parents carried like an egg, while I was just left like rubbish." Aunty Gbemi's voice holds so much resentment.

Mum is beginning to lose patience. "Gbemi, what brings all this stuff now? *Ki lo mu gbogbo eleyi wa* now?"

"You are the cause!" Aunty Gbemi bursts out. "How dare you be asking me why my daughter spends nights in her fiancé's house? So what? My daughter is marrying a whole big doctor when your daughter is still single at the big age of fifty!"

There is a painful silence before Mum speaks. Her voice slow and quiet. "Fine. Since you have said what has been sitting in your stomach – I have heard you. Are you feeling better now?"

Aunty Gbemi sighs. "Anti Mi. You are the person who makes me say these things. Your daughter is—"

"Don't you dare talk about my daughter," Mum snaps.

I push open the sitting-room door and they look up in fright. They have both clearly forgotten that I have a spare key and can let myself in – any time. I just stand there looking at them with no hint of the anger I feel reflected on my face. There is a mixture of guilt and shame heavy in the air between them, but I see no remorse on my aunt's face. Instead, she hisses in disgust, picks up her handbag, and walks out with her head high, slamming the door shut.

Daughter looks at mother and mother at daughter.

My voice is deadpan. "That was interesting."

Mum looks away. "Please do not start your own drama. The doctors say I need lots of peace in my life and my family do not seem to understand that. There is Gbemi accusing me of being jealous of her and her daughter..."

"Why would you be jealous of Aunty Gbemi?"

"How old are you again? Five or fifty? Why do you think she would say that, eh? Her daughter is half your age getting married to a doctor and you—"

"Enough!" The word is out of my mouth before I can stop it and Mum looks at me as though I have slapped her. I might as well have done. No Nigerian daughter speaks to her mother like that. Ever.

I swallow and say quietly. "You are ashamed of me."

Mum turns off the TV and stares at me. "Is everyone in this family trying to drive me crazy today! Why would you ask such a stupid question?"

Why do Nigerians love to answer questions with more questions, pray tell?

"When Kike went to Nigeria to get married, who was it who begged me not to come to spare myself the embarrassment from family members asking questions? You were the one that was embarrassed, Mum," I continue.

"So, you can read my mind now?"

I look at her for a long time and then shake my head. "So have you eaten?" That is what we do in our family when we want to change the subject and avert World War Three brewing. It usually works.

"I had breakfast and was going to cook some yam for dinner," she tells me.

I walk past her to the kitchen without a word and then I hear the TV. Mum is immersing herself in more family drama in another soap while the one we are both literally living in will no doubt continue for another episode, featuring Aunty Gbemi.

On the way home I think of my mother's sister. She is six years younger than my mother but always tries to tell Mum what to do.

I always sensed that Aunty Gbemi's resentment of Mum was down to some kind of childhood thing between them, but I could never get anything out of Mum. Now my suspicions have been proved right.

I have a memory of Aunt Gbemi sobbing as she sat on our old sofa, with Dolapo next to her and lots of suitcases, which filled up our small flat. It was a good job Dad was in Nigeria sorting out his new business at the time. That is what he'd told Mum, anyway. What we all believed. If he had been around, he would have bellowed, "What is all this town council load?"

My father had decided after almost twenty years of marriage that he wanted to start a business in Lagos. After much discussion and misgivings from my mum about leaving his family in London, Dad headed off with lots of hope and a large amount of money taken in equity on the house.

A year later he celebrated the birth of his son Oluwatomiwa. His new wife was almost half Mum's age.

"I need a son," he'd said, and that was it. His family in Lagos must have agreed with him, because according to the photo Aunty Gbemi saw, they were all there, bedecked in Aso Ebi and glowing smiles.

His younger sister, Mummy Lagos, as we used to call her when she'd come over and spend holidays with us in London, rang to speak to my mother.

"Congratulations, Ebun. We now have a prince. An heir for my brother."

My mother was silent. There was no need to say anything. She had been relegated to being the London Wife.

So, Aunty Gbemi and Dolapo took our bedroom, I had to sleep on the sofa and Kike slept in the big bed with Mum. I was in my early twenties then, so I asked myself two questions. One, why were my aunt and cousin sleeping in our bedroom? Two, why was Aunty Gbemi not married? The cardinal sin in my mum's book, which she hammered into my head on a regular basis as a teenager – *Any child that gets pregnant before marriage is a failure in life…*

Aunty Gbemi stayed with us for a long time, until she got a man friend to help her move her belongings out. She was happy and smiley because this uncle was going to marry her even though she was almost forty. She had already started calling the man *Oko mi*, so, like Mum, we all assumed it was a done deal that he was to be her husband.

The man was a waste man. It turned out he was already married with three kids back in Nigeria.

Life continued for us.

One day I came home and saw my mum arguing with two big men. There was a van parked outside with furniture, probably removed from other hapless households like ours. Our neighbours stood around staring or watched from the comfort of their windows. Behind the net curtains, of course. Their innate English politeness made them feel uncomfortable about letting us see them staring while the men had come to take our things away.

My mum shoved me and my little sister into the house and shut the door. I switched on the TV so Kike could watch her favourite programme, then I went to the windows and watched what was happening outside. I couldn't hear a thing but my mother was still talking to the two big men.

About half an hour later, the men left and Mum got us our dinner and then got on the phone, speaking in Yoruba, to Aunty Gbemi. I couldn't hear much but I did get the word "bailiffs" being mentioned several times in the conversation.

In the end, the matter of the bailiffs got sorted. Maybe Aunty Gbemi loaned Mum some money. I don't know. But "bailiff" became a swear word in our house.

Even when my father had been around, we were counting pennies and silver coins from the money jar, having a pay-as-you go meter installed in the house, wearing old uniforms, and not having them replaced. Coats and shoes from the second-hand shop, shopping for meat, chicken, veg, and fruit at the African market rather than Sainsburys or Tesco's. There was seldom money for swimming classes, cinema visits, or even the occasional pizza or ice-cream.

"We have to be careful how we spend money if we want to keep this house" was the mantra we had learned off by heart.

Almost twenty years later and my mum, Ebun Sodipo, had not only kept the house but by working hard paid off the mortgage my dad left her with. She had two jobs. One as a carer and the other as a cleaner in the evenings, when Aunty Gbemi would come round and stay with us. So we didn't have nice new clothes or go to Spain for holidays like our friends, or have money aside for treats and trips to Chessington Amusement Park, but we had a house, which Mum tried her best to make a home for us.

The phone calls from Dad became less frequent until they became negligible. Mum prayed herself hoarse for him to come back. Nightly prayer sessions with the church mummies in the sitting room, their noise echoing through the thin walls to our bedroom where we were trying to get some sleep. Eventually, she got a letter through the post. I was too young to realise that they were the divorce papers.

Then one day we heard Dad had passed.

I saw my mum throw herself on the floor and wail. Aunty Gbemi called the church aunties to come and comfort her.

My eyes were dry. I did try to conjure up some memories of the tall, bespectacled, ebullient man who used to buy us ice-creams and carry us around on his shoulders on visits to the park, but they were lifeless, lukewarm, and dim, shadows of what could have been.

Mummy Lagos rang, first to commiserate with Mum and then ask for his pension money to be sent to her.

Then Aunty Gbemi hissed in annoyance. Aunty Remi shook her head and clapped her hands.

I was so proud of Mum when she put the phone down while Mummy Lagos was still talking.

The Sunday before the op I decide I need some positive reinforcements. Church in the morning followed by a visit to my favourite aunty, Remi Adekoya. She is the aunty I never had, much nicer than my real aunt and definitely not a member of the Marriage Monitoring Aunties' Association.

I press the bell and am buzzed into the block of flats.

Aunty Remi has lived on the fifth floor of Seacole House for decades, and the lift is still grimy with dirt and streaks of stuff whose origin I dare not speculate on.

I remember coming here as while I was younger, full of angst about what was happening between my parents as they had their transcontinental arguments about their marriage. Aunty Remi provided comfort, often in the form of a meal. She would always make an extra plate of egg, chips, and sausage or rice and chicken despite her three ravenous boys, risking Mum's wrath for eating someone else's food outside her house.

Commandment No. 11 for the Nigerian Child. Never disgrace your parents by eating food offered by an aunty when visiting their house. Under pain of hunger, starvation, or certain death, do not even look as if you are going to accept that plate of tantalising rice and chicken, because when you get home your parents are going to make you wish you had never been born.

I come out of the lift with a sigh of relief and walk down the corridor, which looks deserted for this time of the day, and manage to avoid falling over the kid's bicycle helpfully placed in front of the door next to aunty's flat.

I knock on her door and smile as it opens and Aunty Remi envelops me in a big hug and welcomes me inside. Of average height, she is a grey-haired, generously proportioned, ebony-skinned lady. Her eyes light up with joy as she smiles at me.

"You remember my address today, eh?"

I curtsy in greeting. "Aunty, it's work o. I'm so sorry. I will try and come more often."

"Try harder. Come in and take off your coat? Have you eaten?"

I follow her into the sitting room that she calls her parlour and sit on the sofa, looking around at the pictures on the wall. The stories of Aunty's life. Innocent and happy as a kid in Nigeria. Wedding pictures with her late husband, school pictures with the boys, followed by wedding pictures with her looking regal in Aso Oke – and another picture with Mum and some other formidable ladies at some church gathering.

At least Mr Adekoya had treated Aunty well. He had been a good husband. He had been a true man of God. Like the Bishop. According to Mum.

Aunty Remi smiles. "I haven't seen you for a long time, so I told your mum to tell you to come and see me."

"I'm sorry, Aunty. It's work and stuff."

"*O ga o.* It is well. What will you eat?"

"I'm fine, Aunty, honestly. How have you been?"

"At my age, every day that God adds is a blessing."

"Yes, Aunty, but you look good."

"It is well. My sons are arranging for me to go private." She manoeuvred herself into her favourite chair which was smack bang in front of the TV. "It's quicker innit."

"Of course, Aunty."

"So how are you – how is work? Your mum told me about this new manager position in this big company."

"It is not such a big company but it's a prominent one. It's a great place to work." I realise Mum has not told her about my op and that is cool.

"I am happy for you. I know that God will cause you to

always excel. I tell people to celebrate all the accomplishments of their children."

"Try telling that to my mum. It is just marriage and children that are worthy of thanksgiving."

"No. It's not like that. Your mum is always very proud of all you do."

"Maybe Mum should be proud of *me* – not just about what I do."

She gives me a pat on the shoulder. "Of course she wants you to be married and settled – which good mother would not want that for their daughter? I join my prayer to hers for that – but I have told her not to let all the gossip and bad mind of people around her pull her down. I do not listen to all that nonsense. Sadly, our society is too much about shaming people. You divorce; you are a disgrace. Your children are not in university – disgrace. Your daughter is barren – disgrace. Your daughter is not married at a certain age – shame and disgrace. It is not fair."

I sigh. "Aunty, I even hate that word 'barren.' It's so sixteenth-century. I hate when I see these prayer lines of women queuing up to be prayed for and they all come out like lost souls. The husbands sit back. It is like it is the women's problem and not the men's. This is where I can't stand our culture."

"It is sad, my daughter. I agree. People that mock married women for not having children sometimes forget how it was like when they were trying to have children. The same women in our church – their mouth is the loudest when they have just become grandparents and they stop attending when their daughters are having problems or doing IVF. Look, I don't want us to lose hope. It's never too late for God."

"I wish I had your faith."

She hugs me. "When you get to be my age, you realise that life is not always as straightforward as we wish for. Not everyone will go to university at eighteen, graduate at twenty-one, get married at twenty-four and have kids by twenty-five. I prayed for a daughter of my own, and He gave me you to share with your mum."

"Aww thanks, Aunty."

"I have my three boys and I have wisely made all my daughter-in-laws my BFFs."

"Aunty! BFFs! Very millennial, Aunty!"

I envy the three young ladies having a mother-in-law so far removed from the typical Nigerian mother-in-law. I think of Bridget at work and her current trials and tribulations with her MIL and wonder why it is an unwritten code or rite of passage for so many Nigerian women to have troublesome mother- or sister-in-laws.

Aunty Remi gives me another little hug and moves off to the kitchen, humming a hymn as she does so.

I look around at the neat clean units and the vase with fresh flowers. Their fragrance fills the air.

"Roses, carnations, tulips, lilies, and dahlias. Who sent those?"

"Oh, just a friend?" she responds breezily, and I hear the sound of her filling the kettle with water.

"Oh."

Aunty Remi comes back into the parlour. "So, as I was saying, do not mind all those people that like mocking people who do not have what they think they should have by a certain time. They think they are God. There are things people do not have control over, like getting married, having boys, or being able to win the lottery and buy a big house in a nice area where there is no crime…"

I smile, knowing that it has always been her dream to leave Lewisham for somewhere like Richmond or Chelsea. I remembered how she and Mum used to take the buses to their cleaning jobs and look at the palatial residences and dream about raising their families in bigger houses in leafy spaces. "I pray your dream comes true one day, Aunty."

"Thanks, my daughter." She embraces me and I hold tight to her and feel a bit foolish because my cheeks are wet.

Aunty Remi smells of love and hope, vanilla essence and the good parts of my childhood that are worth holding onto, and there is a little part of me that wants to capture this moment, just in case I never see her again … because no op is ever 100 per cent risk-free, is it?

Chapter Fifteen

I sit in the corridor waiting for the nurse to come get me, and try to get used to the antiseptic smell and the brisk efficiency of the staff. Vicky and Sam have taken the time off work to be there with me and their presence is very reassuring. We have been asked to arrive several hours before the op is scheduled, to allow the staff to complete important tests.

Mum hasn't offered to come, and I didn't ask her. I did know that she had taken the day off to fast and pray for my surgery's success. Mum hates hospitals. To quote her: God is the healer – the doctors are just doing what He guides them to do. Better to pray instead of standing in cold hospital corridors and be incubating people's germs.

"I met a chap a few weeks ago." I exhale the information I have kept to myself for the past few weeks.

"You met a man?" Sam's blue eyes light up, transforming the slightly reflective mood we have all been in since we got to the hospital.

"Yep. At the Metro supermarket near work. Then again at my mother's church. He had a nice smile."

"Metro Man." Vicky grins. "The man who might have been a date?" she teases, recalling our conversation weeks ago. "So, it was definitely a date, then."

"Yeah."

Luckily, Sam doesn't look too put out that Vicky knew about Jimi already. Instead she lifts her chin heavenward. "Thank you, Lord!" she says.

We laugh, just as the nurse appears.

"Good morning, Miss Sodipo. I need to take you to the pre-op area."

I get up as fast as the fibroids percolating around in my body allow. "Okay, folks. This is it. We will catch up later."

Vicky gives me a nod and a smile. "God be with you, Sis."

Sam grabs me and bursts into tears.

"For goodness' sake, Sam, I'm not going off to war or something." I step back, a bit embarrassed, as I can feel the stares of the other patients and their families. Someone gives me a thumbs-up. With a smile at my friends, I follow the nurse to a cubicle.

I remove my clothing and earrings, putting them in the locker I have been given.

Lord, this is it.

Before I sign the paperwork, they take vital signs, do the nursing assessment, review my medications, and put the IV line in my hand... Lord be with me. Keep me safe. Basically, keep me alive.

Let this op be successful, O Lord. Amen.

I sign the paperwork.

I always fill out my forms with "Miss" because in some silly part of me I still feel that "Ms" is surrendering to never being married. A bit Miss Haversham-ish.

I open one eye and close it. In my head there are these figures in green with masks waiting for me outside the Space Station. It has to be the *Enterprise* because there are lights everywhere.

Where is Captain Kirk? Mr Spock? Scotty. Lt Uhura? Memories of early childhood on Friday nights flit in and out of my mind.

"Sade." Then, louder, "SADE!"

I let out a strange groan that seems to come from someone else's lips. "Yes." Awakening and reality are groggy and indescribably painful.

"Did you leave my womb intact?" I ask, as this has been my worry. That if my insides are too mashed up and I have lost too much blood they will have removed the whole womb. I had signed that in the paperwork before they operated.

Impostor, a mocking voice reminds me. I thought you career women didn't need a man, family or children...

Dr Bassey smiles. "Everything is still in there."

Thank God for this wonderful Nigerian doctor.

During our consultations Dr Bassey had given me a stern talking-to about procrastinating on the myomectomy and had given me a reality check, which had made me realise it was the safest option.

We had talked about this pre surgery and he seemed to

understand my desire to still have a womb at fifty. Unlike the English doctors, who had been so ready to go for a hysterectomy, this skilled Nigerian surgeon has a track record of removing the offending unwanted visitors and leaving the womb alone.

"There is still a small chance that you could have a child through IVF," he'd advised.

"That sounds great, to have a chance – no matter how slight."

He had shaken his head. "Since you wanted children, why didn't you get a donor?"

I'd just nodded, feeling stupid because what would I say? Everything I had ever been taught in my Christian life made me feel this would be an admission of my lack of faith in God.

Right now he is smiling and I nod and close my eyes as they wheel me back to recovery.

———

It is the third day after the operation. Or maybe the fourth or fifth.

I don't remember.

I am just lying here feeling as if someone has cut me in half. The pain in my midriff has been intensifying, despite all the painkillers and injections. Though the catheter is doing its work somehow.

Kike is here. God bless her.

"You've been sleeping for some time. The boys wanted to come but I told them you need your rest," she said quietly.

I nod.

The nurse comes in and looks at the notes in front of her. "Myomectomy. Two days ago. We will have to get you up and walking, you know."

The first thing I do is think about the catheter under my sheets. My oily face and my hair standing up in six plaits – the grey unforgivingly visible without the extensions I usually put in – seem like lesser worries.

I grab the covers around me. "You don't understand. I'm in bloody agony here. I feel as if my insides are out for the world to see. I can't walk anywhere!"

The nurse nods. "Of course, it's not going to be easy … but it's part of your care plan, and working with a physiotherapist is something that is essential to getting you back out there, enjoying your life."

I want to say something, but the firm look in her eyes behind the polite smile makes me realise that she is not going to budge.

"I will give you some time to get yourself ready and will come back in ten. If you could be sitting on your bed by the time I come back that would be great."

I grunt.

She smiles. "That's fine, then." She heads to the door and then adds, "Don't try taking out the catheter. We can do the exercises with it in place."

I close my eyes as she leaves the room, grab the pillow, and roll my face into it.

"You're doing fine, Sis," says Kike. "Soon you'll be home getting better."

As if I hadn't seen enough shame, I now have to take myself – catheter in place, hair all messed up, feeling awful because I haven't been allowed to bathe, because of the stitches across my abdomen – for exercises with the physiotherapist.

I groan, sit up, and my skin tightens around the area of the stitches under my bandage with a searing flash of pain. Then my phone makes a noise, and I realise that the world is still spinning, still toiling, while I have zoned out for a few days.

Kike stands up and hands me the phone. "You got a message." She smiles. "Guess who?"

"Probably Mum."

"Mum was here yesterday. She was crying, you know. You were sleeping."

I'm too shocked about Mum crying to ask about the text. "Mum was crying?"

Kike nods. "The doctors assured her everything was going to be okay."

The last time Mum really cried was when she heard Dad had died. That was over twenty years ago. "Is she okay?"

"Mum is fine. She said she would call you later today to see how you are." She leans forward to look at my phone. "You got a text from Metro Man. Did you tell him about your op?"

Even though I am in pain, the reality of a real-life flesh-and-blood chap caring about me enough to get in contact after this operation makes my heart flip.

"Well, yes. But because he is a client, I needed him to know that I would be out of commission for a while."

Kike smirks, and thankfully the nurse enters and reminds Kike that visiting time will be over in five minutes.

I am saved from further interrogation by my sister, who still can't resist a parting shot.

"I'll leave you to read his lovey-dovey text," she says, with a wink.

"Kike…" I sigh, partly because I'm tired, though.

"*Mr Lover lover*…" She smiles. "I'm telling Mummy."

"Don't you dare!"

She stands up, gives me a gentle hug, and lets herself out.

I check the phone again.

There are ten messages. Two from my mum, the other two from Kike, one from Sam, one from Vicky, and the other three from Metro Man.

Three texts!

MAY 16 12.00 P.M.

> Hi Sade just saying hi and hoping it all went well. Do take care. You're in great hands in the NHS. Best Jimi.

MAY 16 5 P.M.

> Hi Sade hope you are keeping well. Not sure if you've had the op and have no way of phoning anyone to check on you. Wishing you the best. Jimi.

MAY 17 7 A.M.

> Hi Sade. Hope you're well. Probably recuperating now. Please when you get this message send me a text to let me know you're ok. Best x Jimi.

Be still my beating heart. I pick up the phone and type.

Hi Jimi. Op was a success and feeling much better already but still in hospital. Thanks so much for checking. Speak later. Best Sade.

His response comes about ten minutes later.

Great news. My dad's prayers worked! Looking fwd to catching up when you're up to it. Best Jimi xx

Thanks Jimi. Best Sade.

I put down my phone and close my eyes. *Please don't be an undercover Red flag RAG rating person, Jimi. Don't go breaking my heart. Abeg.*

The next day, Sam and Vicky come to see me. The nurse has allowed me a bath and helped me get to the bathroom and put on a new pair of pyjamas. She even helped tidy my hair into two big plaits.

Vicky gives me a big hug while Sam arranges the contents of the bag she brought with her on my side table. A large bottle of Lucozade, grapes, bananas, tangerines, and a copy of the latest Dorothy Koomson book.

"Thank God, Sis. Let's pour a glass and drink to new beginnings."

"You look great."

"Thanks for coming, guys. It's nice having you here. The great news is that they left my womb intact."

Vicky's brow knits together. "That is great. But the really good news is that you are alive and well. The priority is you."

Sam hands round glasses of Lucozade. "Get that down you."

"Thanks. Viva Forever," I toast, and we clink our glasses together.

I take a sip just as the door opens to admit a huge bouquet of flowers followed by my mum. Colourful English roses, carnations, orchids, lilies. The sweet delicate smell filters through the room.

"Wow," I say. "They're beautiful."

Everyone's mouth drops open.

Mum lays the bouquet on my bed. "Jimi Taylor left this at my house this morning. He got my address from the Bishop and asked if I could give them you on his behalf – he wanted to come but I told him you needed rest."

"Jimi Taylor!" Sam and Vicky exchange looks. "Your new man loves a big gesture, ay?' says Sam.

Chapter Sixteen

I have been staying with Vicky for two weeks since the op. While she is at work, I usually lie on the sofa with a blanket drinking soup and watching *Loose Women* and think about my life. I'm glad that I'm here, in Vicky's sensible and motherly good hands, but the flipside has been that while I am trying to recuperate, I am also on the receiving end of her concerns about my "relationship" with Jimi.

Today, after she comes back from work, she sits next to me on the sofa, her gentle brown eyes full of worry.

"Do you know what you're doing, Sis, with this new chap?"

"Nothing has happened so far, Vicky…"

"Listen. I've been your friend for how many years now – almost fifteen – and we've been through each other's make-ups and break-ups. I just don't want you to get hurt. Take it slow. Find out more about this guy before you decide to… I mean, does he go to church? Does he believe?"

I close my eyes. "I haven't fallen for him, Vicky. I mean I barely know him."

Which is true. And, despite Jimi's dad being the pastor, going by his own words, he really isn't a church person. So we don't have that in common. I don't know whether he likes old movies or trips to museums and historical buildings. And does he hate the pervasive elements of Nigerian culture like I do? All I know is that he is a charming, friendly chap with a caring personality, whose smile makes me go warm all over and my heart beat faster. Okay, these are both symptoms of perimenopause, but I have to be honest with myself, Jimi Taylor has managed to imprint himself into my heart, despite my firm attempts to dislodge him.

"Okay, I'm just looking out for you." Vicky gives me a brief hug and gets up to go to the kitchen.

That's the difference between my two best friends. Vicky wants to know whether Jimi has a relationship with the Lord, while Sam is just happy that I am in a relationship, or what she thinks is a relationship anyway. Sam mostly wants to know whether we have kissed yet.

A week or so later and I am back in my own house, a little more mobile and able to look after myself.

No one can ever prepare you for post-op life, where one day seems to blend seamlessly into the other.

I agree with my director at work that I'll work from home on light duties when I come back to my job. We have a huge project coming with one of the galleries in the city, all about regeneration and increasing the buoyancy of the high street, and I want to be able to do some research so that when I return I am prepared.

Apart from work and reading more books from Buchi Emecheta, Frances Mensa Williams, and Dorothy Koomson, to stop myself from snapping I decide to get a notebook and title it *Suggestions for Singles Ministry*, which I will email to Pastor Keith.

1. Could we think of a change of name from Successful Singles?
2. Could we think of well-researched options for getting more men involved in church? Football team, business/career conferences and events, speed dating events, walks in the park? More events aimed at giving singles a chance to mingle, not just pray together?
3. And possibly a social media page on Facebook where singles can chat?

I'm pleased that I am helping singles find a life partner, which will stop them from being frustrated with themselves, their family and possibly their cat or dog. The limitless joy at Finding the One will also project into their work life and make them more productive, which in turn will feed into them becoming happier law-abiding citizens.

Maybe one day I might get an OBE for services to humanity for this. I can see myself in front of the King, kneeling as the sword touches my shoulder.

I can also see my mum in the background shaking her head.

Is this going to find you husband?

Anyway.

I have been given a second chance at life. I compose another list.

Things to stop stressing over
(or guilt tripping myself over at fifty)

1. Guilt about no longer trying to please Mum.
2. Still wanting children, even though I know it is just unrealistic at fifty.
3. Dating toxic misogynists and narcissists for longer than I should have.
4. Being sarky to members of the Marriage Monitoring Aunties' Association in their natural habitats of church and Nigerian weddings, naming ceremonies and funerals. This includes Aunty Gbemi, the Chairman, and the Board members – her two friends Aunty Ify and Aunty Titi – followed by Aunty Sarah, Aunty Bunmi (Mum's relative from Manchester), and Mrs Shobowale, to mention a few who think they are stakeholders in my personal business.
5. Enjoying my own company and being occasionally anti-social.
6. In the past being attracted to tall guys who are 6ft plus and work in finance and have trust funds, without vetting them first.
7. Being attracted to Jimi without finding out whether he shares a love of the things that mean so much to me.

8. Feeling superior to those who don't know what they want to do in life and in their career.
9. Crying after watching *Me Before You*.
10. Eating too many sweets.

A week after I've moved back home, Jimi rings and insists that he must get me back into the outside world again. Apparently, I have to exercise!

"What do you do all day?" he queries sternly. I feel immediately like one of his physio clients.

"I sleep."

"Sleep is good," he says. "You need rest. But—"

"When I'm not working on a few things," I interject. "Otherwise, I watch TV, eat…"

"I'm coming for you on Saturday. We are going to go for a little walk in the park, work those muscles."

"Look, I can't walk that much. I'm just letting you know."

"Trust me," he says, softly. "I'll be gentle with you."

I blush a hundred times under my dark skin. It wasn't exactly *Bridgerton*-worthy but it was enough to make me swoon a little in my own desire.

After Jimi rings off, I just sit there, trying to will my mind to go blank, but it won't.

It's like every time I try and create some level of professional distance with Jimi, he charms his way even deeper into my defences – my very flimsy defences – because when it comes down to it, I don't want to chase him off.

He probably works with female clients like me on a regular basis, so who better to get me back to fitness again than someone who knows everything about working with muscles and tendons?

As for my heart, well, God will always be there to pick up the pieces just in case this doesn't work – as He always is.

The following Saturday, Jimi arrives and informs me that we are going to Greenwich, with the promise of a lovely breakfast in a nearby café if I make good progress.

He is wearing a blue T-shirt and grey sweatpants and I'm wearing my navy blue Lakers T-shirt and matching jeans joggers with my sports shoes.

He bends to brush my cheek with his lips, and I catch his scent again. Clean, strong and masculine. "Good to see you."

"Great to see you as well. So I'm ready. Early mobilisation, as you said…"

Jimi continues. "Yep, it's what I tell my patients. We try and encourage them to get back on their feet with gentle activities like walking, as soon as recovery after surgery allows it. So, let's have a gentle walk."

He helps me walk to his waiting car and I get in. Then all of a sudden I feel daunted, my muscles as soft as jelly. Jimi, in the driver's seat, turns and examines my face and the anxiety that must be there in my expression.

"You can do it, Sade. I know you can," he says warmly. "You strike me as someone who has gone through a few things in life…" His eyes are kind and tender. "You aren't going to let anything beat you."

"Okay," I say. I am determined to try, and Jimi smiles as he starts the engine and we drive to Greenwich.

We arrive at the park and I let out a deep sigh, willing myself to move one leg and then the other outside the car, and Jimi helps me rise, our fingers brushing against each other. Our eyes meet.

"You okay?" His voice is even huskier than I remembered.

"Y-yeah…" My voice is as unsteady as my legs, and I don't know whether my legs are wobbly due to my lack of exercise or because of the effect of standing this close to him, drowning in those sexy dark brown eyes. The morning air is crisp, and I can't stop myself shivering slightly.

He reaches past me, picks up my flowery scarf, and passes it to me.

"Thanks." I tie it around my neck.

"Okay." His voice is back to being brisk and businesslike. "Today," he says, "we'll take our first walk. You can lean on me."

We move slowly, the breeze rustling through the trees, my steps tentative, and he slows to wait for me. Every now and then, I stop and get some rest until the sun peeks through the leaves, and as it becomes warmer I can hear my own laughter echoing with his as we shuffle along. He patiently helps me walk at a slow pace around a small area of the park, my body still sore from the stitches in my abdomen, and encourages me to keep at it. His hand rests on my back as he assists me, his eyes full of compassion and his tone patient yet determined when I occasionally grumble in pain.

Kindness, compassion, and a handsome chap with a greying beard – I am a sucker for that anytime.

Before I know it, an hour and a half has passed.

"Right," says Jimi. "Let's go and get something to eat. You deserve it."

We end up at a small restaurant facing the park and Jimi leans back and looks at me.

"You did really good."

I sip my green tea, trying to feel virtuous but failing because when faced with Jimi, I don't feel very virtuous. "Shall I expect a gold star, sir?"

He picks up his sandwich and bites into it. "Nah … it's early days. I only give gold stars to my most consistent clients or patients."

"Ah…" I toy with my fruit yoghurt, trying to ignore his teasing glance.

"Yep, this has got to be consistent. I will email you a list of exercises to do – breathing, walking … maybe, later, some gentle cycling. It is important that you try and walk every day – even if it's from your sofa to the kitchen – to help you get back to normal quicker."

"You sound like the physio at the hospital."

"Do I sound that professional?"

"Sometimes."

"Good, because if I behave like a friend," he points out, "you will give me a look out of those big, beautiful eyes of yours and start slacking, and we can't have that. We need to get you out of the house back to work so you can get cracking on my event!"

"So is that what we are then ... friends?"

His eyes narrow. "Ah ... she wants me to define things after friend-zoning me for the past few weeks..."

"Well," I bristle. "Just because we're going to be working together... I just wanted to—"

"Sade," he interjects, gently resting a hand on mine. "Let's not try and analyse things at this point. It's Saturday morning and usually I'm in bed – alone, might I add," he says, his eyes never leaving mine, "sleeping off a hard fifty-five-hour week, and yet I'm here with you at eleven on a crisp spring Saturday morning. Exercising. Surely that should tell you something about how I feel about you."

"Er ... okay."

He laughs, his voice bubbling with amusement. "What kind of a dry response is that to me laying my heart bare to you here?"

Oh, God. It's too early for me to fall this hard for him. There is so much I still don't know. So I smile and touch his hand and thrill at the warm look in his eyes. "I really appreciate you coming out like this for me – and for showing how much you care."

"Is that the revised standard version of your response?" he says dryly.

"Spoken like a true pastor's kid." I grin and offer him the plate with my sandwich. "This is the King James Version. Would thou liketh a BLT sandwich? The last one. So thou can understand the favour and regard with which I holdest thou for thou to know that I must discerneth your intentions before I giveth thou my response."

Jimi rocks backwards with his hand on his heart as if in pain. "My lady speaketh now or I shall forever hold my peace and forsake thee and proceed back to Greenwich with haste with a heart broken – which I will lay to your charge."

I try and make my voice serious. "Alas, kind sir. I can give you no further word on this, for I have spoken all my heart and therefore to Greenwich thou must go. Just maketh sure that thou—" I am laughing now and he is laughing, as well "—transport me safely back to Bow where I will retire..."

"Back to your lonely abode," he finishes.

"I'm not lonely, I have lots of friends," I say defensively.

"Female friends." He reflects. "Why do my female friends complain that they aren't dating – when all they do is hang out with other females?"

"Is that some kind of a dig?"

"Only kidding... Look, Sade, I get you. I like you ... I like you a lot. And I'm confident enough to know that you like me, too – even if it's just a little..."

Tongue-tied, I nod and our eyes meet.

"So ... let's take this slow and get to know each other. Is that okay?"

"Sounds good," I say and smile.

Risk analysis is amber – a low level of risk for now. I long for a green rating. Eternal optimist that I am.

Chapter Seventeen

The latest news is bittersweet.

The fibroids removed have been found to be non-cancerous, which is the most important thing. But I have now officially entered menopause. No more monthly visitor. I now begin the first tentative steps into the rest of my life.

I stare at myself in the mirror and apply some foundation to my face, wondering whether I look my age. Yesterday I got on the train home and squeezed myself in between the harassed and impatient passengers, found a standing spot, and then did a quick check to make sure that my laptop and handbag were still attached to my person, and looked up to meet the friendly smile of a young lady sitting in front of me, and I thought to myself, *No... I'm not that old. I don't need a seat. You don't have to get up for me...*

But "You look as if you need a seat," she said, getting to her feet.

That's my line. That's what I say to the older women I

see standing on trains during rush hour, laden with shopping, family business, and the cares of life.

But the fact was, I was exhausted. I really wanted to sit down.

"Thank you so much." I accepted the seat and put my laptop on my knees, feeling my aching midriff and strained feet thanking me. The scar running across my abdomen was healing nicely, but it still hurt when I stood for too long. Yet as the train rumbled on, my mind was thinking – just how old did I look?

Now, staring at myself in the mirror, I realise that something in me still clings to being seen as young, not past it; still relevant despite the grey strands on my head accumulated over the seasons of life that have passed like currents in a rapidly moving sea.

Inside, I feel as young as I did in my twenties. I still have the same dreams, same unrealistic expectations about finding The One. I still want someone to come into my life and be excited about my passions and ambitions. I still want to live outside London one day and I still love eating Haribo sweets.

Not that much has changed physically, apart from greying hair and a little more curve on my once boyish frame, but mentally I am much more cynical – I have become more sarcastic with age, so I am told. I have acquired an MA, considered a PhD but decided against it, become a homeowner, still haven't passed my driving test. I am still single. Yes, and I still love old school R&B, old movies, and good food.

Now my periods have gone, along with the racking pain and monthly stress, but even though they were a pain in the behind, as long as they kept coming I still had a fraction of a hope that one day I would be able to reproduce a little bit of myself on the face of this earth.

Now I am faced with reality.

When a woman loses a baby people give sympathy and are mostly understanding, but who gives any support to the woman who has lost the chance to ever have her own child naturally? Okay, I know there are other ways of having a child nowadays, but maybe I am too traditional for my own good. I want to have a baby in the same way my sister and mum and all the women before them had their children.

I mourn when I watch happy families on TV, when I see my lovely nephews or parents with their kids at the supermarket or on the school run. I mourn by eating lots of the chocolate my colleagues sent while I was recuperating and by binge watching boxsets of romcoms. I mourn while I am back at work, planning, strategising, project-managing, and "getting on with life."

I finish off my makeup and put on my new outfit. Tonight is Dolapo's engagement party at some club in the city. Maybe that is what is bringing on the impostor syndrome thoughts. I really don't want to go, but Mum pointed out that it would be read in the wrong context – basically Aunty Gbemi would say this is the evidence that we are jealous of her daughter because she is marrying a doctor – while I remain stubbornly single, defying all the prayers everyone is making on my behalf. I am happy for Dolapo, but I can do without the constant disapproval.

I have decided to wear my deep plum flared jump suit because I have braids with burgundy highlights. I team it with my open-toed black high heels and am glad that I had treated myself to a pedicure and had my hair freshly braided with a hint of the same Burgundy Mystery Shade that I add to my lips. I pout like one of the Kardashians at the mirror and try to look enigmatic and wonder what Jimi might say if he saw me looking this glamorous. Should I have invited him tonight as a plus one?

Just to see their faces.

Especially Aunty Gbemi's.

The Central in Hoxton is one of the best wine bars in the city, according to Sam. I'm not really an expert on wine, let alone wine bars, as I have been teetotal since as a seven-year-old I tried some of my dad's beer and spat it out in disgust.

It boasts a young chef who was a *MasterChef* runner-up some time back, and specialities such as deep-fried cheese wontons and dipping sauces followed by a cocktail of seafood tossed with fragrant rice. Or sizeable pork belly slabs, with thrice-fried chips. The sweets are good too – mango and passion fruit ice-cream and fresh fruit, or apple and cinnamon crumble and rum ice-cream. I can feel my tastebuds salivating already.

For the second time today I feel a sense of gratitude for life, health, the love of friends and family, despite the fact that Mum rang and prayed wonderful prayers over the phone last week and spoiled it at the end by saying, "*O ni waye asan.*" Basically, I would not come to this world for nothing.

So not being married meant that I had failed my

purpose of coming to this world as a woman in the eyes of some?

I enter the club and peer through the crowds, trying to find Dolapo's party. The man at the door leans forward to hear me squeak out my request.

"Dolapo's party," I repeat, slightly louder this time.

"Okay. Go ahead to the far left and take the stairs." He points to the steps that lead through two floors to the roof.

The engagement party is set in a chic rooftop garden, decorated with twinkling fairy lights, balloons, and lush greenery. The air is filled with laughter and the clinking of glasses as Dolapo's friends gather to celebrate their friend's special moment. Music blares from the speakers and the queue at the bar seems to stretch to the other side of the rooftop.

My cousin's girlfriends are everywhere – in short dresses, long weaves, and cleavage, battling for space as they jostle to take one selfie after another, capturing memories. There are a few young men as well, alternating between looking suave or just plain overwhelmed by the number of women vying for their attention.

I'm genuinely pleased for Dolapo, but feel thirty years out of place. They are probably wondering who let someone's mum into the party.

I scan the crowd for a friendly face or someone – anyone – I know to make small talk with and the next few hours more bearable. Relief kicks in as I spot Kike and wave frantically in her direction.

Then I hear a scream and Dolapo flings herself at me. She pulls up her sparkly blue dress to cover her cleavage and then pulls it down to cover her upper thighs.

"Sade, so nice to see you!"

"Thanks. Great to see you." I smile and give her a warm hug.

"Every time I see you Aunty Sade I have to remember that you're fifty!" Dolapo remarks.

I shoot Kike a glance and her response is to shake her head helplessly.

"Great to see you, Dolapo."

"Loving the plum colour, babes." Kike gives me a hug. "The braids are lovely, too. You are really looking nice." She gives a little shimmy. "I'm looking forward to boogieing down tonight."

I relent. "Well, okay, then. As long as we aren't dancing around our handbags singing, 'I Will Survive', I can manage anything."

"'I Will Survive'?" Dolapo creases her brow as if in deep thought.

I can't resist. "It's an old song by a lady called Gloria Gaynor."

Dolapo looks bored. "Like during the war or something?"

"Hang on a bit." Kike laughs. "A bit more recent ... like the eighties."

"I was born in the late nineties." Dolapo's perfectly chiselled eyebrows knit in confusion.

"The song was the seventies, actually," I add.

"Oh. Silly me. You would know, wouldn't you." Dolapo taps her forehead as if searching for something and as she does so, her cleavage almost falls out. "OK, then. What about some drill music? I can check with the MC?"

"Of course," I lie.

Then suddenly someone starts playing Stevie Wonder's "Isn't She Lovely."

"Oh, that's nice. Who's singing it?" Dolapo wants to know.

"Stevie Wonder."

Dolapo is lost. "Stevie who?"

I smile again. This time it's kinder. "Don't worry yourself. Just another old man that sang a song after the Second World War. Ask your mum. She might know him."

"My mum only likes Yoruba music that is loud. Especially at parties."

Then a couple of young ladies come up and take her away in a flurry of giggles and excitement about what the night still holds in store.

Kike turns to me. "Why haven't you been picking up my calls?

"Just been busy, Sis."

"You are never too busy to pick up my calls."

"Oh, please, Kike, let's not start."

"I knew it. There's something about you. I mean look at you. A few months away from fifty and you're practically blooming."

"Well, at least we can rule out pregnancy."

"Don't change the subject. It's Jimi, isn't it. You've only gone and fallen for him, haven't you?"

"Don't be silly. You're as bad as Vicky and Sam. He's just a client, that's all."

Then Kike's mouth drops open and I turn round, following her gaze.

It's Jimi Taylor, looking effortlessly debonair in jeans with some African print shirt that shows off his physique, toned from regular workouts. The Adire shirt drapes his form, its indigo colour and patterns contrasting with the classic denim of his jeans. He navigates the room with easy confidence, his smile reaching his eyes and lighting up his face when he spots me trying not to look too pleased to see him, while my sister stands there with a silly big grin on her face.

Chapter Eighteen

"We really have to stop meeting like this," Jimi whispers as his lips brush against my cheek.

I straighten up. Of all the clubs in all the towns in all the world, he walks into mine.

"It's my cousin's engagement party. I didn't know you knew her?" I whisper back.

He shakes his head. "I don't. I'm a colleague of her fiancé's. Kunle. He is one of our residents ... and why are we whispering?"

"Er, hello," Kike interjects into our silent observation of each other. "Nice to see you again," she adds warmly to Jimi.

He shakes her hand. "Hi, Kike. How is the family?"

"Ayo is with the children today, but they are all fine. Thanks again for how you helped that day."

"*Ko tope.* It's nothing. I just happened to be there."

I watch as he and Kike talk and then Dr Kunle, Dolapo's fiancé, walks up and welcomes him warmly.

"So glad you could come, sir."

I notice Kunle's subtle implication of respect for his older colleague, and the fact that Dolapo is giving them both pointed glances means that his invite wasn't just serendipity – he has been invited because I am. Even my extended family seem to be giving this the thumbs-up.

Kike's smile broadens. "I have been told you work as a physiotherapist."

"Yes. Currently I'm working as a locum, so that keeps me busy moving around between hospitals. But I'm looking for something more permanent, somewhere to settle down…"

Kike's smile widens. "Settle down … of course…"

There is a long pause during which little sis pointedly looks at me as if to say, *Talk now. Say something because Imma leave you guys to it. I'm hungry.*

She waves and takes her leave. "Well, I mustn't hold you guys up. I will go and get my food and let you finish your conversation."

Dolapo's fiancé looks at me. "Hope you don't mind – there are some people I need to introduce Jimi to…?"

"Of course." I excuse myself and leave them to mingle, and throughout the night I dance and make conversation with other guests, but I'm constantly aware of Jimi's presence, which adds a vibrant energy to the party. I catch him sharing stories that make guests laugh, offering toasts that touch hearts. I watch him interact with my family and friends, and see him in a different light – as a man respected and valued by those I care about.

I am talking to another guest when I see him approach and he greets us both.

"So sorry to disturb but could I have a word with this young lady…"

The guest smiles and moves off.

"Young lady, indeed." I laugh.

He smiles. "You look great, Sade. I've been checking you out all night."

I blink. "You've been busy chatting to everyone else – don't tell me you had time to—"

"I was making conversation, because that's what you do."

"Of course."

He glances around him. "Most of the people here are half our age. My son would fit in perfectly."

"Your—?" I hide my shock, and quickly recalibrate. Of course he has a son. Hopefully he is a single parent, and—

He looks at me, instantly reading my thoughts. "I've been married before."

"Ah." I smile. I can't judge him being divorced. Not with the state of the marriages in my family.

"Come on. Let's get some drinks and food. Then we can find a quieter place to talk," he suggests and I relax.

"Sounds good."

He takes me over to the other side of the roof, which is quieter. There are a few chairs and tables used for private dining and hardly anyone about.

We sit on the balcony and can see the city sprawled out before us – people, cars, and their lives, loves, and problems – like little dots.

"I haven't told you much about me – but I want to," he begins. "When I busted my leg and couldn't get back in the league I kind of went off the rails. Broke my parents' hearts.

Almost got done by the Old Bill. Then I decided to leave home – went travelling around the Far East to kind of straighten myself out. I was in Thailand when my mum died and that really made me hit the self-destruct button."

"Sorry to hear about your mum."

He sighs. "I didn't come home. I can't forgive myself for that – and my dad, for all his position as a bishop, hasn't forgiven me either. I know my brother hasn't. I wasn't in a fit state and I felt it would be disrespectful showing up like that to her funeral. I was involved in all kinds of stuff, drink, drugs, you name it." He sighs and looks at me through eyes that could melt me. "This is the fourth or fifth time I'm meeting you and I'm pouring out my life history to you. I'm sorry. That's crazy?"

"Life is crazy sometimes," I tell him. "And I don't mind listening. If it helps."

"Thanks, Sade. It does help, talking through things."

"Tell me more," I say.

"Are you sure? I don't want to fill your time with my boring history."

"It's not boring. And I don't mind." I lift an eyebrow to lighten the mood.

"Okay, then." He smiles. "So, I was young, in my mid-twenties, and I was in love. I thought love would be enough and so did Karline – my ex-wife. We met while I was in my early 'prodigal' days, and we had lots of fun together, backpacking round the world – Thailand, to be precise – partying, drinks and, you know – I won't bore you with all the rest. Then she fell pregnant and I wanted to do the right thing. So we went back to San Francisco and tried to be grown-ups."

"Tried to be?"

He shakes his head. "I was immature, selfish, and couldn't really be the man she needed, nor the father my son Alex needed. We would have these rows and say the craziest things to each other. Karline's parents were not exactly overjoyed about the marriage, but their negative input wasn't any more contributory to the end of the marriage than the fact that we just had this knack of bringing out the worst in each other. A few years and a divorce later, and I was backpacking again – but this time in Brazil. The country of my hero, Pele. And the rest you know... I was lucky to meet Cyril out there. He was volunteering as a teacher and one day he asked me what my plans were. I just looked at him and said, 'What plans?'" Jimi pauses. "Sometimes life forces you to take a step forward. I was stone cold sober, you know, and reality hit that I was thirty, thinking that I was a rolling stone, and that I needed to get a profession. Be the kind of man that my son could look up to.

"I had always had an interest in sports rehabilitation, which came out of the injury – my damaged knee – I'd had when I was a player and I didn't get the kind of support I needed. That journey I took before I decided to go back to university again and train to become a physiotherapist made me realise what was needed. I loved Brazil and wasn't keen on coming back to London, but six years ago, after working in Brazil with street kids and ex-offenders, I made the decision to set up football academies and give young talent vital emotional and physical support."

"That's amazing," I say, impressed. "What about spiritual support?"

He smiles. "What about it?"

"Don't you think that they might need faith to pull all this together? Who provides the pastoral support?"

Jimi laughs, his shoulders heaving gently. I watch him until he stops.

"You're one of those, aren't you?"

"One of what?"

"One of the Holy Rollers."

"Are you saying I'm a Bible basher?"

He shakes his head. "Don't mind me. I wouldn't put it that way." He wrinkles his nose. "Okay, I might have said but I don't go to church myself. Not on a regular basis. I go to see my dad now and then – like the day you came to St Thomas's. But to imagine going on a regular basis would be bloody torture."

"I take it you are not a fan."

He leans back. "Where do I start? Why would I need to go to church? It's a construct set up by man to be able to tell his congregants – mostly women – how to live their lives. I know you may think that sounds like something out of Philosophy 101 or the Karl Marx handbook but I no longer believe in man-made religion. Sorry."

"Christianity isn't a religion."

"Really? So what is it?"

"It's a relationship between God and man."

The silence from the man next to me tells me all I need to know.

He sighs. "The last thing I want to do on a day like this is debate religion, politics, or the meaning of life."

"Oh, so you have special days for debating, then?"

He laughs again. A sound that started deep in his belly

and explodes from his throat. Despite our difference of opinion, it has been a long time since I have heard a man laugh like that, totally at ease with himself and the world, and it sounds good.

This is a man who is comfortable in his skin. Who has put the work in to get to that place. A place I have spent so long trying to reach myself.

"I like you, Sade Sodipo. I think we are going to be friends," he says.

"I hope so." I pause. "But there's something about me that I need you to know straight up."

"Go ahead."

"That my faith is very important to me. You don't have to believe what I believe but it's helped me get through a lot of crap in my life."

He nods and smiles. "Of course. I'm sorry. I shouldn't have sounded off like that," he says, running a hand over his head.

"That's okay, and thank you."

"So, we good?"

I allow my lips to relax into a smile. "We good."

"Anyway, enough of me… Tell me about you."

Me. I hesitate for a minute. "I like to make things happen. I used to be a dreamer but I soon realised the world doesn't have time for dreamers."

"That's funny. I used to be a dreamer, too," he admits.

"I like processes. I like to make sure things run smoothly. I hate it when things that should be taken care of are ignored. I gave my pastor advice recently. I think I created more work for him and probably for myself."

"How so?"

"We have this singles group in church that's mostly women. The few single men avoid it like a plague. I was trying to make some suggestions to get some men in."

Jimi smiles. "Ah. The perennial quest to get men in the church."

"Yeah. You're a man ... give me some advice."

He laughs, his deep voice pleasant to my ears. "Hear her! 'You're a man ... give me some advice'!"

"That didn't come out right, did it?"

"What can I say? Men can't be bothered to go to church. It's full of women who are pumped full of a philosophy and fairytales about finding a happy ever after with 'The One.' Who are waiting for a Prince. And when he shows up, a bit worse for wear, with a few knocks here and there that life has thrown his way, on a three-legged donkey instead of a horse, they behave as if life has cheated them. Life isn't a Disney movie."

"Hey, you're generalising," I challenge.

"Okay, *some* women want perfection. Men can only give reality. Christianity perpetuates this myth of being perfect so..." He looks at me. "You look like I did when I found out that Bambi's mum died."

"Oh, come off it."

"Don't get me wrong – I know Kunle is crazy about your cousin and they look like a lovely couple and with any luck they will have a fantastic marriage but ... so many of these weddings are just formality. The family are more excited about the chance to dress up and parade themselves. The bride and groom are just going through the motions."

"And I thought I was cynical."

Jimi's smile is a bit wry. "Sorry to burst any romantic illusions you might have."

I shrug. "Nothing wrong with believing in love and happily ever after."

There is a slight sadness in his eyes. "I did once. If I ever do this again – and that's a big *ever* – it will have to mean something. If not, it's too much of a sacrifice to make... Some think I'm a bit of a Jack the Lad. My wild-child days are over now – anything else would be seen as a midlife crisis – but I'm not interested in doing what society or faith expect me to do when it will not make me happy."

I fall silent for a minute before I say, "I feel a bit jealous actually. You went out there and lived life on your own terms, made your mark..."

He smiles. "I feel like my life is now fitting together like a jigsaw puzzle, but back then I just didn't know where the pieces were. I thought they were in being in the top league, then I thought they were in sex, drugs, and getting plastered. Then I met Karline and thought it was in trying to be a good husband and father to Alex. Then I failed at that..."

I nod. "I grew up with dolls and being trained as a kid how to develop the attributes of being the perfect daughter, perfect wife. Any mistake, and my mum would say, 'Don't go and disgrace me in your husband's house,' and I'm like, 'Mum, I'm only eleven!'"

We both laugh.

"That's our parents for you. I grew up being primed to fulfil my father's lifetime obsession of me becoming a doctor..."

"But you wanted to play football."

He spreads his hands in surrender. "You see my father's frustration. My mum understood. My dad was disappointed. It was like I had killed somebody."

I shake my head. "My mum wasn't too worried about the educational bit with me. I did well at school and got a 2.1 in Business Studies. Then became an admin officer, progressed to personal assistant. Then I turned thirty, and everything changed. My friends started getting married, Mum's friends' daughters started getting married. Then my younger sister got married, and my mum started ramping it up. You see, her dream is that I get married to a someone who isn't like my dad."

"Your dad?"

"Someone who ups and leaves, then starts a new family in Lagos."

"Oh…"

"Yeah. I don't like the term 'dead beat' but…"

"I'm sorry you had to go through that."

"He's dead now." I look down at my manicured nails. The pain is still there, though. Kike speaks about it sometimes while I shrug it off. The inability to acknowledge pain runs like a river through the lives of the women in our family.

We fall silent again and I look at my phone, noting the time.

"Well, we really had better be getting back."

"Before we go back there—" he gestures towards the other side of the roof "—and we forget about today and get absorbed by life and all that hustle, I just wanted to say that I really enjoyed talking to you. I always do."

I find myself smiling as we both stand to our feet.

"I mean it," he persists. "You have that rare gift of listening without judging and I thank you for that."

I feel something in my throat but I can't find any words.

"I like being around you," he says simply.

"Well. I like a good chat, me."

He looks me in the eyes. "No, don't do that, Sade. Don't minimise yourself or this… We like each other. We like each other's company." His hand reaches for mine and draws me closer until I am looking up at him. "And I'm attracted to you. Have been from that very first time I saw you buying those crisps and a tuna sandwich."

I laugh and he smiles.

"You're beautiful, funny, brave, passionate about your work, and devoted to the people you love – and there's so much more about you that I want to discover."

No one has ever said that to me before. My eyes fill with tears because I am emotional about this man with his kind eyes and that gift he has of reading my mind. But he doesn't share my belief in marriage or, most importantly, God, and I feel such a hypocrite. Because for all my independence, my body is crying out to be held and made love to as much as my mind is yelling for intelligent and creative conversation, and my heart that loves Jesus is yelling NO.

"Discover?"

"Yes … like this." I feel the air thicken with anticipation as he leans in, his lips brushing against mine – gentle but passionate – a mixture of confidence and restraint as my fingers find refuge in the folds of his shirt and he pulls me closer, his hands running down my back and resting on my waist.

Then Jimi lifts his head, rests his forehead against mine,

and whispers, "I've been thinking about doing that since the day we met. I thought to myself, wow. I wanted to get your number that day in the supermarket, and I tried to be clever and ask for your business card instead. I was cooling my feet waiting for a call, playing it off that I'm looking for a project manager, and then who decides to catwalk down my dad's church aisle – on one of the few days I decide to show up – an African queen in a headwrap and trousers looking like a cool glass of India Arie. You."

Heat engulfs me and it isn't menopausal.

Cool glass of India Arie. So, he liked me back in March.

We kiss again, and this time it's a fusion of longing and surrender as I step closer into his embrace, but we hear the footsteps and laughter of some other guests coming closer and Jimi lifts his head, looking at me, and I realise that my heart is beating faster than it ever has.

A couple of partygoers walk by and give us the thumbs-up and we give them a sheepish smile.

"Busted by a couple of twenty-year-olds." Jimi grins at me when they are out of earshot.

"Imagine that," I manage, and am amazed at how normal my voice sounds. Stay calm. Crack a joke. Straighten your hair and your newly bought outfit. Pick up your beautiful new purse that seems to have dislodged itself from your person and fallen to the ground. "I think we had better be heading home."

He blinks and then smiles slowly. "I am not really that kind of guy… Anymore," he adds. "I'm getting a bit too old for that."

"Oh, no – I didn't mean…"

His lips twitch with laughter. "I'm kidding. I know what you meant. But are you okay?"

"Yeah. Of course. Why wouldn't I be?" My voice sounds stiff, even to my own ears.

·He is quiet now as we walk back to the others.

"How are you getting home?" Jimi asks.

"The same way I came. I'll get the tube."

"I can drop you home, if you like—?"

"No!" I say, abruptly.

He frowns. "Did I do anything wrong back there? I'm sorry if—"

"No, Jimi, you didn't do anything..."

"I can't let you get on the tube by yourself at eleven p.m. when I could drop you off myself." His voice is patient yet firm, as if he is talking to one of his patients.

"I'm capable of getting the tube home at night," I respond with a flounce of my head and a steady step in the opposite direction. "If I'm quick enough I can get a train home before the station closes."

We turn and find ourselves facing my cousin and her fiancé. From their expressions, I have a strong feeling that they heard every word of our very first argument.

"Aunty Sade! So, there you are," says Dolapo. "We were wondering if we should send out a search party. Sis Kike was trying to find you but had to go home..."

Chapter Nineteen

Jimi again offered to give me a lift home, but instead I hitched a ride to Mile End with one of Dolapo's friends and managed to get a bus to Bow. All the way back I remember our kiss, how it made me feel, and wonder why it has freaked me out.

When I get in a message pings on my phone.

> Call me as soon as you're home. Jimi.

It was midnight, so I send him a text.

> Sorry I left like that. Rude of me I know. I owe you an apology.

He responds immediately.

> Not good. Sade. Not good.

I know. I'm sorry.

I will let you take me out to lunch to make it up to me.

Sure. I owe you one. ☺

Next week?

I can't do next week.

Just make it soon. If not, I will come and drag you out of your yard, girl. Don't make me have to come to the 'ends for you.

Ha. What's wrong with us Eastenders.

Goodnight Jimi.

Sweet dreams, Sade.

I take a morning off work to have a meeting with Pastor Keith at church.

"Sit down, Sade." Pastor Keith smiles and I wonder whether he will still be smiling at the end of the meeting.

"Good morning, Pastor Keith. Hope you and the family are well?"

He nods and leans back in this armchair. "They are all well. So how are you doing?"

"Oh, I'm fine."

"Haven't really had a chance to catch up with you after the break-up with Simon."

"No." I don't really want to talk about Simon.

"So how do you feel about that? Do you think you have moved on?"

I shrug. "At the time I was p— I was angry. Now I don't feel anything."

He raises an eyebrow. "I sense that you have some healing to do around that."

I look at him. "Pastor, I didn't come here to talk about Simon. I've been doing a lot of thinking in the meanwhile, as well as counselling, and I'm looking to my future and not the past now."

He folds his arms. "I am glad to hear it."

I can see the relief in his eyes that I am not going to burst into tears. "I wanted to speak to you. I can't blame the church for the number of single women – all I ask is that they are given the consideration and emotional and spiritual support that other members of this church are given."

Pastor Keith removes his glasses and starts to polish them. "We have a whole department – it's called Successful Singles – to cater for your needs."

My voice is matter-of-fact. "Sorry, Pastor. The actual name itself is an oxymoron. Most singles don't want to be single, and many like myself have spent years manoeuvring a lonely life successfully, trying to pretend that we are happy being perpetually single. I think we really need to provide a healthy atmosphere for singles to mix and make church more man-friendly."

He puts his glasses back on and his voice sounds dry. "I

hear you, Sade but you can't blame the church for the lack of men."

"I am not blaming the church," I persist. "It's just … if I was a guy, what would make me step inside and hang around? Successful Singles meetings are full of women from thirty-five to sixty years old sitting down looking eagerly at the door for when the next man walks in. The meetings are full of discussions on how we can be better singles, so let us normalise Christian Black women falling in love and dating in their twenties and thirties, and older, and having families. I go to work and my colleagues are discussing weddings and dates while the majority of my Black female single colleagues are dreaming of one date in a year."

"The Bible doesn't say that everyone should be married, Sade. I wish I could promise you all husbands, but you know with the current statistics out there – there are not enough men. It is just a fact of life and one that women are going to have to deal with." The defensiveness in his voice rises as his brow furrows and he runs a hand over the bald patch on his head. "I will have you know that Sister Mary is doing an admirable job with the singles team."

I blink. "Sister Mary has been married twenty-five years and doesn't have a bloody clue – and she doesn't listen to anyone's suggestions."

His blue eyes freeze. "Please don't swear."

I bite my lip. "I'm sorry, Pastor Keith. I guess I feel strongly about this. Mary's idea of events is bussing a group of forty women and six men up to Blackpool pier for the day. Or organising a Christmas ball, for which we spend good money getting glammed up to go to a swanky event in central London, and pay sixty pounds a ticket. A lot of us professional women: lawyers, doctors, engineers. And just a handful of men show up."

His lips twitch and then he looks sober. "I can see you have some strong thoughts on this and that is understandable. You also must see that the elders group, youth group, children's church, and young-marrieds group are also very important and need our support."

"I know that," I say. "But why can't we have a monthly prayer group where the church prays for us to meet partners, as well? And it would be great to have a men's group where you and the other elders mentor and talk football, business opportunities, relationships, and the wealth of knowledge that you have from years of marriage."

Pastor Keith adjusts his glasses again and shuffles some papers. "Well, this is the end of our catch-up. I have my eleven-thirty meeting waiting outside. I will have a look at the suggestions you emailed and discuss them with Pastor Sandra. I'll pray for guidance as to where we go from here." He nods at me, implying that I should leave.

Feeling stupid, I get up, thank him for his time, and shuffle out to get the train back home.

I really shouldn't have used the word "bloody" when talking to Pastor Keith. But the more I think about it, except for that, I wouldn't take a word back.

Chapter Twenty

A week later and I get a text from Jimi. He is going to be at Dolapo's traditional wedding in two weeks' time. I guess, instead of lunch, we are going to see each other there.

Yes, that's us Nigerians for you. Sam asked me one day why we need to have three marriages when one would do. You see, we don't do things casually. When we do something, we go for it in a big way.

In Yoruba culture, wedding ceremonies are a blend of traditional and modern practices, typically consisting of three distinct events. The first is the civil wedding, often accompanied by a reception, where the couple legally formalise their union in the presence of family and friends. Next is the traditional wedding ceremony, the *Igbeyawo*, a vibrant celebration rich with culture and tradition, symbolising the joining of the two families through age-old customs, blessings, and the exchange of gifts. Finally, the "white wedding" takes place in a church, reflecting

Christian influences, where the couple exchange vows in a formal religious ceremony.

So if I ever do get married to anyone, I will be having three weddings! The trick is, I need to find someone first innit!

Let's catch up, Pastor Sandra's text says. She's invited me for breakfast in the posh café not too far from church. So Pastor Keith must have said something.

It is nice of her and very unexpected. I can't say I am that close with her. I view her from afar because she is my pastor, because she is busy with the work of running the ministry alongside Pastor Keith, and she is a wife and mother. Apart from our Christian faith, we have very little in common.

"I just thought it would be good to have a little chat. I didn't know about your surgery until I saw your friend Vicky and she happened to mention that you had been off work for a couple of weeks. I know it was some months ago – but things have been so busy…"

I shrug as I stir my Earl Grey and watch the cinnamon and sugar dissolve. "It's no big deal. A routine op." I am so glad to be able to walk around again and do all the things I loved doing, now that I have the energy to be able to enjoy them.

Pastor Sandra nods. "I just wanted you to know that we love you and we value you. Also, we saw your suggestions and felt they were quite interesting."

The waiter arrives with plates of warm buttered toast, accompanied by crispy bacon and perfectly poached eggs.

Pastor Sandra clears her throat and goes on. "Pastor Keith told me about your conversation, and we did give it some thought. A lot of thought. I know it took you a lot to tell him how you felt about things."

I sigh. "I have a confession to make. I have been at Living Waters for almost twenty years and have given my all to the church for years – like so many single women – but we seem to be treated like an afterthought."

Her blue eyes fill with concern. "I'm sorry you feel that way."

"When I found out about the multiple fibroids and the doctor said that if during the op there was so much bleeding or damage to my womb, they would consider a hysterectomy, I couldn't come to terms with it. I thought to myself – what do I have to offer any man apart from my ability to have a child? Irrational, of course, but that was how I felt and there is no teaching from the pulpit or any kind of emotional or mental support on this. We are totally ignored until we succumb to the flesh or get pregnant, and I can tell you that, to be very honest, if I were to get pregnant, I would be the happiest person in the world right now."

Pastor Sandra's voice is even but firm. "But you are not married, and you know that would be a sin. The Bible says—"

"I know what the Bible says," I interrupt. "I have had a painful rehabilitation, couldn't walk properly, and discovered a month after the op that my periods have stopped. Right now, I am taking day by day as it comes.

Apparently, according to the *Daily Mail*, career women can't have it all."

"I don't really know what to say."

"I know I really shouldn't believe everything I read in newspapers."

"No. That's not what I meant."

My eyes meet hers. "What would you say if I told you that there are many women in church who show up every Sunday with bright smiles, who feel exactly the same way?"

"But no one says anything?" Pastor Sandra blinks. "If people don't talk to us as their pastors, how will we know how they feel?"

"They don't want to disappoint you, especially as you seem to believe that we should be totally content, sold out for Christ, devoid of feelings for the opposite sex."

"We – I mean, the singles department is meant to be supporting you all."

"My friends have been there for me, and an amazing family friend, Aunty Remi, as well. They helped by being there, by praying for me, making cups of tea, and listening to me rant on about being single and childless, and they didn't tell me that this was God's plan and I had to like it or lump it. They hugged me, cried along with me, and helped me realise that my life counted and that the best was still ahead for me."

Pastor Sandra sips her tea. "I don't think we have ever said singleness is something that you are stuck with, that you need to get rid of or endure. It is for most people just part of life's journey."

"Well, this journey has taken me on a detour that I didn't

expect, and it's taken a bigger chunk of my life than I would have wanted."

Pastor Sandra acknowledges this. "Pastor Keith told me that his initial response was to be on the defensive – but on due consideration we are open to working with you to see what we can do better. We have the singles ministry here for you all, and many activities. It is not our fault that men don't seem to want to attend those events. But we have prayed and we both feel that more can be done."

"Well, that sounds good," I say.

Pastor Sandra puts down her tea. "You know, I used to look at you and feel that you had it all together."

I laugh. "I'm just a great actress."

Pastor Sandra gives me a small smile. "I appreciate you being honest with us like this. It is the kind of feedback that we need to hear. I confess I've forgotten what it is like to be single."

"I guess you've also forgotten what it's like not to be able to have sex," I say dryly.

There is laughter from her. "Well. I do counsel singles before they get married and that is something that features heavily on their minds, but after they get hitched, they realise that sex forms a much smaller part of their lives than they envisaged. I do realise that we haven't fully considered a lot of what singles have to face, especially the women, if they want to have children in the future."

I put my own tea down. "I'm the first daughter of a Nigerian woman – I'm amazed that I have not succumbed to the pressure and settled for some DIY relationship concocted by my family members."

"I had no idea you were all dealing with this pressure."

"But we are, Pastor. Some of us are mature single women who feel ashamed to acknowledge our fears of growing old without a partner and with no kids. Then if you happen to be Nigerian – just ramp all that up by a hundred per cent. We don't want you to have all the answers. We just want to know that you care."

Pastor Sandra smiles. "We do. Do you mind if I have a quick prayer with you?"

In the middle of a crowded café? People might think we are kind of weird but who cares; people think that about Christians anyway. So I nod and she picks up my hand and we both bend our heads.

"Lord," she whispers. "Help Sade to realise that she is loved by you. Loved by us all. You are the only one that can answer her prayers, and those of all our ladies in church, for life partners that will complement them and be blessings to them. Father Lord, fill her with your joy and your peace in the meanwhile and lead her to your perfect will for her, in Jesus's Name."

"Amen."

I feel a peace well up in me.

A week before Dolapo's big day, Kike and I go to the dressmaker to get our outfits for the wedding. I try mine on and realise that staying at home and grazing on too many snacks has added a bit to my waistline and hips – but at least now I actually have a waistline!

Kike nods as I stand in front of the mirror, running my

hand over the mermaid-style cut of the skirt that fans out over my feet.

"I like this. Really gives you a shapely look."

"Really."

"Yes. I always thought you were a bit too slim. You are probably a size twelve now, like me."

"I'm more a ten, actually."

Kike shimmies in front of the mirror and pats her stomach. "I've been doing lots of exercise to shift my baby belly."

My lips twist. "The twins are now ten. What baby belly?"

"Watch it," she warns, wagging her finger. "I'm off. See you downstairs."

The day of the traditional wedding arrives and we get to the hotel, which is beautifully decorated, the tables set out with rows of chairs. In the middle there is a table with golden plates set with the essentials for the ceremony such as honey, kolanuts, yams, and bottles of expensive wines. There is a suitcase which will be full of several sets of Aso Oke and other materials for the bride. All this will form part of her dowry, which is integral to a typical Yoruba traditional marriage ceremony. Aunty Gbemi has given the groom and his family a list of all the dowry requirements.

Mum is already there, looking elegant in her grey and pink lace, seated with Aunty Gbemi and the rest of the family – which consists of two uncles and Aunty Bunmi – who have travelled down to London from Manchester.

The groom's family sit on the other side of the hall, dressed in dark navy and silver. The groom's friends sit around him in white robes and dark navy caps.

Mum gives me a small nod of approval. "Hmm. You are looking beautiful today. This outfit really suits you. The tailor did a good job. All you need is to get your Gele properly tied. There is a woman in the toilet doing the tying for just five pounds."

"Wow, Mum. Did she tie yours?" Kike asks.

My mum snorts in derision. "Five pounds for a head tie. God forbid. It is you people that do not know how to tie head tie that can pay that kind of money. When my hands are still useful – why will I not tie my own head tie? What a nonsense!"

We head for the loos and join the long queue of women waiting to have their head ties done.

Afterwards, I emerge with a headache but head tie firmly in place. Kike has had hers done, too.

"You look fantastic!" Kike exclaims when I complain about the headache. We are walking back into the auditorium when I see a tall dark gentleman striding towards me, his white Atiku outfit and navy cap marking him out as one of the guests of the groom.

Jimi Taylor is in the building.

I look pointedly in his direction, my insides leaping all over the place like an excited puppy. He waves and walks towards us.

My hands grip my silver purse as if it is a lifeline. The memory of his lips seeking mine and giddy anticipation, the longing for the forbidden, darts around my head.

Kike shakes her head like she does when dealing with

her sons or her husband and whispers as he walks towards us, "For goodness' sake, Sade, I mean, have a look at that. Premium husband material."

Jimi stands in front of us looking handsome and regal in his robe. "Hi, ladies."

"Hello, Bro Jimi." Kike adds the term of respect reserved for a brother-in-law and I shoot her a warning glance. It makes me cringe. I make up my mind to have a word with my sister later.

"What are you people doing out here?" The sharpness of the query interrupts our greetings, and we turn to see Aunty Gbemi standing in front of the entrance to the hall, her face tight with impatience. "Kike and Sade. *Awon Ebi?* You are needed inside with our family. The Alaga is getting ready to start!"

Aunty Gbemi is perfectly made up in a grey and pink Aso Oke wrapper and Buba. Her silver head tie and matching shoes and bag complete the ensemble.

"You look wonderful, Aunty," Kike coos.

Aunty Gbemi's tight lips morph into a smile as she walks off. "Thank you."

Jimi pulls one side of his Agbada over his shoulder, mouths the words "See you later" at me, and then goes into the hall.

Kike winks at me and I grip her by the hand and lead her away.

"Tone it down, man," I tell her.

"What did I do?"

"What's all this Broda business?"

"Look, I only called him Jimi when he was a stranger but now…"

"Now what?"

"You guys have snogged, innit." Kike grins. "He could potentially be family!"

My eyes narrow. "What are you on about? It's so early in the relationship."

"Stop looking so guilty. Dolapo saw you and Jimi kissing."

"So." I shrug, trying to look casual.

"I have never ever seen you this defensive about any guy before. I think Jimi is perfect for you. If you see the way he looks at you when you speak – as if you're the only one in the room."

"Stop, Kike." I frown. "Jimi is never going to be your brother-in-law." I know what I know and I don't want to get anyone's hopes up.

Her smile falters, then she nudges me. "Never say never, Sis."

_____

I make it into the hall while the Alaga is officiating and telling the guests some jokes about how the bride and groom met.

My mother and aunt give me some looks as I ease myself into a chair. Then I just sit there and stare ahead of me, the words of the MC going over my head.

So Dolapo has seen us kissing.

Oh, my days.

A couple of hours after the Alaga, who is also the MC, chairlady, and comedian of the day, has heckled the groom and his friends as part of the entertainment for the wedding guests, to the background of dancing, music, and lots of laughter – there is a break for food.

Kike is being annoying, wanting to know the details on Jimi, and though I tell her to forget it, her shoulders heave with quiet laughter.

"I think you've pulled."

I bring out my fan from my purse and fan myself. "Slow down, girl. I hardly know the chap."

She drags me towards the food area. "Like I said before. Did you see how he looked at you when he came into the foyer?"

"No.",

"He looked at you like he was looking at a cool glass of water in the desert. I don't even think he would have come if it wasn't for you. He doesn't do social events."

"And how do you know this?"

Kike smiles. "I have my own intelligence-gathering sources. Which will remain secret for now. Look, have a nice time, smile, and stop being so serious. Let's go and get something to eat. I'm starving."

I lower my voice. "I just have this fear that any member of the Marriage Monitoring Aunties' Association – who are present today – might poke their nose into my affairs and spoil my chances." Inside, I'm trying to pull myself together. It's early days. No one knows anything and I want to keep it that way. I don't even know what this is – let alone how to explain it to anyone else.

"Let me tell you – that guy is serious about you," Kike declares.

I roll my eyes, but can't stop the rush of sweet heat through my body. I like this guy, I mean really like him, and even if I can't admit it to my sister, I can't keep lying to myself.

We head for the serving point and look over what is available. There are silver serving points for pounded yam, Efo Riro and Egusi stew, Asaro, jollof rice, and large slabs of chicken, fish, and beef. The savoury aromas tickle my taste buds and I feel my stomach rumble. Then I hear a deep voice behind me comment, "Lots to choose from, isn't there?"

I turn around and it is Jimi standing there, with an empty plate in his hand.

"Hello again," I say, sensing there's something on his mind as he looks at me intently.

"I'm glad I've got you to myself," he whispers. "I need to ask you … what happened that night?"

"I don't get you?"

"After we kissed, you just checked out … disappeared…" His eyes are warm yet there is a hint of steel in the tone of his voice.

"Look, I'm sorry—"

"If you don't want me to kiss you again … just say." I look up and see the challenge, the teasing, in his eyes.

"You are my client, Jimi," I whisper, trying my best to look stern. "I've been trying to keep things professional between us."

Jimi adjusts his *Fila* on his head and looks at me for a long time and says nothing.

"What?" I stare at him.

"You are an enigma. Your eyes say one thing and your lips say another."

I don't know whether to be angry or take it as a compliment.

"I'm off to get some food," he adds, swiftly changing the topic. "I think I will try that yam pottage and have some fish. My favourite meal."

"I might try that, too."

Suddenly Kike is back, grinning from ear to ear as she looks at us like a proud parent. And then Jimi stands there, making small talk with my sister instead of getting his food. This is unreal.

Eventually we all go and fill our plates with food, and get some drinks, and are walking away from the serving point when I hear it.

"Jimi!" It is like an accusation.

He looks away from me and in the direction of my mum, who is staring at him as if she has caught him doing something wrong.

"*E Kasan ma.*" Jimi bows before the older woman in respect and her lips soften in approval.

I know she is thinking to herself, *At least he still remembers his culture.*

"*Kasan.* How are you? I was wondering that we do not see you in church any more. Then a month ago I saw you at the back and I said to myself, 'This is good. Bishop will be pleased.'"

Jimi's expression is unreadable.

Mum clearly has more to say. "It is well o. It is good to see you. Make sure that you come to church more often. Bishop needs to have you around more," she adds, with a glare at me, before turning to greet some people behind her.

Jimi and I look at each other.

"I think that's your mum warning me off you," he says, with a half smile.

"Sorry. My mum…"

He shakes his head as if he is having a secret joke with himself. "No worries, Sade. I understand these things."

He takes me by the hand and leads me outside the reception, where it is quieter.

"Are you coming to the church wedding next week?" he asks.

"Unless I want to be hung, drawn, and quartered."

His face lights up. It was something that started from a twist in those lips of his and spread up until it filled his eyes and his shoulders shook. "A dry sense of humour. I like that."

"It helps."

"I wasn't going to that wedding but I will make sure I change my shift." His eyes meet mine. "As long as you are sure you're coming?"

"But I didn't think you liked weddings?"

There is a distance in his eyes as if he is thinking of another time. Another place. "I have nothing against them. It's when they become a pageant that I lose interest."

Then he grins and laughter comes back into his voice. "You had better get back inside the reception. We don't want a repeat of last time…"

"What happened last time?" I really can't figure out what he's talking about.

His eyes darken as he looks at me. "Do you really want me to show you here?"

Realisation floods through me and I remember everything about That Kiss. I get up. "I had better go."

He is grinning. "See you next week, Sade."

Chapter Twenty-One

A week later and it is a lovely sunny morning. The kind of morning that you dream of for your church wedding day, the third wedding in Yoruba culture.

One of the advantages of being my age is that no one can manipulate you into being a bridesmaid. You have now earned the right to be called an Aunty of the Day and not be expected to serve guests. You have also earned the right to sit with church mummies and other aunties and look at the antics of PYTs as they strut around in clothes that are too tight, revealing a flash of cleavage or thigh, and with eyelashes sweeping the floor.

The colours for the day are aquamarine, gold, and cream. The idea is to get something close to these colours. It is mainly for the ladies. There are not many instances of men being expected to arrive at a church or a country manor in Surrey wearing a suit in any of those colours.

I have got a dress that I thought would do the event justice from a boutique in Westfields Stratford that specialises in evening and day wear. I found myself an aquamarine brocade off-the-shoulder silk day dress that flatters my new slim waist and has a full skirt that swishes against my ankles when I walk.

"It's very fifties," the shop assistant said.

"I'll take it," I said. And then looked at the price and hesitated.

"Oh, but it really flatters your complexion." She'd given it the hard sell, bringing out a gold gauzy chiffon wrap, costume gold jewellery, and an exquisite fascinator that she added to the dress.

A cheeky move, but it worked on me!

The church is packed with relatives, friends, and some gatecrashers who have no idea that Aunty Gbemi has placed a bouncer at the reception hall so that non-invitees do not get a place at the exclusive wedding lunch she has planned. Dolapo has a really good job as a pharmacist and has split the cost with her fiancé.

The church hall is decorated with roses, lavenders, and magnolias, and their scent mingles with the anticipation.

Dolapo walks down the aisle with her dad, who has shown up for the occasion from Lagos and for one day is playing the role of proud father. Mum said that if there was a contest for the most irresponsible father in the world, Dolapo's dad would win first prize. With her daughter marrying a doctor, Aunty Gbemi is happy enough to be icily gracious to him, even though he left her to bring up their daughter single-handed after he legged it back to his wife and family.

My cousin, the bride, is beautiful. Her hair is piled high on her head and secured with a pearl-encrusted tiara, and, to my surprise, she has decided to wear a modest gown with a high neck and a bodice encrusted with mock pearls. It billows out as she moves and makes her look princess-like as she almost floats down the aisle on her dad's arm to her groom. Behind her are five bridesmaids in aquamarine off-the-shoulder taffeta gowns, with the groomsmen in cream jackets and black trousers.

I take a quick glance at the crowd, hoping that Jimi is there as promised. Anything to make the long day worthwhile. I can't spot him amidst the faces of friends and family, so I have no choice but to turn around and wait for the wedding to commence.

The bride stands at the altar with her groom and faces the pastor officiating the wedding and my lips curve into a secret smile.

The pastor welcomes the congregation.

"Dearly beloved…"

_____

After the bride has danced out with her bridesmaids and groom to the accompaniment of Michelle Williams's "When Jesus Says Yes, Nobody Can Say No", the family gather for pictures.

As people assemble, I feel someone tap me on the shoulder and turn to see Aunty Bunmi. She lives in Manchester, which means I don't get to see her that much, thank God. A key member of the MMAA, she has been calling and sending messages and prayers on WhatsApp for the past year regarding marriage.

I curtsy in greeting. "Good afternoon, Aunty Bunmi."

Aunty Bunmi's eyes are dark with disapproval. "You are too big to pick my calls, eh?"

"I am sorry, Ma."

"Hmm. I have some things to say to you."

I am silent. Aunt Bunmi is always ready with a long lecture about husband-finding, my ability to have children, and how to cook perfect jollof rice that isn't soggy.

"Hi, Sade."

I turn and relief floods through me at the sight of my rescuer. I stop smiling.

Can't let him see that I'm that pleased to see him. Might be seen as being too eager.

Jimi is dressed in a smart grey suit, which looks similar to the one he wore the first day I met him. His tie is grey with aquamarine dots.

I am aware of my aunt standing there staring at us, and sense her demanding an introduction. But my mouth refuses to oblige. I don't want her in my business. Then, like an angel from above, one of my relatives appears to inform her that she is needed in the photoshoot for the senior-aunties slot with the couple.

"Make sure you see me before you go, Sade. I am not happy with you o," is her parting shot.

"I will come and find you, Ma."

I watch her leave and turn to Jimi.

He is laughing. "You are going to see her, aren't you?"

I shrug. "Maybe. Maybe not. Until I meet my aunt at the

next Great Fat Nigerian party, I've bought myself some time. Phew. Thanks for saving me from another inquisition from the MMAA."

He looks confused.

"MMAA – the Marriage Monitoring Aunties' Association."

He chuckles. "Interesting. You had that look in your eyes that just said HELP!"

We laugh, and then he gives me another look and smiles. "Well, Sade. You look stunning. That colour really suits you."

"You don't look too bad yourself," I say. "So, how's things?"

"Busy. You know how work in the hospitals can be. What about you?"

"Same. I'm in the middle of several projects, so it's like having several meals on the boil at the same time."

"I know the feeling."

Kike appears. "I need to get Sade for a family picture." She puts a hand on my arm. "But I will return her to you."

Jimi gives me another warm all-encompassing look. "I'll be here waiting."

Kike steers me away and flutters her eyelashes. "Hmm. I am not saying anything."

I find myself fussing around with my bag.

Kike nudges me and grins. "I can see it in your eyes, Sis. They are all bright and shiny. You like him, too."

"You make me sound like a Labrador," I scoff. "Of course I like him. He is a nice guy, but it's early days so do not be getting your hopes up – and please do not say anything to Mum…"

195

"She was muttering something to me about it a couple of days ago," Kike admits.

We are nearing the podium to take pictures and wait as the bride and groom finish their shots with the groom's family.

"What did she say?"

"Something about Jimi being the black sheep of the family and not wanting you mixed up with him."

I roll my eyes. "I'm fifty years old – she really should give me credit for a little judgement. I can look after myself," I grumble.

The photographer makes a call for the bride's family and we go forward.

After the pictures I return to where Jimi is still waiting.

"I just saw your mum," he says.

I frown. "She didn't say anything, did she?"

"Not really. She asked about my work."

I am silent, wondering what Mum is up to.

"Let's go inside and join everyone," Jimi says. "We can catch up later?"

"Yeah. Let us do that."

Two hours later, I'm sat at the table with Mum and Kike, watching as the MC makes another call-out regarding the bouquet. I have already eaten and am bored silly. Usually by the bouquet call, I am out and on my way home. Things often start going downhill from that point at weddings. People have eaten, the cake's been cut, and the embellished or redacted story of how the couple met has been recounted. People are now ready for a little single-woman shaming.

Beyoncé is blaring from the loudspeaker as the ladies run to the dance floor.

> *All the single ladies*
> *All the single ladies*
> *All the single ladies.*

The MC yells on his microphone for all singles to pay attention. There is one aunty here, Mrs Onabanjo, who has written a book called *How to Get Married in a Year* and she is sowing ten copies into the lives of all the single women that are first on the dance floor.

I spot her, resplendent in gold and red lace and a huge gold head tie, as she walks majestically to the stage amid a scramble to the dance floor by some young ladies.

Mr MC is smiling. "Let's clap for her. Mrs Onabanjo has been married successfully for twenty years and she has put a book together to help some of our ladies here." The MC gives her the mic. "Tell us in few words what this book is about. The title is very interesting."

"Thank you, Mr DJ."

"Please. My name is Solomon."

"Thank you, Mr Solomon. This book was written out of concern for some of our single ladies. Yes, it is wonderful that our young women are acquiring degrees and buying homes and cars but they must not, in their bid to get a career, neglect that the main aim of every God-fearing woman is to be a successful wife and mother." Mrs Onabanjo adjusts her glasses so she can scour the crowd for her target market. "My book talks about how to dress and comport yourself, how to speak respectfully to your intended and especially your in-laws-to-be, how to cook and how to make your man fall in love with you, so that he will put a ring on it."

"Tell them!" shouts out one church mummy to the claps of several others in the audience.

"Thank you, Madam Onabanjo." The MC takes the mic from her and she stands there still soaking up the limelight with her blinging outfit. "You can take your seat, Ma. Thanks again for the books."

Mrs Onabanjo slowly steps down and as she does, she almost loses her balance coming down the stairs with her high gold heels and the room falls silent with anticipation until one of the male guests helps her and she makes her way to her seat.

The MC starts to give out the books to the eager ladies pushing to the front of the queue, which is lengthening by the second.

Dolapo comes out in her second outfit: a cream and gold lace strapless ball gown that shines like the overhead chandeliers. She is holding the bouquet like some kind of javelin.

"Okay, now, ladies, let us get back to business," calls the MC. "Come out to collect the bouquet or we will name you one by one!"

My lips tighten. That sounds like a threat to me.

The MC is warming to the theme, his voice getting louder. "Folake, come out o – your mother said you should come and be leaving your father's house for your own husband's house. Come out and use this bouquet as a point of contact for your miracle! Besides, you all need this book – especially those of you that are looking at forty!"

Single shaming.

"Anybody who does not come out is not happy about the celebration taking place o. We will mark you out as one of the jealous ones o."

Blackmail.

"Eniola, come and catch flowers because your own flower is fading fast."

I am sure that qualifies as an insult.

There is a ripple of laughter in the room. A twist in the lips of the smug marrieds sitting there waiting for the singles to line up. Out of the corner of my eye I see some of Dolapo's friends and other young ladies beginning to make their way to the floor.

The MC ramps it up. "Amaka, Janet, come out and stop pretending. We all know you are both single."

More laughter.

For goodness' sake. It is like a Roman amphitheatre. I stand and pick up my purse.

"Sade. Are you not going to collect the bouquet?" Mum eyes me.

"Mum…" Kike's voice is tired.

"I need to get some fresh air, Mum." My lips are set in a firm line.

My mother looks at me over the rims of her glasses. She wears them occasionally for reading and for being able to see better. "Fresh air?"

I don't look at her as I walk off with brisk purposeful steps towards the door, catching some speculative looks as I walk past the tables of wedding guests until I exit the great hall and stand outside, looking around.

I see Jimi standing feet away, looking out at the expanse of trees, gardens, and flowers that surround the manor, and walk over to meet him.

"You had enough too, ay?" he says, still staring at the view but with a half smile on his face.

"Uh huh."

We both stand quietly for a moment. Close but not too close, just enjoying the beauty around us. I glimpse a deer disappearing behind a tree.

Then Jimi breaks the silence by pointing towards the lake. "Fancy a bit of a walk to the gazebo? Get into the shade."

I look at my heels. *They are not made for walking on grass. They cost me a pretty penny but...*

"Why not."

We walk and talk, breathing in the fresh air and the sun blessing the day.

"So, one wedding done and dusted."

I allow my lips to relax into a smile. "Yep. Lovely wedding."

I hear my phone go off in my bag, and grapple inside to check it.

"Just in case someone is wondering where I got to..."

His lips twist wryly. "I don't have anyone in my life that tells me what to do any more."

I decide to ignore my phone. "Do you want someone to tell you what to do?"

"Nah." He grins. "It is a brilliant feeling. A benefit of middle age."

I envy him. It's true that the older you get, the less you care about the self-imposed structure of societal norms and expectations. Especially trying to live up to your parent's rigid code of What a Good Nigerian Child Ought to Be Doing at Fifty and Beyond. But of course, it's easier for men.

"I still find myself trying to please my mum," I admit. "Although the older I get the less I care about trying to live my life according to anyone's expectations.".

"I could never please my dad," Jimi sighs. "But it is what it is. I think we have both learned to accept ourselves as we are."

"If only my mother could accept me the way I am."

He turns to me, and I shake my head.

"Marriage and motherhood are everything, for women particularly, in our society, you know that. My mum feels I've left both a bit late."

"You can get married anytime."

"But you can't have children anytime."

He sighs. "Is that something that you think about?"

"I used to, but now..." I shrug. "I've accepted my reality."

"Being a parent is a wonderful thing – but it's also a road of challenge, hard work – sometimes with little appreciation or thanks or even acknowledgement."

"That tough, eh?"

"Teenagers are a tough lot and when you are trying to be a long-distance dad – co-parenting with an ex – it makes it almost impossible."

"Sorry, here I am, going on about my issues."

"Don't be sorry." Jimi pauses. "I don't know why our society makes women like you think that you are at a disadvantage because you are single. I look at you and wonder if all the guys around you for the past twenty years have been blind."

My throat is dry, and we stand there looking at each other.

"Sade, I…" he begins.

My phone goes off again, but I ignore it.

He glances at me. "Aren't you going to get that?"

"Nah."

"It might be urgent."

"What can be that urgent?"

But whoever it is is persistent, so I find my phone and am about to mute it, when I see who's calling.

Jimi's lips twist. "It's your mum, isn't it?"

I nod and drop the phone back in my bag again. "I'm bloody fifty years old and she is trying to police my life like I'm a kid."

"I can understand why. She does not want you mixed up with the kind of person I used to be."

I look at him and shake my head. "She means well, but…"

"You do not have to explain anything, Sade. It's cool."

The phone sounds again. This time its wail is more plaintive, like a baby needing to be fed.

Jimi tries not to smile and it annoys me that it makes him even more attractive. "I had better get you back to your mum before she sends out a search party," he says, and we head inside.

"He has a son, you know!" Mum can't help herself as I get into the Uber with her.

"Mum, can we drop this." The fascinator is giving me a headache and I take it off my head.

"I have to say my mind. Jimi was following you all over the place today. He has a son with an Oyibo woman."

"So? He has a son – what's the big deal?"

"*O gboro mi.* Jimi looks like a ladies' man. I don't want anyone deceiving you, especially now."

"Especially now what?"

"I met this very nice young man at the reception. Lawyer Ade. That's why I was calling you. I wanted to introduce you to him. Especially as you were looking so presentable today."

"His first name is Lawyer, ay?"

Mum doesn't find this funny. "No, his first name is your father's family name. Do not be asking me stupid question! Your Aunty Bunmi brought this man to the party to see you and we could not find you. I do not know where you were. Probably running around after this Jimi boy like a teenager, I am sure! You'd better not disgrace yourself. I have said my own."

"Mum…"

"And this Jimi, you think you have feelings for him? You, this girl – you think you know everything!"

"I hardly know Jimi. We have been discussing work and other stuff."

"You do not know him. Beware because sometimes things that are shining can blind a person's eye – if you do not know! See this Ade. I know him. I know his father. I know his mother since she was—" Mum lowers her hand

"—this little. I can get any information you want on him. He is a good God-fearing man. But this Jimi, he denounced his father, his faith, and refused to even show up for his mother's funeral and you are making puppy eyes at him. He does not even return his brother's calls – and his brother is a big lawyer in Nigeria. A Senior Advocate of Nigeria, for that matter. Jimi is not even a doctor despite going to medical school. Imagine the waste – just to end up as a physiotherapist!"

I am so glad that the car is stopping outside Mum's house. "We're home, Mum. Let me help you inside…"

She opens the door and shakes her head. "Do not bother. All I have to say is that a word is enough…" She gingerly manoeuvres herself out of the car.

"For the wise. I hear you, Mum. I will check up on you during the week."

She nods and I watch as she walks towards the door, a diminutive figure in her grey and pink outfit, her huge silver head tie and bag.

"You should listen to your mum," the Uber driver chimes in. "I wish I had my mum here to give me advice."

I close my eyes. How selfish of me. At least I have a mum. "How long has it been since she passed?"

"She is not dead or anything. Just abroad. In Turkey."

My lips tighten into a firm line. "Please take me to Alderbury Crescent, E3 2TY."

The driver keys it into his satnav and is silent for the rest of the journey, which suits me. I do not want to hear any more unsolicited advice from him, or anyone, tonight.

Chapter Twenty-Two

S trange.

Yesterday I was sitting on a bus and could have sworn I saw Bishop Taylor and Aunty Remi coming out of a Nigerian restaurant together. One of the nicer restaurants along Kent Road. I wanted to mention it to Mum, as I thought some small talk might cool the air between us, then I decided against it. Mum has not answered my calls for a week.

I am so worried that I phone Kike today to ask if our mother is still in this earthly realm.

"She's fine, Sis."

"Why is she being so difficult?"

Kike sighs. "She is just worried that you might miss your chance with the lawyer, but I'm Team Jimi all the way and I told her that you are an adult and she needs to chill."

"Did she listen?"

"What do you think?" Kike pauses. "So, when are you seeing Jimi again?"

I sigh. "I don't know. He sent me a text asking me how I was and all that but he's busy at work at the moment."

Kike's voice sounds eager. "I like him. He has a touch of Idris about him. Kind of bad boy turned good." She giggles. "Or trying to be good. It is up to you to find that out."

"He has a son."

"How old?"

"I dunno."

"Come on, Sis. Do you expect a guy of forty or whatever to—"

"Forty-five."

"Okay, forty-five. Do you expect a man of that age to have been a monk for all these years? Not everyone is like you."

"Thanks, Sis, for putting it like that. I feel much better now."

"Do not get me wrong, I admire and respect your stance of waiting for the right person. In fact, I wish society could see that there are people out there that are prepared to stand up for their values – no matter what it costs them – and I know what your beliefs have cost you."

Yeah. Marriage and children.

"Okay. You can get off your soapbox now before I start playing 'Jerusalem.'"

"Don't kid about it, Sis. I'm proud of you, and the guy that you marry will be honoured that you respected yourself enough to think, I don't want to do this with someone that doesn't value me, and know that's bloody rare nowadays."

"I feel like a freak. Also, I must carry it around like a secret."

Kike's turn to sigh. "It's sad that you feel ashamed for something that you should be appreciated for. It is your life and yet people want to hate people for doing what's best for them. Sis, I don't know whether Jimi is the one. All I know is that ever since he showed up, you look happier. You look more alive and there is a sparkle in those eyes."

"I do need to go to the opticians, though."

"You are a joker, Sis. I see the way he looks at you ... like he's eating you up with his eyes."

"That's what you see?" I laugh. "You watch too many romcoms and soaps, babes."

"Whatever. You know exactly what I mean," says Kike. "Look, Hubby has just walked in so I must dash. Will catch up later. Let me have the latest regarding Jimi."

"Okay, Kike. Laters."

On the way back home, I bump into Sam going off to the West End. Says she is meeting up with Martin to watch a show somewhere along Shaftesbury Avenue. From the way she lights up, and the mischievous glint in her eyes, I can only assume that Kike has dropped some gossip. Sam gives me a hug like a proud mother. I swear that she has a tear in those big blue eyes of hers.

"I'm off to get me hat," she teases.

"Calm down, dear. It is not that deep. We have had a few chats and gone out a couple of times. Exchanged numbers and bumped into each other at a wedding. Period."

Sam puts a hand to her chest. "I'm so happy for you."

"If you don't stop with this Mrs Bennett stuff, I swear I will stop talking to you. Now, be a good girl and run along."

Sam flutters her eyebrows. "Jimi. That name sounds so sexy. I heard he looks a bit like Idris. I love that dark brooding look with the hint of grey and possible inner bad boy. You know I'm a Luther fan."

I listen to Sam rabbit on and wonder how my life will be if this doesn't work out. My friends are already planning a whole wedding in their heads about someone whom I like but still feel slightly undecided about.

"Enjoy the show. Must dash." I give her a hug and a wave as we go our separate ways.

"You got a minute?" Greg sticks his head round my door.

"Sure." I get up and follow him into his office. I take the seat across from him.

On his desk, I see glossy marketing material with the name NuChance on the front cover.

Greg follows my eyes to the magazine cover, then leans back in his chair.

"I confess I'm at a total loss regarding putting stuff together for this NuChance event. I thought maybe your deeper knowledge of the issues these youth are dealing with would make you better placed to win us the contract."

I smile. "Thanks for the opportunity."

"Great." He sounds reassured. "We have two of the patrons coming to see us on Friday." He looks at the screen in front of him. "One of them is Cyril Peters. He used to play for Liverpool back in the late nineties. Brilliant but got dropped due to a knee injury. And the other is a chap called Jimi Taylor. He was in the youth team for Aldery City FC. He was another professional player – suffered a double leg fracture after a game with another youth side – early 2000s or something. I can't remember exactly."

"Yes, he's talked about that," I say.

Greg lifts an eyebrow, but smiles.

"How do you know him?"

"He is a friend."

Greg's eyes narrow but the smile stays in place. "Just to be clear here. Are you dating him?"

I take a deep breath. "Kind of…"

Greg steeples his fingers. "Do you think this could pose a problem going forward?"

I shake my head. "Of course not. You know me. Professional all the way. Work always comes first. I've proved that."

Greg nods. "I will expect your professionalism in this. Make it work, Sade. It is good publicity for the company to be seen to be working with this charity. It is all about social value. It can't hurt us to get involved in this. You know the big money is in the corporate sector, but working with charities shows our caring side."

Yeah. Inner city disadvantaged young men are really top of the corporate agenda nowadays.

Greg's phone rings and with a nod I'm dismissed. I walk back to my office biting my lip.

At my desk, I check my phone and see a text from you-know-who.

Jimi.

> I know this place that does great
> Caribbean food. What are you doing next
> Friday night?

This time I don't hesitate.

> Nothing much. I like Caribbean food.

I wonder if I can get a nice dress in two days.

Chapter Twenty-Three

Next morning at work, Bridget rings in and tells me that she isn't feeling that well but will come in later. I tell her to work from home, but she insists on coming in anyway.

I am at my desk working away when she arrives a couple hours later and pops her head round the door.

"Hiya…"

She walks in, sits down and sighs. "I'm so sorry. I spent yesterday sticking needles into my abdomen for the IVF and have been having headaches and nausea."

"Oh dear…"

Bridget closes her eyes. "My mother-in-law has been staying, and last week she cornered me as soon as her son had left for the office and knelt in front of me. She was sobbing that I should please, if I really love her son, leave him so he can marry a real woman that can definitely have children – before she dies of a broken heart. Can you believe this woman?"

I look at Bridget. When I first met her, the girl was sharp, from her perfectly coiffured hair to her manicured nails and her Karen Millen tailored suits in bright pinks and greens. Now, in her eighth year of marriage, she has lost weight, cut her hair, and wears black and grey most of the time.

"What does Emeka say about all this?"

"He just says he is tired of trying to referee between us and that she is his mother and what can he do? Although when I told him about the latest stunt with her kneeling down and begging me to leave him, he did reprimand her. She went home a couple of days ago and I have started another round of IVF. At least without her being there I can have the peace and quiet I need. Hopefully this time we might be successful. It has been tough having all these people in the house."

"What do you mean, 'all these people'? I thought it was just your mother-in-law."

"His sister invited herself over for a holiday, too. Sister-in-law number one, the eldest, who must be called Sister Esther, arrived unannounced with four kids under the age of ten in our two-bedroom house. Even though I'm working full-time, she would routinely demand four different breakfasts for the kids. You can't believe it. One wants cornflakes. Another wants egg and toast. One wants porridge, and the other wants yam and beans. Guess who was meant to get all this prepared before leaving at seven every morning? Me. All the while, Sister-in-law stood over my head and barked out instructions like a drill sergeant. I could not wait till they all left for Lagos with Emeka's mum. Now I have the house back to myself and can plan."

My voice is firm. "Can't Emeka put his foot down and

tell his family that they can't treat you like an unpaid servant?"

Bridget shakes her head. "Esther has two housemaids in Lagos. She is used to ordering people around. Besides, no one says no to her in the family. It is a taboo."

"Well, I hope you at least get some peace and quiet now. You so deserve this. Both of you."

I feel for Bridget, having to deal with a Nigerian mother-in-law. I had heard stories from my mother and her aunt as well as their friends about how they had been treated by their female in-laws when they were younger in Nigeria, their culinary and home-making skills monitored and criticised.

I sigh. "Sometimes people put culture above reason. My dad would not rest until he had a son. It broke up our family. His family planned the whole thing. They even found a wife for him, according to my mum."

"So you have a half-brother."

"Yeah. My mum saw him when she went to Ibadan for Dad's funeral. He'll be in his mid-twenties now. He lives in Lagos with his mum."

"The evil that men do. And then they leave it for their children to deal with."

"I feel sorry for my half-brother. Dad just wanted to have an heir," I say.

"That is what my mother-in-law keeps repeating. 'My first son must have an heir.' She has three other sons o. For your father – I guess he probably must have considerable properties that this son stands to inherit."

I bite my lip. "Not really. There is the house in London, but he has no rights to that. My mum has fought hard to pay off the mortgage on it, and me and my sister helped her out when we started work. She's only just become mortgage-free in her early seventies."

Bridget huffs. "The sagas in the life of the average Nigerian woman sha..." She gets up. "I had better get back and let you have your lunch. I will send you the costs for the project with the libraries we were speaking about."

I nod. "Brilliant," I tell her with a smile, and get back to typing out a report, half my mind on our conversation and the seeming conspiracy against the childless woman in our culture.

***

I bump into lovely Aunty Remi at Stratford later that evening. She has had her hair freshly done and is wearing a pink and lilac patterned dress.

"Aunty Remi?" I say, a bit surprised because Stratford is nowhere near her neck of the woods. Especially late enough for Thursday late closing hours.

"I just came to do a bit of shopping at Westfields." Aunty Remi smiles and leans forward to give me a hug.

As I hug her back, I sense something is a bit off. She keeps looking around her and fidgeting with her bag.

"You okay, Aunty? You look as if you are in a bit of a rush."

She nods, a bit too fast for my liking. Aunty Remi never rushes anywhere. "You are right, my daughter. I am in a bit of a rush. My friend is waiting for me. I will see you later."

"Right ... okay, Aunty."

"See you soon," she says and turns in the opposite direction.

A few minutes later, I turn around and see her and a man walking towards Westfields. He is too far away for me to make out his face, but I can see he is a tall chap and they are walking very close together. Then I watch as he takes her hand in his.

Wow.

Aunty Remi has a man friend. Boyfriend. Lover. Whatever.

The evidence was all there. Looking very charming today in a pretty outfit complete with fresh coiffure and heels higher than the sensible church-matron pumps that she favours, that gigantic bunch of flowers in the house when I visited months back, looking furtive when she saw me – like a teenager caught tiptoeing back home from a party or illegal rave by their parents.

Aunty Remi is in her late sixties. I am thrilled that this woman who has suffered after losing the love of her life and has struggled like my mother to look after her children has now found love. Hopefully.

I decide to keep it to myself, but in the meanwhile, good on Aunty Remi. Woo hoo!

When I get home I start a text to Jimi.

> Hi Jimi – Thanks. Next Friday sounds great. Just to confirm that I will be the account manager handling your contract at Ryder & Hamilton. We can discuss over dinner later on Friday and go over the deliverables.

I look at it and wrinkle my nose.

It's dinner though. Not a business lunch.

I delete the text and start again.

> Thanks Jimi. Looking forward to dinner next Friday. Caribbean sounds lovely. Let me know where you want us to meet. I will call you back to discuss some of your plans re the NuChance Foundation and send some dates for a possible meeting at our offices. Best wishes. Sade x

I delete the "x."

———————

I have a date. Okay, maybe it's more of a business dinner, I tell myself.

Jimi rings as I am waiting for my train to work. His voice is as crisp and as fresh as the croissant I have just picked up for breakfast.

"How are you this morning?" His deep voice sends all the wrong (right) messages to my brain this morning.

"Fine, thanks. And you?"

"Great. Got a full day. It is what it is in the medical field. I got your message about Friday and I'm looking forward to dinner. The restaurant is in Peckham and does wonderful food. Cyril recommends the curried goat and coconut rice. And their rum ice-cream is legendary, he says."

I laugh. "Well, I can't really resist that, can I? Did you get my email about meeting at the offices next week?"

"Yes, just checking with Cyril and will get back to you," he responds. "So how is your mum? Your sister."

Er. Mum is mum.

"Mum's fine. Same old."

"She had words with my dad about us, you know," Jimi says, and he seems to be laughing at this.

"She never."

"I get this abrupt phone call from Dad about not embarrassing the family and not taking advantage of the daughters of key members of his congregation."

I close my eyes. "For goodness' sake."

"I assured him that my intentions towards you are very honourable. I can't promise what will happen after you have had a glass of wine, but…"

I am silent. Flirty banter isn't my thing. In fact, I don't even know how to flirt. This is why I need to get the PYTs in to give other women advice in the church. This is now a matter of urgency. I don't want Jimi reading my awkward silences as a lack of interest in him. Now that I have established that I *am* interested in him.

"Sade? Are you still there?"

"Yep?"

"You know I was just kidding." His voice holds a tinge of concern.

Now I laugh. "Of course. I don't even drink anyway."

I can imagine him stroking his chin in that way he has when he is trying to figure me out.

"So, you are totally without any kind of vices at all? You are a beautiful woman whose life revolves around work and church. You don't drink, smoke, or indulge in flirtatious banter or anything in the slightest bit improper. I'm intrigued, Sade Sodipo, and looking forward to getting to know more about the real you."

"This is the real me. Live and direct." Take it or leave it, too old to change it.

"Yeah, right."

I see the train arrive and people moving towards the doors.

"My train's here, Jimi. See you soon."

"Can't wait."

Chapter Twenty-Four

J imi comes for a meeting at our office on the same day we are to go for dinner.

I take one look at myself in the mirror. Long braids tied into ponytail: check. Makeup on point. Subtle but effective. I am wearing my new white blouse with a flirty bow at the neck, tucked into slimline flared tan trousers with tan high-heeled sandals. Added linen jacket for presentation purposes.

One deep breath and I walk into the conference room and see Greg, Jimi, and Cyril at the table, deep in conversation. Cyril is tall, light skinned, and balding with glasses. After introductions and handshakes, I glance at Jimi, whose smile is polite and totally professional. He is smart in a navy-blue suit; no tie today, just a plain white shirt. His handshake is firm and strangely reassuring.

"Good morning, Sade."

"Good morning, Jimi," I respond with an equally

professional smile as his hand envelops mine. I can feel Greg's eyes on us.

I turn to shake Cyril's hand as well.

Cyril nods. "Good morning, Sade. Nice to meet you. I have seen your proposals. Now let us see how you are going to bring it all together."

I walk towards the screen.

Before I know it, the presentation is over. And it seems to have gone well.

Greg shows Cyril and Jimi out of the office, while I stay in the meeting room, looking out at the skyline and the imposing buildings along the Thames.

Soon, Greg walks back in, his face impassive.

"Well?" I look at him. "How do you think it went?"

Greg's face breaks out into a huge grin and he fist-pumps the air as if his team has just won the Champions League.

"They love us. We got the contract. Jimi seems especially impressed."

"Fantastic news. Now the work begins. I had better let the team know."

"Really well done with that presentation. Just how I like it. Straight to the point. Well researched and it flowed seamlessly. I knew you could do it."

It is a good feeling getting praise from the boss.

"By the way, I am organising staff drinks next month at The Tap – my favourite watering hole. Sorry about the pun." Greg is walking to the door, opening it for me to precede him. "It's going to be after work. Will be nice to see you there. I want no excuses."

I rarely go to staff drinks. Last time they had coincided

with an evening prayer service in church. And before that there were countless other reasons I couldn't go to departmental shindigs. To be honest, I am not a pub person. Drinking after work and musing over colleagues, having post-mortems about work, work, politics, and work after 6 p.m. is something I've always given a miss.

Yet everything is about balance, and career networking will do me no harm, so I decide I will go to The Tap. Apparently, the odd celebrity pops up there now and then. Who knows, I might bump into someone famous while nursing a mocktail.

———————

That evening, I almost trip over my high heels as I walk out of Peckham station. I know I should have taken the lift.

The restaurant is on the High Street.

"You look lovely." Jimi bends to brush his lips against my cheek and I am glad I changed into my African print maxi dress in the loos at work and piled my long braids into an updo that shows off what I have been told are my best features: my high cheekbones and my dark brown eyes and long eyelashes.

The restaurant is a rustic traditional eatery getting lots of good reviews. There are prints of azure seas and sandy beaches, delicious seafood and carnival dancers. The cream walls create a spacious feel, even though every table is occupied and the place is busy. A mixture of blues, reggae, and R&B filters through the atmosphere.

The server welcomes us warmly and hands over the

menus, then asks us about drinks. I go for the mango and lime delight and Jimi asks for a sarsaparilla drink.

"Great news about the contract," I say. "Thanks for trusting us with your project."

He smiles. "You were great this morning, I must say. You and your team know your stuff and I know you guys will smash this out of the park. Cyril is also impressed with your proposals ... and that, my dear, ends all talk of work. We are *not* talking work tonight. It is a chance to talk about fun stuff, not what we do nine-to-five. I did warn you."

I laugh.

"You can tell me how the NuChance project is going next week in an email... Tonight is ours."

I smile at the way he says "ours."

The menu arrives and I choose seafood patties for starters followed by rice and peas and grilled chicken and the famous mango and coconut ice-cream he has told me about.

"What will you have?" I look up and see he is watching me.

"Cyril recommended it and I know he knows his food – I will have the meat rotis for starters followed by the oxtail, white rice, and salad," Jimi declares.

"Sounds good."

The starters arrive quickly, succulent and grilled, the aroma tantalising as we tuck into them.

"So, what don't I know about you?" Jimi smiles. "Apart from the fact that you are a good project manager, a good daughter, and stunning."

"Does anything else matter?" I laugh and so does Jimi.

"You like living alone?" he says.

"I do," I say. "Or rather, I'm fine with my own company."

"Sign of a healthy mind," says Jimi. "And you own it, or rent?"

"I own it." I shake my head. "I remember when it was going through, Mum telling me it would 'deter possible suitors.'"

Now Jimi shakes his head. "Our parents are a pair, aren't they? When I came back to the UK, my dad was so excited that I was pursuing a medical career that he hugged me. He hasn't hugged me since I fell down and hurt my leg in the park at about eight years old or something. But when I told him I was studying physiotherapy he lost it. Like, 'How can you study some of the same electives as a medical doctor but not be able to use the title Doctor?' he roared, before he put on his clerical collar and went off to preach the gospel at his congregation."

I frown. "I don't understand. Why can't you call yourself a doctor?"

"It is something I've tried to explain many times to people, and we discuss it a lot amongst ourselves as practitioners. Some say yes, I would say no. A physiotherapist specialises in the diagnosis, treatment, and management of patients with mobility issues because of illness, injury, or surgery." He pauses to take a sip of his drink. "A medical doctor is a professional who's completed a degree in medicine and surgery, has studied at med school, and has expertise in a number of specialities: cardiac medicine, gynaecology, paediatrics... Once I've completed advanced studies, I can call myself a doctor, but it really is no big deal to me. I have other motivations and carrying titles on my head is not one of them."

"You know how Nigerians obsess over titles. If you do the advanced training, you can add Doctor to your name and get your dad off your back," I suggest.

"Maybe. It's not in my project tray right now, but if and when I do it, it will not be to please anyone else but to enhance my patients' treatment. Anyway, Dad is calming down nowadays. We are having less arguments and he is in a better mood. At first, I thought it was because he was getting on, but guess what – he is in love. My man is dating! There is this 'special' woman he has been seeing."

The mains arrive piping hot and we waste no time in tucking in.

I pause between mouthfuls and ask, "What else do you know about your dad's new lady friend?"

"Not a lot." Then Jimi laughs. "My dad has more of a dating life than I do – no wonder I had to even the score by asking you out."

"Charming. And here I am thinking it is because I am 'an absolute stunner.'"

"You know that you're all that and more besides." He winks at me. "So, regarding this woman. She is a member of his congregation, and very pleasant. I went to see Dad a while ago and met her there in the sitting room sipping a cup of tea with him. She knew my mum and spoke fondly of her. I do not really remember her from when I was young, to be honest, but she has a kind face."

"So, you think this is serious then?"

"My dad has not dated anyone in the past fifteen years. My brother has hinted that a few of the church mummies have tried to get in there with kindness and covered dishes of cakes and jollof rice, but he has remained polite and distant. He is not the philandering type any more, but if he was, he would have a field day in that congregation. I mean you can almost smell the adoration of the older females for him. I am glad this lady has taken him off the market, to be honest. He seems a lot happier. She got him to get himself checked out with the doctor, eat properly, sleep more often, and actually go out and have fun. Can you believe that they went off to Westfield to watch a film the other day?"

"Westfield?" I say. "In Stratford?" I feel a prickle on my skin.

"Yep." Jimi grins. "I just love it when I see OAPs living dangerously! He warmed up to me and told me that he is planning to ask her to marry him. He says he asked her about three years ago and she said no then but he asked her early last year and they have been dating since. He asked my permission and wanted to know if I minded if he gets married again. It is not that he has forgotten my mum but he would like a chance to experience happiness again in his old age. I gave him the thumbs-up, of course. So did my brother, Femi. Now Dad has started googling the cost of a cruise to the Caribbean for two of them. It is a surprise for their honeymoon if she says yes."

I remain calm. "So, when do you think he will pop the question?"

"She turns seventy next month, so he thinks he'll do it then. Now that he has made friends with her sons. Dad is a fast worker, man."

I smile. "So what's her name?"

"Remi. Remi Adekoya."

Ah. Seeing them from the bus, coming out of a restaurant months before. It must have been them having a rendezvous for two. Aunty Remi's newfound bubbly joy and fashion makeovers. The flowers in her kitchen. The weird look on her face when we bumped into each other at Westfield.

Wow.

I realise I haven't said anything.

"Sade? Are you okay?"

I nod. "I am just reeling from the news…"

He frowns.

"She has been an aunty to me for as a long as I can remember," I say. "I adore her, and though it's a bit of a surprise, it could not happen to a nicer person. Aunty Remi deserves a good man, a man of integrity who loves her and takes care of her. She does so many things for so many people. Charity work with the homeless and children with special needs, serving on the church board. I think she will be a wonderful pastor's wife."

"Ah, Sade. I can see how much she means to you."

"Yes. She's like a second mum. She has three boys, so I suppose I am the daughter she never had."

Jimi is beaming, but he leans forward. "Please, do not say anything to her about it. In fact, it is meant to be a secret from everyone. Dad says he will tell his parishioners after he has spoken to her."

"I fear many hearts will be dashed." *Including my mum's.* One thing to find out that the Bishop is dating and then, double blow for Mum, it is her childhood friend.

"Hope there won't be any drama or wig pulling."

"That was so wrong and sexist," I reprove.

"Okay. I am grovelling now. Is my apology accepted?"

"I'll think about it."

"Don't give me that stern look out of those big, beautiful eyes of yours."

"Moi?"

"Yep."

"Oh, come on." I roll my eyes.

"So how are you feeling, after your op? Are you keeping up with the exercises?"

I shake my head. "Not so much. I've been busy…"

His voice is serious. "Never be too busy for your health. I don't want to nag but I've seen so many women that are guilty of looking after everyone but themselves…"

I nod. "I should have had the surgery years ago and saved myself a lot of pain…"

"So, why didn't you?"

I stare at my glass. "I was scared."

"Scared? Of what?"

"It's silly, I know, but I was scared that they might take out my womb and leave me totally unmarriageable in the eyes of most Nigerian guys, or most guys generally, who want children. Ridiculous, I know – and I pride myself on taking charge of my own life."

"Any man that makes having children a prerequisite to having a successful marriage doesn't know the meaning of love. I thought it was meant to be for better, for worse?"

"Are you actually Nigerian?" I narrow my eyes.

"My friend, shall I show you my Nigerian passport?" He laughs and then sobers. "Look, the most important thing is that you are much better." He puts a hand on mine and looks into my eyes. "I know it's not fair. It's not a fair

227

world. You are fantastic, Sade. It's not your fault that no chap has realised that yet. Let everyone else that tries to make you feel small go take a flying leap. It's not what they think that matters. It's what *you* think. Don't let them squeeze you into their boring mould. Don't let them do that to you. Please."

My eyes meet his and I feel that foolish giddiness again.

"I was dating this chap – Simon," I muse. "I thought it was going somewhere… But it didn't work out. His mum didn't like the idea of her son marrying a woman in her forties."

"That's his loss. A grown man should not let his mum decide who he marries. What's up with that?"

I smile. "I know. Pathetic, isn't it."

Jimi laughs, then shakes his head. "Promise me that you will always be you, Sade. Don't change for anyone."

No man has ever said anything like this to me and it makes my heart flip.

"People want you to be a bad photocopy of another copy of someone else's bad photocopy – so they can classify and file you under their definition of what you should be. I'm single because I enjoy being me, and maybe I'm too old to change, or even want to change, into the person whoever I'm dating at the time wants."

"You're such a romantic."

"You're such a cynic."

"Romantics get hurt. It is a tough world out there and no one is really who you see on the surface. Besides men can get hurt, too."

"Really?"

His lips twitch. "I want to stand up for the rights for all

the misunderstood, unappreciated, and unloved men of the world."

"Oh, please. You know that most of the wahala in relationships is from men."

I watch as Jimi pretends to look hurt while looking incredibly adorable.

"That is so … sexist. I'm appalled," he says, and we both laugh before he shakes his head. "Okay, hear me out," he adds. "We all have masks we put on to protect ourselves. You've probably been hurt enough times to fortify yourself against any predatory male. I put mine up after my divorce. That is what my therapist told me."

He pours us each a glass of water.

"When did you start seeing a therapist?" I ask.

"When I first came back from Brazil. It was while I was studying for my physiotherapy qualifications. I thought to myself, if I was going to be of help to anyone, I needed to sort myself out. Get rid of the weight of expectations, of being the first-born son who had disappointed the family, the pain of being compared with a younger brother who did everything right, the guilt of not being there for my mum when she was ill. I told my dad I'd started therapy and he said I was too old for 'that nonsense' and that my problems were nothing that some prayers and Bible study couldn't sort out. More or less, 'Pull yourself together and get on with it.'"

I smile wryly. "That's how we deal with it in this country. Stiff upper lip. And in Naija, we just pray it away or pretend it's not there, bury it under our Agbada and big society shindigs."

"Exactly." Jimi nods. "Then there was my divorce and

my son. My ex didn't let me see my son for years. I had to go to court to get access. Things are much better now. I mean he is a young adult. Comes over on holidays from San Francisco sometimes."

"Wow, that's a lot to deal with."

He smiles warmly. "So, I really felt that I was the common denominator to a lot of people's pain. I had a lot of stuff to unpack. Stuff I didn't want anyone else to deal with. The counselling was thorough and regular. It really helped. I started a tentative reconciliation with my brother Femi, who for a long time thought I was the scum of the earth. He lives in Nigeria and is doing well. Big house. Fantastic job. He always thought I was jealous of him, but didn't understand that I was actually happy for him and his family. I'm happy doing what I'm doing and happy doing me. And I think he is finally starting to believe me. And then there's Dad, who used to think I was a ne'er-do-well. But now, five years later, we are making baby steps towards having conversations without yelling at each other."

"So things are getting better."

"I hope so. Femi allows his children to call me Uncle Jimi now. I'm no longer deemed a bad influence."

"Jimi, that's a real achievement," I say. "You've worked hard to change and work on yourself." I look down at my food, realisation hitting me. "Maybe my problem is that I've stayed the same. Gone to the same church, played it safe with my career – do you know I once wanted to live in the States and study international relations? It would have allowed me to work in different countries influencing global policies. I could have travelled the world like you."

"Why didn't you?"

"My mum wanted us close. Ever since my dad left, it has been the three of us. But the thing is, even though I did the 'right thing' I still failed to meet Mum's expectations of me. I still disappointed her. I should have just gone for it instead of worrying about leaving her here."

Jimi sighs. "One cannot live life trying to live up to anyone's expectations. When my marriage was going down the pan, I was trying to keep it together because of expectations from my dad – saying 'Thou shalt not divorce' – and from her parents, who thought their daughter had made the mistake of her life by getting with a black guy. It was hard for Karline. I guess she was trying to referee both sides. And I could hardly expect her to choose me over her parents." He smiles. "Anyway. She's married again now. To a banker. The kind of guy her parents wanted for her in the first place. In every possible way, I am happy for her."

"You mean that from your heart?"

He nods. "I am getting on with the rest of my life. My work as a physiotherapist and this project with Cyril are things that really inspire me. I want to try my best to help younger people find what they are best at doing and not waste time playing Russian roulette with their lives like I did."

"You know what, Jimi Taylor? You're a good egg."

"And you, my dear, are an absolute star. How is your food?"

I take another forkful and close my eyes. "Delicious."

"We are going to have to do this again, and next time we won't talk about our deepest dark secrets. We can talk about fun stuff."

"Define fun stuff?"

"Anything apart from dark deepest secrets," he says with a smile. "So, how about it?"

I flutter my eyelashes and realise that it comes naturally. "Depends. What do you have in mind for our date?"

He winks at me. "That will be my surprise."

I smile and watch his eyes darken.

I take a sip of water. "I'll look forward to it."

"Me, too," he says, and his voice is like warm, melted velvet oozing over me.

Chapter Twenty-Five

On the following Sunday, I join Kike and her family at church. Afterwards, we see Mum.

Mum and I haven't really spoken much since the wedding. I think she's probably still annoyed that I am getting quite friendly with Jimi, but I decide to front it and carry on as if all is normal.

At her house, we are welcomed by the delicious smell of fried plantain. Kike's twins run over and hug Mum and her face transforms. Brightening up like twenty years of stress and grind have been taken off. I realise she's reliving and correcting her motherhood journey through those two boys.

Then Mum turns to go into the kitchen, leaving Kike and her husband with the children, and I join her.

"How are you?" I ask.

She grunts, focused on turning the plantain in the new non-stick frying pan I got her for Christmas. It took years to get her to throw away her old one... She truly is of the waste-not-want-not generation.

I move over and gently take the fork from her hand. "Mum, I'll do that. You can go and sit down."

"I was frying this before you knew how to say your first word." She doesn't look up, turning one golden brown plantain onto its side to make sure it is well done.

"I know, but now we are here – you don't have to do it."

"Do you know that the Bishop has not been returning my calls since you and Jimi started going out?" She releases a sigh.

I lean against the kitchen door and stare out at the next-door garden. Like Mum's, it has now reached equatorial proportions. I swear I see a giant fox scuttling around in the foliage. I make a mental note to get a handy man in to give me a quote. Mum has never been much of a gardener.

"Did you hear what I said, Folasade?"

I take a deep breath. "Mum, Jimi and I are just friends – I don't see what the problem is – and as for the Bishop not calling you—" I bite my lip "—I didn't know you exchanged phone calls that often anyway."

Mum frowns. "He is my bishop. He has said I can call him anytime I have a problem. He knows I am all here with just my God now. He has always been very helpful when he can, calling me to see how I am, sending me a card at Christmas with good wishes. Once he arranged for the church to organise buses to pick me up to bring me to church – you know, that time I hurt my leg in 2015."

I nod. "That was 2018."

She picks up the bowl and loads the frying pan with more pieces of plantain and the oil sizzles. "Anyway, you know what I mean. I know how he has suffered since his wife, Sister Fola, went to be with the Lord. Such a great woman. She was a great mother to her boys. The youngest has done so well and settled in Nigeria – a top lawyer there, you know. A Senior Advocate of Nigeria – recognition of the highest order." Her voice lowers. "Jimi, on the other hand, has always wanted to do his own thing. He would have made a wonderful doctor, but it was this football in his head. Now he is doing therapy of the leg or the arm – I don't know which."

"Mum – Jimi is entitled to do what he feels best for him. He is a big boy now."

"You people like to do your own thing. That is why he is where he is in life! How can a person go to university and study physiotherapy and not have the sense to realise that he could add a few more subjects and become a doctor?"

I sigh. "He doesn't want to be a doctor. He is happy being a physiotherapist."

Mum shakes her head. "Can you imagine when people ask a parent at a party, 'How is the physiotherapist?' instead of 'How is the Doctor?'? It does not carry the same respect."

"Mum…"

"Anyway, he is not in his father's good books at all. So, finding out that my daughter is going out with a son that has caused my dear friend the Bishop a lot of pain – how do you think I feel?"

"Frankly, whoever Jimi dates is not really his father's business. He is forty-five."

"Forty-five and not a doctor. And he has a son who lives in America, far away from him. I hope the boy's mother does not stop him from reaching out to his grandfather here. You know these Oyibo women and their wahala."

I shake my head. "Jimi is in contact with his son, Mum.

I don't think the boy seeing the Bishop will be any problem. And Jimi has great prospects."

Mum gives me a hard glance. "So, you seem to know a lot about Jimi for someone who is telling me, 'Mum, we are just friends.'"

"Well, friends talk to each other, you know," I tell her. "Like you talk to Bishop Taylor."

She seems to stiffen, then pulls herself together and holds the fork out to me. "Anyway, I've said all I will say on the matter."

I turn to attend to the plantain, trying to make sense of our conversation as she walks out of the room.

———————

We have a delicious meal and watch TV with the boys, but on the way home I can't stop thinking about how Mum is so proprietary over Bishop Taylor. The look in her eye when she said "my dear friend" worries me. Does she have feelings for him? I am concerned, especially since I know his heart is with her best friend, Aunty Remi, and who knows what will happen when Mum finds out about that? But I won't get involved. I'll let Aunty Remi tell her when she is ready.

Chapter Twenty-Six

I meet up with the girls for lunch and Sam immediately jumps in with her questions about Jimi.

I roll my eyes, smiling. "I just knew it – when am I going to get a break?"

Vicky crosses her arms. "Come on. You know we aren't going to sit here and just pretend that we don't know you two are dating."

I sigh. "You know it's early days and we're not really a couple-couple ... or something like that."

Sam grins. "I am just happy that you are *dating* again. He is definitely an improvement on the last one."

"As I said, it's early days."

"There is this new buzz about you nowadays. You smile more, laugh more, and are less sarky. It must be love." Sam puts her hand to her heart.

"As long as you're not rushing into things," Vicky says, but with a smirk.

Sam nods. "I mean, if Sade's boyfriends were like

237

buses – it would have been like the whole of London buses' staff going on strike – for years."

I shake my head. "Sam, I just love your way with words."

Sam chuckles. "What about sex – have you had it, or talked about it, yet?"

Trust Sam to go in for the kill. "Whoa."

But Sam continues in her usual no-holds-barred way. "I am just being realistic. That is the part of the relationship most guys are interested in. I mean, after a couple of weeks Martin had already—"

I cough. "Nothing's happened romantically, except a kiss."

Vicky arches an eyebrow.

"I mean, there is definitely a vibe," I clarify. "Chemistry. But we're both a bit old for all that teenage stuff. We talk about intellectual things, politics, music, and enjoy a mutual dislike of tradition, convention. I think we're just taking it slow and learning how to be mates."

"Hmm." Sam shakes her head. "From what you say, that guy fancies you. It is only a matter of time before sex becomes something you will have to deal with, and the subjects of tradition and politics will be the last things on his mind then."

"I know." I hesitate. "It's just that I have my beliefs and he doesn't believe in anything. We haven't – I haven't told him about how I feel about that side of things. I know it sounds stupid but I still believe that some things are special enough to keep till after marriage. You know what I mean?"

Vicky and Sam both nod.

Then Sam sighs. "It's this church thing, isn't it?"

"We've been over this, Sam."

Sam looks at both myself and Vicky. "I don't understand how you guys do it. I mean don't you…"

Vicky chuckles. "Of course you want to but you discipline the mind and learn how to work on other parts of your relationship. Karl and I have agreed. Sex is reserved for marriage."

"I just don't want her to lose this guy," Sam continues.

"Hey. I'm still here," I add.

"I mean, didn't you…" Sam shakes her head. "What about Simon?"

"Simon was willing to wait."

Sam falls silent.

"Go on, say it, Sam. My unrealistic ideals are keeping me single."

"Well…" Sam puts a hand to her forehead.

"Look, guys, "Vicky interjects. "I'm sure you'll sort it. I know you, Sade, and I have faith that you will let God guide you."

I smile back. "Good advice." Vicky obviously has more faith in me than I do myself.

"Anyway," says Sam. "How's everything with your mum?"

"She's fine."

"I mean, what does she feel about Jimi?" Vicky persists gently.

I heave an almighty sigh, "Let's just say, like everything else about this relationship … it's complicated."

Chapter Twenty-Seven

Yesterday Jimi rang and suggested we go to the British Film Institute to watch an old film. He had it all sorted out plus dinner at a restaurant close to Borough Market.

I was impressed. "I never knew you were into old films."

He laughed. "I seem to remember you said you liked old movies – you know, film noir and all that stuff – and then I saw that Alfred Hitchcock's *Vertigo* was on and it just felt like a good idea."

"It's a great idea," I said, smiling at my phone. "Looking forward to it."

At the BFI, we snag some good seats and munch popcorn as we watch James Stewart and Kim Novak navigate heights, vertigo, and smokescreens. I feel warm all over. Not just because it is a balmy August night, but because this chap went out of his way to research films I like when I told him film noir from the forties and fifties were my favourites, and secondly because he is sitting so close to me that I am getting the occasional palpitation.

When his hand links with mine as Kim Novak falls to her death, I lean into him and ask in a whisper if he's scared.

"Nope," he whispers back.

I am staring at his profile, trying to make out the expression in his eyes from this angle, when his face turns to mine, as if in slow motion, and like a blurred dream our lips meet. Heat rises from my stomach to my chest as his lips gently explore mine, and my heart decides to skip a beat as the kiss deepens, inflaming every part of my body. Neither of us pulls away, and before we know it, the lights have come back on and people are getting up to leave.

"Get a room, mate," I hear someone say with a chuckle, and Jimi's lips curl into a smile as he finally lets go of me.

After a tapas dinner near London Bridge, we walk to the train station, comfortably not saying much; in fact, Jimi seems lost in thought.

"What are you thinking about?" I ask him.

He shakes his head, smiles. "Just that my son rang me today."

"Oh, that's great, Jimi." I smile back.

"Yeah, it was great to hear from him."

"But?" I query, sensing there's one coming.

Jimi shakes his head. "Well, he was all set to do his Masters in London, and I was really looking forward to it, but now he wants to take a gap year. In Thailand."

"That doesn't sound like a bad idea," I say carefully.

Jimi's tone is serious. "It's not, in principle. I would always encourage him to see the world. But I guess I want him to get his education out of the way before he does that. He was so set on coming to London soon, but suddenly he's changed his mind." Jimi pauses. "I can't help thinking that his mum is behind this."

I decide not to probe into that. I'm not getting involved in his relationship with his ex. Instead, I go for pragmatism.

"On the other hand, if he does some travelling before he studies, he gains some life experience, and some perspective?"

"I just don't want him to—" Jimi stops.

"To make the same mistakes you did."

"Exactly. He is so young. I just want everything to be perfect for him. You know…"

"That's natural. You want to protect him from the big bad world. Like our parents wanted for us. And we end up hating them for it."

Jimi laughs. "True. My dad – in his own way – was trying to save me from the consequences of my own choices, but—" he nods "—that's futile. It's inevitable that we will make mistakes."

"All part of growing up," I say. "You've grown into the kind of person who can guide your son and be there for him in all the right ways."

"That is sweet of you to say. My ex would say I was a crap husband, and she was right. But I am trying to be the best dad possible. But when we spoke, my son accused me of being just like my father, I just don't want to admit it."

"Hmm." I smile. "On this occasion, maybe he was a little bit right."

Jimi chuckles to himself. "You know, my mum used to say that."

"I'm in great company, then," I say, and he grabs my hand and squeezes it as we enter the station.

———————

At work the next day, I notice that Bridget looks more like herself. Her smile has returned.

"Hubby looked me in the eyes yesterday and promised me that it was just going to be us now. He says he knows it has been difficult over the past few years with the in-laws. We're going to concentrate on us, on the family we want to have, going forward. I just pray things work this time with the IVF."

"I'm praying for you, too, Bridget. You so deserve this. Both of you do."

She eyes me. "And I hope things with this gentleman work out. I can tell you really like him."

I sigh. "One of the main reasons I like him is that he is as un-Nigerian as I am. I don't have to try and live up to traditional expectations. He just lets me be me. I don't have to worry about pleasing his relatives, or him scoring marks on my cooking or anything…"

Bridget smiles. "He sounds perfect for you."

"It's easier talking to you about things. You are not so in awe with the idea of being in love, like Sam, or too practical, like Vicky, who as good as gets out the Bible and cross-checks everything in my new 'relationship' to see if it lines up."

"And does he share your faith? I know it's quite important to you."

"That's a big one. No, not really, and sometimes I wonder if I'm trying to cover up the real me." I laugh. "The me that is a total wreck without my faith in God. That has been the main constant in my life over the years. The only thing that hasn't let me down."

"Listen, if he loves you, he will want you to be yourself. Don't try and hide any part of you. You got to unpack the bags when you get home, if you get me. Is Jimi 'home'?"

"I hope so. I want him to be, so badly," I admit.

Chapter Twenty-Eight

Pastor Keith likes my recommendations and wants me to meet with Sister Mary to discuss implementing some of them into the Singles Ministry.

Sister Mary has been married for thirty years and believes that the best way of supporting single people in their forties and fifties is to tell them to forget about marriage and concentrate on being good single Christians. This is a woman who believes that a Successful Singles event is one where ninety per cent of the attendees are women, and she hasn't forgotten that I was the one who complained first.

I pick up the phone and call her.

"Good evening, Sister Mary."

"Evening, Sade. Pastor told me to expect a call from you."

"Has he discussed anything with you?"

"Yes, a little. I'm afraid I have been too busy really to go through all your recommendations. All two pages of them."

Okay, so it had been double-sided. "Oh. No probs. I know things are busy."

"Look, I will be honest with you. We are in the trenches here. It is okay for you to sit at home and go over my head and give suggestions, but I can tell you from years in the Singles Ministry that most of those ideas are not practical! This is not a Christian dating agency."

I close my eyes and press on. "I hear you, but suppose most of the women and the few men we have want to be like you – have successful married lives that are godly."

There is a long pause, during which I can hear pots and pans clattering about. "Listen, Sade. I am preparing dinner at the moment for my family. I can't discuss this over the phone. Let us say we meet up after church and have a meeting. Right now, I have a family to take care of."

"Sure," I say. "Be assured that it is not my intention to undermine you in any way. I just want to be part of the solution. I want to make singles feel great again."

Did I just say that?

"Fine. We will speak on Sunday," Sister Mary says crisply, and terminates the call.

I go to see Jimi and Cyril in their offices – they have a couple of rooms in an office block for creatives in Hoxton. We have a brief discussion on key project expectations and requirements. We lay out milestones and objectives, and address their business goals.

After a lengthy discussion we arrive at the decision that the best bet for this new sports charity will be fundraising through community events such as a walkathon or a sportsathon. Raising awareness and funds whilst building support with patrons, so we will hopefully increase fundraising and recognition within the community.

We finish the meeting and Cyril thanks me, then Jimi walks me to the lift.

"I forgot something the other night," he says as the lift arrives and a few people disembark.

I stare at him. The lift pauses and then the doors close.

I can see his eyes blink as he puts his hands in his pockets and looks down at me. "A goodnight kiss."

I glance down the corridor to see if anyone is around. "We kissed during the film."

"Yeah. I remember." He looks at my lips as he says this.

I can feel my heart thumping again.

His eyes move up to settle on mine. "Maybe we can do it again sometime?"

I am aware that my cheeks are hot, and all I can do is nod.

"Great," he says, grinning, as another lift arrives.

"Call me," I tell him as I get in, and he nods.

His grin, stretching from ear to ear, makes my heart do a somersault as the lift door closes.

I show up at church for my first singles event in a long while. I see a few women and a couple of men who look embarrassed to be there. I also spot two other members of the Successful Singles committee team: Chioma, a thirtyish social worker who is in the choir and Margaret from the ushering team. I can't make out her age, but the strands of grey in her hair probably mean we are in the same age bracket. I like Margaret; she is one of the most cheerful members of the ushering team and is known for her big smiles and warm handshakes as she welcomes visitors to the church. They are the long-suffering members of Sister Mary's team, and they have some news for me.

"Sister Mary has stepped down from the team," Chioma announces with a grin.

Margaret looks hopeful. "She says that you will be taking over?"

"What?" I shake my head. "No, no – that's not my remit. I just have some ideas, that's all."

"To be honest," Chioma's voice lowers, "we were quite happy when she gave us the news. We have been tearing our hair out hoping for new ideas – I mean, look around you. There is hardly anyone here."

"What are your plans for tonight?" I ask, stunned.

Margaret shrugs. "I don't know. Sister Mary said we were going to pray for missionaries abroad."

This is my calling. I spring into action. "Okay, let's have a networking session where everyone gets to know each other. I will pop down the road and get some soft drinks and biscuits."

Suddenly Chioma hugs me. "I'm so glad you're here, Sade. I feel as if this department needs some fresh ideas."

I feel embarrassed. "Er, okay. I will just pop down the road."

Later, on the bus home, I'm joined by Margaret, who lives in East London as well. We discuss the evening and how we can organise exciting and different events that might attract some more singles to join. As soon as I get home, I add them to a new list on my iPad.

1. Karaoke, games. Live DJ lip-synch battle with gospel music.
2. Professional network night – get some speakers to give professional development advice. Probably will volunteer myself and get some others.
3. Organise community involvement – possibly football club and get locals involved – maybe I could ask Jimi to put in an appearance. Cheeky, I know, but maybe I could go on a charm offensive. Offer to kiss him or something.

I delete the last sentence.

Chapter Twenty-Nine

At work, another NuChance project meeting with the team yields more progress. We negotiate free hire of a football pitch in return for publicity, and get Jimi and Cyril to talk to their old friends, some local and national celebrities – go through their agents and ask them to play for a small fee or free. We sort out the merchandising, PR, and social media and it's all looking good.

That afternoon, I get a text from Jimi.

> How are you doing? Great meeting today.

> I'm well. Glad you think so. ☺

> So, when do I get to take you to that Nigerian restaurant I was talking about?

We didn't discuss anything about a Naija restaurant?

We are now. 🤭 Trying to get another cheeky date. Can't blame a guy for trying.

I'm sure I can fit it in, in between working on your launch.

Talking shop isn't allowed. Just two hours of your time.

I hope the food is good.

It is. It's the 404 on Kent Road.

Oh, I saw your dad coming out from the place with Aunt Remi about a month ago. I should have guessed then that something was up.

My dad is in love. Apparently, it just catches you unawares.

Really? Like a disease?

Yep, and symptoms include making a guy take temporary leave of his senses.

You're scaring me with this red-pill angle.

It's costly emotionally, too. As the less emotionally connected of the species, for guys it can be like asking a fish to walk down the High Street.

Wow, that's quite an analogy. You're very philosophical tonight.

When I'm with you, I like to show you my philosophical side. If I don't, you might leg it.

I like you just as you are.

You don't know all of me yet.

You don't know all of me yet, either.

That's why we need another date.

Okay, you've convinced me. 😌

I promise you won't regret it. Their food is on point.

If I start putting weight on with all this food…

You'll still be absolutely stunning.

You and your sweet mouth, eh.

So, the kiss was that good ay.

I hover over the keypad.

OK. I had better get back to my shift, Jimi. Break's over.

Aw, you spent your break flirting with me. 😌😄

Bye, Jimi x

Goodbye, Sade xx

Making Singles Meetings Fun Again!

Over the next few months, my strategy for Successful Singles kind of works.

We have had speed dating, professional networking, and a crazy-golf trip, which pulls more men in. Plans are also underway for a Seventies Night with afros and bell-bottomed trousers and platform boots – the latter making Mum grimace.

"Orthopaedic shoes," she said when I asked if she'd kept hold of hers. "I was happy when the fashion died."

Chioma and Margaret have reported that there are more men joining the group in church as well.

One night Cyril joins. I had no idea he was single, or a member of our church, but then Jimi told me that he had lost his wife about five years ago and he has been on at him to get back out there. Cyril is a really nice guy and his manners are impeccable. He works for the charity full-time and like Jimi has put a lot of time and money into it.

He and Jimi invite me to accompany them on a local school visit, where they speak about their current work with youth and how it is impacting lives.

For the first time in my work life, I feel something stir in me. A passion for helping and working with young people. I make a mental note to get my DBS form done and offer to volunteer.

Men with purpose. Wonderful.

One man with a purpose can change the world. Start a movement.

I so like the idea of that.

In fact, it is one of the things I long for in a life partner: a man with a mission. I mean, a guy who's passionate about people and things other than himself, what's not to like?

On that note, Jimi asks if I want to go and watch football. His old club, Aldery City FC, are playing Leyton Orient.

"Um, okay?" I smile. "I don't really care that much about football, but catch me during the Euros or Olympics and you will not recognise me. I instantly become a football pundit debating sidekicks and shouting at my TV."

"That's my girl. See you Saturday."

There is a capacity crowd at Brisbane Road. A sea of Leyton Orient kits and the blue and yellow for Aldery FC. The rivalry is friendly but fierce, and bragging rights fill the air.

We arrive half an hour before the match and enter the stadium through the turnstile to get ourselves hot drinks and burgers before kick-off.

The atmosphere is tense. We sit with the away crowd on the Main Stand, which is full of yellow and blue banners, and notice Jimi getting a few looks.

"Hey. Aren't you Jimi Taylor?" says one vociferous supporter.

Jimi grins and sticks out his hand. "Nice to meet you, man."

"I knew it was you. Wasn't it about 2000 or 2001 you played?" says a grey-haired man nudging his friend.

"What you doing now?" says his mate.

"I work for the NHS. It's less stressful than playing for Aldery FC."

"Up Yellows!" They start chanting their football anthems.

"I really appreciate you coming out with me today." Jimi smiles in that beguiling way he has that keeps me wanting to have fun and put off discussing serious topics with him till another day. I never want that day to arrive.

I give him a carefree smile. "I'm up for new experiences, me. Imagine never going to a football stadium before, at my age."

He grins and brings out a little wrapped package from his bag.

"Just a little thank you."

I open it and find a yellow and blue scarf and hat.

"Aw. Thank you," I whisper, and our eyes meet.

"I gave my missus one of those when we first went out," a male voice interrupts our reverie.

I turn and the middle-aged man behind us is giving us the thumbs-up. Sitting next to him is, I assume, his wife, along with some kids who look like grandchildren.

"No, we are just..." I start to say, before a roar erupts through the crowd as the two teams come out of the tunnel together followed by the officials and the mascots.

As we sit there waiting for the first half to begin, Jimi links his hands with mine and we sit there like an old married couple.

Chapter Thirty

Date number four – or is it five? I'm losing count – and Jimi insists that we go to a karaoke bar nearby.

"No way."

"I heard you say you used to sing with the choir. And that you like old-school R&B."

"Not the same—" But Jimi shakes his head and leads me by the hand into the bar, where a good number of people are sitting at tables with snacks and drinks, facing a small stage with a microphone.

Jimi and I find a table at the back and he goes off to get drinks while I listen to the young lady on stage, who is going for it with all the strength she possesses. In the wrong key.

He returns with the mocktails.

"Drink up, then we are going to show them how to do it."

"Says who?"

Jimi grins. "The last time I did this I was drunk in a bar in Phuket. So I'm making my apologies already."

A man gets up and gives a slightly drunken rendition of Aerosmith's "Don't Wanna Miss a Thing" complete with air guitar, and there is anaemic applause when he finishes.

I freeze. "Jimi. I don't think I can do this."

His eyes catch mine and he smiles for reassurance. "It is just for a laugh, Sade. We aren't going for a Grammy."

I look at the crowd and back at him. Didn't I say I was open to all kinds of different experiences? Maybe getting booed by an audience is one of them?

"Come on." His eyes challenge mine. "It'll be fun."

I can see a young man giving us the thumbs-up to signal it is our turn.

"Fine." I take a deep breath and we get up and walk towards the stage. Jimi steps up first and then gives me his hand, pulling me beside him. He hands me the mic and whispers, "Just look at the screen or at me and go for it."

I close my eyes as the beats start from the instrumental part of "Ain't No Mountain High Enough." It's the Marvin Gaye and Tammi Terrell version.

When Jimi starts singing, his melodic tenor voice is an expected but nice surprise. I hear people clapping and see the encouragement on faces, and I smile into Jimi's eyes as I sing my own lines.

In a flash, it's over, and Jimi is helping me down while the audience claps and whistles for us.

"We did good, huh?"

"One of the good things about being forced to join the choir as a teen."

"Pastor's kid here. So was I. Besides, Motown classics are my favourite. I am old-school, me."

Me too.

We sit down and he orders us each another mocktail. There is a buzz between us tonight. I can't explain it, but something about the combination of the song and looking into each other's eyes... Something has shifted.

Later on, Jimi walks me to the bus stop, his hand in mine, the busy streets full of night owls like ourselves. For a while, we don't speak, each filled with different thoughts that we are still trying to process.

"Great night tonight," Jimi says finally.

"Yeah. I never knew you had the back catalogue of *100 Motown Hits* stored away in your hard drive."

"Ah ... lots you don't know about me. So, what's your fave Motown hit?"

"Where do I start? I love 'Respect' by Aretha. It's iconic. Marvin Gaye, too."

"'What's Going On?'?"

"That one, and 'I Heard it Through the Grapevine.'"

He is looking at me again. "Okay. Let's play this quiz before your bus gets here. Five more minutes. Let's see how much you know your Motown. Are you up for it?"

"Of course. You give me a few words and I tell you the artiste?"

"You're on. Let's go. 'Don't Stop Till You Get—'"

"M. J."

He gives me the thumbs-up. "'Chain of Foo—'"

"Aretha Franklin."

He claps his hands. "This girl knows her Motown. OK. 'Midnight Train to Georgia.'"

"Gladys Knight and the Pips."

"'End of the Road.'"

"Boyz II Men."

I look up as the 425 bus arrives all too soon. "Ah, and here's my own midnight train to Georgia." I sigh.

Jimi grins. "Too bad. But thanks for a lovely evening."

"Thank *you*. For forcing me to do karaoke."

He laughs, takes a step forward, and lightly kisses me on the cheek.

"We'll have to save our next proper goodnight kiss for next time."

A subtle glow infuses me and spreads out into my thoughts as I mumble a hurried goodnight as the bus arrives and I get on with a wave.

As we move away, I see him standing there waving with that self-deprecating smile he has. I wonder how he is going to get back to South-East London.

Chapter Thirty-One

Over the next few weeks, I find myself drawing closer to Jimi, though work has ramped up, including what I'm doing for the NuChance event, so we only get to squeeze in a couple of dates amid meetings at either his and Cyril's office or mine to talk through progress.

I'm happy with how things are going, though there is still a part of me that's holding back. Despite Jimi having the emotional intelligence and broad mind I've always craved in a partner, I'm scared to invest in him 100 per cent because I'm not too sure what his reaction will be when I unpack my fears and expectations for this relationship.

Tonight I am heading for our much-delayed work drinks at The Tap, organised enthusiastically by Greg. A showpiece of minimalist modern architecture, The Tap overlooks the river. From the balcony there's a good view of the riverside path below, and the bars and cafés that have sprung up over the last decade. If you look down, you can see all the city types sipping wine and toying with snacks as they make small talk and network on a sunny London evening.

Greg is in an ebullient mood, buying the first round of drinks for everyone in the team.

"Mocktail, Sade?" he asks, handing me a drinks menu, from which I choose something bland with orange juice and cranberry.

As Greg heads off to the bar, I look around. The place is a celebrity hotspot, and though my brain tells me I am not interested in anything so shallow, I find myself scanning for anyone famous. I spot some girls that look like they're auditioning for *The Only Way Is Essex* and a footballer who's been in the news recently.

I also notice an intriguing dark-haired beauty with long black hair and green eyes cinched into a red dress and gravity-defying heels, sitting at the bar sipping a cocktail and scrolling through her phone. *Is she famous?* I wonder. She looks the part.

A long hour later, as Greg is tipsily updating everyone on the company's performance, I am half listening to the terms "deep-dive", "leverage", and "drill down", hoping that once he's done we can call it a night and go home.

To my relief, colleagues start collecting coats and booking Ubers, and I head to the ladies before I leave to catch my train. As I move past the tables, my eye catches a couple sitting at one, and my heart jumps up in my throat.

It's Jimi, and he's with the stunning woman I saw earlier.

I freeze, knowing I should move before they see me, but

my legs are trembling. I wonder if I'm having a panic attack.

The woman in the bright red dress is laughing, flicking her dark hair over her shoulder as Jimi smiles at her.

I have to get out of here, I think, and turn, forcing my feet in the direction of the lift as the hot sting of tears burns the back of my eyes.

Jimi's never promised me anything. Many times, he's tried to manage my expectations, saying I don't know him fully yet. He's never once said we are exclusive.

I am an idiot.

I stand there in the lift, my emotions plummeting with every floor.

I only have myself to blame. The red lights have been flashing all along. Reformed bad boy – when maybe the bad boy never went away – emotional and life baggage, a broken marriage, reluctance to conform to convention when it comes to relationships. Doesn't believe in God. I know all this, and yet I've fallen for him.

The lift stops and a blonde woman enters, glances at me.

"Up or down?"

"Down," I mutter, searching in my bag for tissues, and I see her rummaging in her bag and passing me some.

"Whoever it is, they aren't worth it, babe. I can guarantee you that."

I want to reply, but words seem to choke in my throat and all I can do is mumble my thanks as I dab at my face, trying to restore my features to the blank canvas I need to make my exit.

She gives me the thumbs-up as we reach the ground floor that leads to the exit and I hurriedly make my way out, when I hear someone call my name.

I look up and it's Cyril.

"Oh, hi, Cyril." I manage a breezy wave.

He is staring at my face and I wonder whether my mascara is smudged.

"How are you?" he asks. "Good evening?"

Terrible, I think. *The worst.*

But I nod. "Great, thanks. How are you?"

"I'm well."

"Good." Suddenly, I can't think of what else to say.

"Are you okay, Sade? You loo—"

"Fine. I have to get my train," I cut him off, seeing the confusion on his face. "Later, Cyril."

And I flee into the night.

On the way home, my brain attempts to think more rationally. Seeing Cyril at The Tap provides a bit more context for Jimi's behaviour, perhaps. Maybe the beautiful brunette is just a client or a sponsor … or maybe she's just a friend. They weren't kissing or holding hands, after all. And even if there is romance involved, what right do I have to get angry over it? The terms and conditions and even nature of our relationship have not actually been defined.

By the time I get off the train, stoic, resilient Sade has replaced the Sade who was vulnerable and hurt.

A text comes from Jimi before I go to bed, but I don't read it. I am too tired. I need to pull myself together. I've been single for too long and it's made me latch onto the first half-decent guy that came along. And my reaction when I saw him with that woman was just fear talking. The fear of going back to life in the single dating pond. It is what it is, and I feel stupid for building it up to be anything more.

No, there is something missing with Jimi. It's our foundation. I think about all of our dates, all of the laughter and banter and fun, and I realise we haven't spoken enough about all the things that really matter, mainly the issue for me of dating a man who isn't supportive of my faith.

Maybe tonight has been the wake-up call I need...

Chapter Thirty-Two

Next morning at work in the project meeting I determinedly put last night's events aside and throw myself into efficiency mode and my to-do list.

First on the list is the NuChance launch.

"Is everything in place for the event?" I demand, looking at Bridget.

She nods. "Food and drink sorted with the caterers."

"What about the venue? All confirmed?"

Bridget looks up from her laptop. "It is. At the town hall. The auditorium there is wonderful. There is also a great outside space at the back for the match. Also, it's great for transport – close to several central London Underground and Overground stations."

"Great." I am relieved. The plug is that we are organising an event with some retired footballers playing a charity match against a team of youngsters from the local Pupil Referral Unit and other places – to boost their confidence, help mental health, and raise funds to support young athletes who face setbacks due to injury. It is our first opportunity to introduce NuChance to the media.

Bridget gives me a thumbs-up.

"I have had only three celebs from the list Cyril gave me say they can't make it. Everyone else is keen because it is for a good cause."

I breathe out. "All systems go."

———————

Just before lunch, our receptionist rings through to me.

"I've got Jimi Taylor here in the foyer to see you."

"We don't have an appointment," I say, coolly.

"Oh."

I look at the time on my phone. Maybe this is a good thing. Time for lunch and a candid convo. I really cannot keep running away from reality.

"Okay. Tell him I will be down in a few minutes, at noon."

Ten minutes later I pack my hair back into a ponytail, straighten my smart navy-blue trouser suit, add a hint of lip gloss to my lips, check my face briefly in my makeup compact, and head downstairs.

The foyer is busy as usual with guests waiting to meet people for conferences, project meetings, and business lunches. Jimi is sitting in a chair working on his iPad, but looks up when he sees me coming. I can't make out his expression, but his eyes have a slightly speculative glint.

"Jimi," I greet him professionally. "Nice to see you."

"Hi." He is looking into my eyes, as if he's expecting some kind of explanation.

I can't even explain what's going on to myself, mate.

"I'm sorry I didn't get back to you last night," I say. "Got a lot on."

He stands up, reminding me how tall he is. I see a flash of fire in his eyes that softens as he looks at me. "I was worried about you."

"Why?" I feign confusion.

"I saw Cyril last night. He said you looked upset."

"Oh, right." I shake my head. "Family stuff, Jimi. Nothing to do with you."

My tone is harsh, I realise, and my heart crumbles a little as I see the bewilderment on his face.

"Look, can we go for a walk outside or something?" he says. "Maybe grab a coffee? I don't want to take up too much of your time."

I sigh. "Okay. Coffee sounds good."

So we walk out of the building through the glass doors and head for the colonnade, both of us ignoring the crowd of office workers, tourists, and the world around us. This is the first time we are together and neither of us can think of anything to say.

He gets two coffees from the kiosk on the corner and we walk to the nearby gardens and sit down on a bench.

"Cyril said you looked as if you had been crying." Jimi looks ahead of him as he speaks.

I am about to repeat that it is none of his business, but his tone is so caring I can't bring myself to.

"That's a bit of an exaggeration," I say quietly.

"For the record, that lady was one of our prospective sponsors. We – Cyril and myself – met her for a drink to discuss it. It's just 'client liaison.'"

"You don't have to patronise me, I know what client liaison is."

"I didn't mean to sound patronising," he says, and looking at him, I can see he's hurt.

I sigh. "Look, I'm sorry. I admit I jumped to the wrong conclusion, but what else was I supposed to do?"

He shakes his head. "Give me the benefit of the doubt, maybe?"

We are both silent.

I venture, "Look Jimi. I like you. I like you a lot – probably more than is good for me but—"

"Charming. Am I some kind of poison you can't resist?"

I run a hand over my head. "No, I didn't mean it like that. I mean, maybe things are going a bit too fast. I jumped to a conclusion, and I'm sorry about that, but it has made me realise that, despite how fun it's been spending time with you, I don't know you that well and we have not taken the time to discuss the important things."

I glance at his expression and see he's frowning, but I continue.

"Obviously, we know we are attracted to each other, and we've bonded over our mutual dysfunction, but I have values I can't compromise on. Like I take my faith seriously. And I believe in marriage and you, well, you don't."

Jimi sighs. "You want to wrap us up in a neat little bow, but life's not like that," he says. "Yes, I have my reservations about the church. I grew up as a pastor's kid and we PKs have our own scars. I grew up watching Dad say one thing on Sunday and live another way for the rest of the week. Yes, he is a changed man now, but my mum did not have it easy and neither did Femi and I. We were the perfect family on the outside, but away from Sunday service, it wasn't quite like that."

"I didn't know," I say quietly. "Mum's always thought your dad is a saint."

Jimi half smiles. "What she sees is the new improved version. I just wish we could have seen more of that growing up. And as for God – when Mum was ill, I fasted and prayed. Man, how I prayed, asking God to please fix it so that she would get better. I bargained with him that I would stop drinking, stop doing drugs, if he would just look after her. But she died. That's when I lost my faith. I told God that I had no use for Christianity anymore and I have never looked back." He takes a breath. "Will I ever change how I feel about that? Who knows. I might, and I might not. But I'm not going to start going to church again just because I'm falling for you."

I put down my coffee. "Falling for me?"

He looks me straight in the eyes. "I'm too old to be faffing around. You heard what I said."

My throat is dry at the intensity of his gaze. "But you don't believe in marriage – and I don't believe in premarital sex."

Jimi shakes his head. "Sade. I am ambivalent about marriage. I've told you about mine. It was hell, though I don't excuse my part in making it so. Will I ever want to do it again? I can't make any promises. I can tell you that I care about you, I'm attracted to you, and I know you feel the same way—"

I cut in. "This has to stop, Jimi. I don't want to hurt you and I know you don't want to hurt me. We just believe in different things and – because we care for each other –

maybe it's best we go our separate ways now, before we get into this too deep." I swallow, because every word I've spoken hurts.

"You really want that?"

"I think it's the best thing."

"That's not what I asked. Look me in the eyes and tell me you want to lose what we have, and I will walk away."

"That's not the point."

"Then what is the point?"

"I've just told you."

"About your faith? You can still have that. I don't care, as long as I have you in my life. I just want to love you. I don't bloody care about anything else."

Oh my days.

So I decide to go for it. "Jimi, you don't understand. I'm fifty years old and I haven't had a serious relationship with a man before. I know that's a lot to take in."

He shrugged. "So…"

"You don't get it." I face him and shake my head. "Let me spell it out for you. I haven't slept with anyone before because as a Christian I feel that should be reserved for marriage. And marriage for me has to be with someone who shares my beliefs, so we have a bit of a problem… Do you see where I'm going on this?"

He is silent and then he turns to look at me. His voice is low and serious. "Okay. That is a bit of a surprise but it doesn't change anything. I still love you and I know you love me. We can take each day a step at a time and work things out…"

"Jimi, the fact that you still feel we can work this out, despite what I've said, makes me realise that you don't understand how integral it is that I be with a man who shares my faith. Not someone who stands on the sidelines while I go to church and isn't part of it. I just can't imagine sharing my life with someone who doesn't fit spiritually."

"You are so implacable on this. Look, we are just different people at different stages of our lives. It doesn't mean we can't see where this goes – explore possibilities."

"I'm too old to want to wait and see where this goes." My voice sounds tired. I am looking through him, past him, to months and years ahead of a situationship, and I can't seem to see any resolution. Anything tangible.

He is frowning now. "It looks like you've made your mind up, and all I need to do is sign off on it. I thought we had a connection, Sade."

"Yes, we connected physically and, yes, in the soul arena, too, but spiritually – it's like trying to mix oil and water. Try as hard as you can – they can never blend. I would hate a time to come when we would drift so far apart that we become strangers to each other."

Jimi is shaking his head.

I keep talking. "I'm sorry things haven't worked out, but this doesn't affect my work on your event. I do not think this should stop us from collaborating on a fantastic day for NuChance. I really believe in what you are doing."

My words sound forced and unreal even to my own ears.

His lips twist bitterly. "Maybe you believe in NuChance, but you don't believe in me. Even though I know I can make you happy. I can hold you in my arms and show you what you have been missing all the years you have sat in the same church with these same chaps who do not seem to

271

know a good thing when they see it. You want to walk away from the past few months we've shared together, because I don't share your faith."

"There is also the fact that you don't want to get married," I finish simply. "We are just too different. In the end, emotions, chemistry, and sharing great banter just are not going to be enough to keep us together. Let me release you so you can find a nice uncomplicated woman who isn't as goofy as me."

"Suppose I just want goofy," he says simply.

The silence stretches between us. The only sound filling the space is birdsong. Jimi finishes his coffee and I notice that the supermarket where we first met is just across the road. It feels kind of symbolic that we should be sitting just a few metres away from it on the day we are parting.

He sighs. "Okay, Sade. I hear you. And, of course, I would prefer that you continue with the launch – you and your team have done a lot of work on it, and besides," he adds, "you did make sure we signed a contract. To get out of it now, with less than six weeks to go, will entail considerable financial losses on our part, and that would not be feasible for a small charity like ours." He gets up and tosses his empty coffee cup in the bin by the bench. "I will leave you alone. See you in a few weeks at the launch."

I watch Jimi walk away, his tall frame disappearing into the crowd, and feel loss like a deep ache that seems to reverberate through me. I had been holding onto a whisper of hope that maybe, just maybe, God would find a way for us. But God isn't some kind of magician and it is the best decision to walk away.

"It is a far, far better thing that I do, than I have ever done."

My favourite passage from my grammar-school days comes to mind – from the tongue of Sydney Carton in *A Tale of Two Cities*. He kind of reminds me of a Dickensian Jimi. A guy who wants to do good but sometimes wrestles with his past mistakes.

Chapter Thirty-Three

As the days pass, the NuChance launch becomes even more my focus, a welcome distraction from the turmoil of my emotions.

In a couple of weeks, it will be done and dusted. And so will Jimi Taylor.

———

Pastor Kevin calls me.

"I'm hearing good things about the singles meetings."

"We've all pulled together," I tell him. "And we've rebranded it as the Inspired Network."

"Interesting. We have quite a few new people joining the church enquiring about some of the programmes. I am impressed."

"Thanks, Pastor. It is a great team and I think we might be able to get some of the men to join the leadership team. The idea of a football team lured them in."

"Brilliant. Chioma tells me that you know a former footballer."

"Well…" I begin, hesitant, "I used to—"

"I'd love a chat with him. Maybe the church can support that? We have a lot of youth that would be keen and maybe some of the oldies as well. Myself included. I love a bit of footie, me…"

I find myself fudging an introduction, muttering something about Jimi being very busy, and end the call feeling sad and frustrated. Jimi would have been perfect to help with the church football club. Especially with his experience of supporting young people with mental and physical challenges. But it just wouldn't be appropriate. Any interaction with him just has to be professional from now on.

The following week, I am at my desk when Cyril calls. Seeing his name flash up on my phone, I check the time. It's nearly 7 p.m. and I've lost track of time. What's Cyril doing calling me this late?

"Cyril, hi," I say. "I was going to check in with you tomorrow. Everything's on schedule for the launch."

"That is not why I'm ringing," he says, concern in his tone. "I mean, it's not a professional call."

"Okay."

"It's about Jimi. He hasn't been himself lately – been behaving like a bear with a sore head." He pauses. "I know you two aren't dating anymore."

"Yes," I say. "We decided to call it a day."

Cyril sighs. "You mean *you* decided to call it a day."

My hackles go up defensively.

"I thought he explained about the client," Cyril adds.

I take a breath. "I don't know what Jimi's told you, but that isn't the reason. We don't share the same life goals or values... We want different things, Cyril."

His voice softens. "Look, I know Jimi isn't perfect, and he has his views on certain things, but you're one of the best things that has happened to him, Sade."

"I..." I don't know what to say.

"Okay. Can't blame a guy for trying," Cyril says, despondent.

This is excruciating. I decide to change the subject.

"Did you get my email about the food for the launch and the guestlist?" I say.

"Er, yes, I did. But food is Jimi's area, not really my forte. And with the final guestlist, you will need his sign-off."

"Of course. I'll contact Jimi, then. Soon."

It is my job to say yes to things that I'm asked to do. Project managers are expected to do the impossible and come up with viable solutions. But calling Jimi is not something I want to do, not right now. I'm afraid of what I might say.

"Thanks, Sade," Cyril says. "I'd better go. Speak soon."

I end the call and decide to delegate the task to one of my project officers, who can email Jimi and get his approval on the final guestlist, as well as the operational plan and the catering. I put it on my to-do list for the morning.

———————

The next day, I email Bridget first thing and fill her in. A couple of hours later she emails back to say Jimi has approved everything. Perversely, I feel my spirits drop. So that's it, then. What was I expecting? For Jimi to insist on speaking with me and declare his undying love? No. Seems like he is behaving impeccably. Respectfully and professionally.

And it only makes me miss him more.

Chapter Thirty-Four

On Sunday morning, as I'm getting ready for church, I get the phone call I've been half dreading, half expecting from Mum.

"Sade," she says. "Did you know about your Aunty Remi and the Bishop?"

I hesitate, then: "Well, yes, but I only found out very recently," I say carefully. "Are you all right about it, Mum?"

"All right about it? How could my dear friend do this to me? She knew that the Bishop liked me first."

"Oh." I knew Mum might be put out; I didn't realise she had such strong feelings for the Bishop. "I didn't know you felt that way about him. Perhaps you should have told him." I look at the time on my phone and see it's only an hour till the service at eleven. "Listen, Mum. You've always wanted Aunty Remi to find a nice man to take care of her. Can't you be happy for her?"

I hear Mum practically hiss in irritation. "I will have words with her. This is not how things are done. She has kept a secret from me. What kind of a friend is she, sef? All these years that we have been friends and she has deceived me!"

I have visions of two grey-haired women having an argument or even slapping or shoving each other in the vestry of St Thomas's.

"I have to leave for church soon, Mum. But please don't fall out with your best friend over a man. Try and be glad for her."

Mum sniffs. "Hmm. Just because you now have a man for five minutes, you think you can be giving advice?"

Ouch. Mum always delivers with the precision of a sniper and it hits the target.

"Anyway. Just be careful of the Taylor men. They are good at breaking hearts."

I don't tell her that doesn't matter anymore. Instead I shake my head, and with one last plea to be civil at least to Aunty Remi, I pick up my bag and leave for church, which has never felt so appealing. I need to be in a place where I can hear God louder than I can hear the issues competing for space and attention in my head.

Later on that evening I get a phone call from Aunty Remi.

"Hello, my darling."

"Aunty Remi, how are you? Is everything okay?"

"I am not happy, my daughter. You will know about Bishop Taylor and I. Your mother is very upset with me. She will not talk to me. Imagine that. Me and Ebun have been friends for over forty years and she wants to fight with me over man."

I feel slightly awkward. I am so happy for her, but I feel for Mum, too. The last thing I want is to be caught between the two women I love.

"She'll come round, Aunty. Give it time."

"No." She sniffs. "I tried to greet her twice and she pretended she didn't hear me. I will stay in my house until Ebunola returns to her senses."

"Aunty, please…"

But the line goes dead.

I close my eyes and sit for a minute, thinking.

All Aunty Remi has done is fall in love. She has grabbed hold of happiness, not let it slip through her fingers. If that doesn't meet with Mum's approval, then I guess it's just tough. Mum should have been more proactive if she likes Bishop Taylor that much…

Suddenly, something slides into place.

Isn't it about time I seized hold of my own happiness?

Chapter Thirty-Five

I t's the day of the NuChance event.

With my project officers on hand to make sure it all goes smoothly, we welcome the celebrity footballers. Despite it being October, the weather holds out, and it feels more like late summer than early autumn. Not too cold, and – importantly – not raining.

The sun casts a hazy glow over the football pitch as the match is about to begin, and the air of anticipation intensifies through the crowd. The guests, a mix of fans, sponsors, and local supporters, settle into their seats chatting excitedly. Colourful banners representing the cause NuChance is fighting for – the empowerment of young people through sports activities – hang from the bleachers.

As the celebrity footballers and the younger unknown players battle for possession and goals, the victory in the end gets the assembled crowd up on their feet and roaring. I glimpse Jimi and Cyril standing, shouting, laughing, and commiserating in the directors' box and connecting with investors and high-profile sponsors, and I feel a sense of satisfaction.

I have done my job, and that takes the edge off the pain I still feel at seeing Jimi.

With the match over, everyone turns their attention to refreshments. The caterer has outdone herself with hamburger sliders, sandwiches, and sausage platters, and there are natural fruit drinks from our sponsor, Spring Dream, as well as tea and coffee on tap.

I take a few pictures with the celebs while trying to stay focused on ensuring the rest of the event goes off in line with our schedule. I walk round making sure that the young people – the focus of the event – are being looked after and see Cyril standing watching me with a happy smile on his face. He gives me the thumbs-up.

"Thank you," he mouths, and I smile back.

Eventually all the guests, sponsors, and investors have left, the lights are dimmed, and the echoes of the day's excitement have faded. I am about to leave when I see Jimi standing by a window, looking out into the night.

I approach him hesitantly, coughing so he isn't surprised.

He turns and gives me a polite smile.

"Hi," I say. "It all went well, I think, don't you?"

He smiles. "You guys did a brilliant job tonight. I have a

list of contacts from all the networking we did. I've talked so much that I can hardly remember what I was talking about."

I smile, happy that he is happy. "I can tell you, from the buzz generated, the guests were really impressed."

"Again, thanks for all you put into it. I will definitely recommend Ryder & Hamilton to anyone who needs top-notch project management."

"Thanks. That's much appreciated."

He hesitates. "I've been meaning to catch up with you."

"Oh..."

"Yeah. I've been thinking," he begins, his voice slow and deliberate. "Cyril mentioned some help with this football club at your church he wants to be involved in. The pastor is trying to set up a team."

My heart beats faster. Jimi attending *my* church. Possibilities dance in front of my eyes but I shut them down. "That sounds great. It would be amazing if you could help us out. Our pastor would be over the moon."

"This isn't a ploy to get back with you... I just want us to be friends again. Can we at least do that?" He is standing close enough to pull me into his arms and far enough for me to easily move back to create some distance if I want to.

"Of course." My voice is breezy, hiding my inner longing.

"It was tough not contacting you – knowing you were a phone call away, but having to hold myself back," Jimi adds quietly.

I want to tell him I have been feeling the same way, but instead I clear my throat.

"Thank you, Jimi. Thanks for backing off and letting me

try and make some sense of things," I tell him. "I needed to figure out what I want in a relationship. Maybe I was expecting too much – trying to mould you into this perfect package, when I'm far from perfect myself. You're a good man, and you've demonstrated that you care about my feelings and my values. I had no right to put all that pressure on you."

Jimi takes a step closer but then stops. "Sade. Thing is, I gotta work out the whole God and marriage thing, and I know I'll get there. But I have got to want those things for myself. Not just because I want you in my life."

I nod. "I respect that."

It wasn't a grand resolution, nor a declaration of undying love. But it was a beginning, a tentative step towards understanding and acceptance.

Chapter Thirty-Six

Jimi and Cyril made good on coming to the singles event and helping set up the football team, and the response from the guys in church and even from the locals has been amazing. It's meant more new male faces in the congregation. Pastor Keith is very pleased, as, I'm sure, are some of the long-suffering females.

A couple of weeks after the NuChance event, Jimi comes to Sunday service and afterwards goes for a chat with Pastor Keith. I can't help asking him what it was about, but his response is vague.

"This and that," he says with a smile. "Don't worry, he didn't thrust the Bible down my throat. He was very approachable actually. I had a lot of questions about some of the things that have been on my mind, and he tried to answer them as best he could. I told him I wasn't into church in any shape or form and he didn't try to persuade me. In fact, we spoke about football most of the time.

He offered to pray for me and I felt it would be rude to say no so I let him pray."

"Okay, sounds good," I say.

It's a start, isn't it?

Two weeks later and I am sitting in front of Pastor Sandra in the church office.

"So, what's happening with this Jimi? It was nice that you introduced him to Pastor Keith after service the other day. I talked to him, too. He seems like a nice chap."

"He is," I say. "But you know he does not believe in God?"

There is a silence, in which I am ridiculously hoping she will come up with the perfect solution for me and Jimi. I look up and see her looking intently at me.

"Sade," she says softly. "I see how much this man has entered your heart. And I see how much you are struggling for guidance on your future with him."

I nod, feeling tears coming.

"I could counsel you against a future with him because he isn't a Christian, but I've been doing this job for years and I've come to the conclusion that telling people what not to do only pushes them further in that direction."

I look at my hands.

Pastor Sandra sighs. "Just what do you want from Jimi?"

"I want him to be 'the one'," I say. "It's true. I've fallen for him. I can't keep on deceiving myself. We are just friends for now – but I know we both want more than that.

It's getting more difficult to resist what is staring us both in the face."

"You want him to be your knight in shining armour and chase away all your single blues," she says. "And Pastor Keith tells me he's on his own journey. He can't be all you want him to be. Don't put that expectation on him. I've seen you both at the football matches the last few weeks. I just don't want you to get hurt."

"I'm a big girl."

Pastor Sandra nods. "I know. She isn't the one I'm worried about. It's the little girl that dreams of her happy ever after, deep down inside, that I'm trying to protect."

I am silent.

"Jimi seems like a great guy but you can't put the weight of your expectations on a man to make you happy. You got to find your own peace first."

I am coming to the conclusion that she is right.

Yes, I think, fervently. *He is a really good man and I can't pray him, wish him, or nag him into being a model Christian so I can get him up the aisle. I have to find my own peace in God and let everything else sort itself out.*

Chapter Thirty-Seven

A week of revelations. First of all, Dolapo is pregnant. I found that out by accident at Westfield, which was packed, with more schoolkids in the food court than customers shopping in the swankier shops on the upper levels.

I was just leaving Zara when I saw her coming out of a shop with Kunle, pushing a trolley of baby stuff. I stepped behind a pillar to avoid being seen.

In my culture, women's pregnancies are meant to be shielded from potentially jealous female relatives who are unmarried. It actually makes it worse to not be told. I wouldn't say humiliating, but it is a kind of dishonesty.

I looked down at my M&S bag with continental salmon for one, salad pack for one, bottle of Ribena for one, solitary French roll, small tub of olive oil butter, and pack of Braeburn apples, and tried to squash any feelings of self-pity. But my carefully curated independent life seemed in that moment to be unravelling.

The thought that I have been holding out for someone who doesn't exist is weighing on my mind. All around me, people are embarking on family life – at work, Bridget has announced she's pregnant, too – or committing to each other, like Sam and Martin, who've just got engaged.

I arrive at Aunty Remi's house for lunch. Over the past couple of weeks she's reached out to me more, and she's exactly the person I want to see. Warm, non-judgemental, and a wonderful cook. And I really need some TLC.

"Sade, my darling!" Aunty Remi opens the door and steps out to give me a big hug. I can smell the delicious aroma of fresh Efo Riro stew and know I am in for a treat.

"Hello, Aunty."

"You've just missed Jide. He was here with my granddaughter."

Jide is her eldest.

"Aw. How is she?"

Aunty Remi brings out her phone and proudly shows me pictures of Olamide, her cute five-year-old granddaughter.

"She's gorgeous, Aunty."

"Isn't she just."

She puts away her phone and ushers me inside to her parlour, then bustles about getting me a drink. As she places it on a table beside me, she plumps herself down on the settee next to me.

"How is everything?" she asks. "Where do you stand

with young Jimi? Bishop Taylor tells me that Jimi is not quite himself right now."

"Oh?" I shake my head. "We're still not together, Aunty."

"What a shame? And he has done so well to turn his life around."

"I know." I wince. Even though I feel proud to stand up for my values, it all feels a bit flimsy in the face of everyone's bafflement at my decision.

"He is such a nice chap," Remi goes on. "I have known him since he was a little boy. Always loved his football, did Jimi. Used to be in the choir, too." She sighed. "Then life happened to him."

"Aunty, I am proud of him, you know," I tell her. "He's a wonderful person."

"Not wonderful enough, though?" She lifts an eyebrow.

I shake my head and switch subjects.

"So, how are things with you and Mum?" I ask. "She doesn't talk to me about anything lately."

Aunty Remi sighs. "Still the same. I wonder if she will ever forgive me."

"You and Mum just need to have a good chat – to iron things out."

Aunty Remi nods. "I wanted to tell your mother about me and the Bishop. But I couldn't until I was sure, until I had prayed and he had proposed marriage. I had to know it was serious, you see? What was the point of boasting about something that might fizzle out?"

"I see that." I smile at her. "And I think Mum will too, eventually."

"Yes. I do so hope my sister Ebun will soon celebrate

with me." Aunty pats my knee. "Now, go to the kitchen. There is vegetable and fish stew and Fufu waiting for you. Olamide loves it. I am so happy that they are teaching her to appreciate our food and not that nonsense pizza and chips that young people are giving to their children nowadays."

I smile, because I know how much Aunty Remi loves my mum and I know that, somehow, they will sort it out.

That evening, I call Sam, who is all in a tizzy. Talking non-stop about wedding plans and dream honeymoon locations.

"Mauritius is the place for me," she says, her head already on some beach surrounded by blue skies and white sands.

"Sounds wonderful," I reply.

"Sorry, Sade. I'm just going on about myself. Dare I ask about you and Jimi?"

"Nothing to say, Sam," I tell her. "It's fine."

"Hmm."

And the doubt in Sam's voice echoes the doubt in my own heart.

Chapter Thirty-Eight

A few days later Jimi calls me and tells me he has been invited to Kike's husband's fortieth birthday party this coming weekend.

"Your sister invited me," he says. "I just wanted to give you the heads-up."

Nigerians can never miss out on the opportunity to party and Ayo is my man. A lovely brother-in-law and a great dad and husband.

I am taken aback. "Oh. I didn't realise you were friends with Ayo."

"You don't you want me to come? I get it." He sounds hurt.

"No." I try to laugh, to soften the air. "I mean, yes, of course I don't mind if you come. It will be nice to see you."

"Likewise," says Jimi. "Looking forward to it."

The following Saturday, Ayo's birthday party is going well – everything is in place, from the decorations to the food and the live band. Kike and Ayo look great – very regal in matching turquoise and gold Aso Oke outfits as they move on the dancefloor.

I circle the hall, giving out little gift packs from the celebrant to the guests, when I spot Aunty Gbemi sitting at one of the tables with the other members of the Marriage Monitoring Aunties' Association – Aunty Ify and Aunty Titi, Mrs Shobowale and Aunty Sarah. All they need is Aunty Bunmi and the quorum would be complete. They are all wearing matching turquoise lace and gold head ties, white lace outfits, and sour expressions.

I can't avoid them, as I need to give out the gifts to everyone in the hall. Aunty Gbemi looks at me from the top of my head down to my feet.

"Sade *bawo ni*? Is this your own dress?" she says, obviously not impressed that I have refused to buy the turquoise and gold Aso Ebi and have opted for a long turquoise halter-neck dress, which I've jazzed up with gold accessories.

"Good evening. I'm fine, Aunty Gbemi."

She nods curtly and looks down at the plate of Amala and Egusi stew in front of her.

Aunty Titi, with her bleached face and dark lips, looks at me intently.

"We see you have found man," she says.

I ignore her and hand out their gifts.

"Don't you know him, Titi?" puts in Aunty Ify, whose fake eyelashes made her look like a Disney character. "He is the Bishop's son."

"The one that married Oyibo," Aunty Gbemi clarifies. "Not the one that is a big lawyer back in Lagos?"

Mrs Shobowale shakes her head and stops eating. "Jimi Taylor. Isn't he divorced?"

"Yes o." Aunty Ify nods as if I am not standing there.

"Anyway, at your age you can't afford to be choosy," concludes Mrs Shobowale, going back to her meal.

I want to walk off and leave them to their gossip, but Aunty Gbemi won't let me go that easily. "I can see the man likes you. You just need to make sure you don't chase him like all the rest."

"Chase him?" I respond coolly.

"Yes. Your mother told me you have been chasing men," Aunty Gbemi chided.

"That's not true." I look at them. Aunty Gbemi is a single parent. Aunty Ify and Titi have husbands who are perpetually in Nigeria – in fact, I have never met them – yet they have several children between them. They made bi-annual trips to Nigeria to see their hubbies, until they had their quota of boys and girls. Aunty Sola's husband is here in England, but he hardly ever attends their church and has what Mum terms politely a roaming eye for young ladies.

They are all lonely and bitter and sad, whereas I am just occasionally lonely and sad and not yet bitter.

Aunty Gbemi continues. "Would I lie on my very own sister? Somebody buying a house and reading big book – is that not chasing men? I've told you, men do not like clever women—"

"This one does." I hear a deep voice behind me and turn to see Jimi standing there. He has a warm smile on his face as his eyes hold mine as if I am the only woman in this room.

Aunty Gbemi's hand stays suspended in the air between the mound of Amala on her plate and her open mouth.

Jimi bows his head slightly in her direction. "Good afternoon, Ma."

Aunty Gbemi nods. *"Bawo ni.* Jimi, how are you?"

"I'm fine, Ma." He puts his hand into mine. "By the way. Sade is beautiful, smart, and intelligent. Do you know that she heads up a department at her workplace? She manages a team of about ten people and a huge budget. Her boss sees her as a big asset to the company. He told me so himself. If not for her, our charity event would not have been such a great success."

He then takes the box of gifts from my hands and gives me one of his best smiles. "Let me assist you, babes," he says, his voice tender, dangerously so.

"Praise da Lord!" Aunty Gbemi stares at me as if she is seeing me for the first time.

Aunty Ify picks up her phone and stares at it and Aunty Shobowale focuses on her plate of food.

Stifling a laugh, I let Jimi tug me away.

"Thanks, Jimi," I whisper. "That was very gallant."

He shrugs. "I just happened to be walking past and overheard them talking rubbish about you. I couldn't let that pass."

I chuckle, a bloom of heat spreading through me. "Aunty Gbemi will get her own back on me for this, but I will be ready for her. Are they still staring at us?"

"I wouldn't look back if I was you. It spoils our kick-ass image."

We giggle as we walk away and mingle with the other guests.

———————————

The next day Kike phones, on the pretext of thanking me for helping at the party. The real reason for the call is revealed within about a minute.

"Aunty Gbemi told Mum that Jimi jumped to your rescue when she was interrogating you. She was very impressed, apparently."

I laugh. "I was on the verge of giving her and her cronies a piece of my mind when Jimi shut them up. Politely, of course – but they knew he saw through their nonsense."

Kike chuckles. "Can you not see how much he likes you? Methinks he is a keeper. Pray you get him to the altar and marry him soon."

My good humour fades a little. "It's not that easy."

"Yes, yes. So you say," says Kike. "You gotta get things resolved, you know. Because it's obvious there's something strong between you still."

"I know," I say. "I know."

Chapter Thirty-Nine

Church service is just about to start, but I am in absolute shock. One of the single ladies in my team has passed away, suddenly. Margaret, the lovely friendly usher, who was so happy that something was being done for the singles in the church, had an undetected heart condition and died in her sleep.

We were the same age. Occasionally we would say a quick hello, or exchange talk about work or our shared aspirations of life, love and motherhood, and then go back to our single lives. Once, when we got the same bus home, she'd jokingly informed me that she was probably the only virgin in the village. I had been too embarrassed to say anything about myself.

All the waiting. All the praying and all the serving in church – and that was it?

Margaret is dead – just like that, without ever knowing what it was like to have children, to feel a lover's heart beating next to her, to fully experience the joys and delights of a marriage.

While I am trying to process this, I see Simon and his girlfriend's faces appear on the announcements screen.

Simon Okolie and Nneka Chibuike will be getting married here at Living Waters Church on the 6 of December.

Something cold wraps itself around me and squeezes. Whispering into my ears, mocking my efforts to ignore it.

———

For days afterwards, I am in a daze. Questioning everything I have ever believed in. Margaret died without ever experiencing the love and companionship she had longed for.

I battle with grief and introspection. I realise that life is unpredictable and fleeting, and the thought of living mine without ever experiencing the fullness of love and happiness weighs heavily on me. I remember the moments I shared with Jimi, the way he made – makes – me feel alive and cherished. Things I have never felt with another man.

One evening, I make a decision. I pick up my phone and send a message to Jimi inviting him over for dinner to thank him for his occasional work with the church football team. It is a bold move, but driven by the realisation that I don't want to live with the regrets of "what if" anymore. I am tired of fighting this inevitable pull between us.

We have a lovely meal and sit on the sofa to watch a nice innocent documentary and chat about everything and anything, and the chemistry sizzles between us.

It is when he mentions seeing Dolapo and her hubby in

some restaurant that my face must have registered something.

"Hey," he says. "You look so far away."

I shake my head. "Sorry."

Jimi's eyes are kind and gentle as he kneels in front of me, holding my hands. Then he reaches out and touches my face. "What's all this about, Sade?"

My eyes mist over and all I can see is the soft tender look in his eyes and the fact that we are inches away from each other and then I lean closer to him.

"Sade," he begins.

"Just hold me ... please." I press myself against him and wrap my arms around his neck. And he takes me in his arms. I want to stay like this for ever, feeling cherished, like someone really cares.

"Is it that aunt of yours that is always chatting nonsense? Has she said something? If so, I can go have a word?"

I shake my head.

"So, what is it?"

He pulls away gently and looks down into my eyes.

"Sade, you do know I'm really attracted to you, and so being close to you like this ... it is doing things to me that..."

I kiss him, then, and he snatches me close, returning the kiss. He is stroking my hair, my neck, his hands leaving a trail of fire wherever they touch. "I don't think a kiss is going to be enough," he murmurs.

"Good," I whisper and he nudges my chin up with his thumb to kiss me again.

"Oh, Sade," he whispers as my heart thumps in my

chest, and, closing his eyes, he kisses me again, pulling me closer.

His lips tug at my ear. "That first day I saw you standing there looking so beautiful…"

I smile and flutter my eyelashes as his eyes darken with the same passion I'd seen glinting there the night of our first kiss. His lips hover closer to mine again, as we fall back on the sofa.

"Are you sure about this?" he whispers.

I nod as his hands move to the front of my blouse, opening each button one by one. His eyes still fixed on mine.

I close my eyes, feeling a wave of shyness, not wanting to answer the question in his eyes – are you okay with this? – but I reassure myself that he is a man and men don't ask too many questions at times like these … or do they?

"I have a scar running across my belly."

His eyes are full of tenderness. "It doesn't matter, Sade. Everything about you is perfect."

"You haven't seen my toes yet."

I want to tell him about all my imperfections, but he kisses me again and I forget all about it, revelling in the feel of his body against mine, and I know that I am closer to understanding the mystery of sex than I have ever been before.

"It is my first time," I whisper.

Jimi strokes my hair from my face. A kind of unfathomable look on his face that I can't decipher. Is it reluctance? "I know. Which is why I want to be sure you want this. I know how much it means to you."

He DOESN'T want you so stop making a fool of yourself! a

voice within me mocks. I sit up. "I've put you off," I say, all the momentum of desire coming to a screeching halt.

"No. Of course not." He shakes his head. "I just want you to be okay, that's all."

I sit up and pull my blouse closer over my chest. "Fine."

He looks confused. "Sade, please don't be like this. You know how much I fancy you."

"I think you'd better go," I tell him.

Jimi stares at me for a minute before he sighs and gets to his feet.

"If that's what you want," he says.

"That is what I want," I repeat coldly as I turn my back to him and stare at the wall. *Did I really just throw myself at a guy like that? Am I in my right senses at all?*

"Bye, Sade." His voice is as cold as mine.

The door closes behind him and I have never felt more alone.

In reality I have to get up the next morning and stare at myself in the mirror and wish so hard that I could press the back space button and delete all my actions of the last twenty-four hours but alas ... no success.

I check my phone several times in between meetings, hoping for a text from him, but nothing comes.

I've really messed this up.

_____

A week later, I've thrashed the whole thing out with Vicky and Sam about ten times – both of them adamant I got the wrong end of the stick and handled things really badly. Then Jimi texts while I'm at work.

> Can we catch up soon? Need to have a chat. Best Jimi.

Now is my chance to apologise for how stupid I was that night. I suggest a café not too far from work, and try not think about how it reminds me of the losing team in *The Apprentice*.

Jimi walks in wearing a smart suit. He is coming from a meeting with a donor and wants to look the part. He is polite but a bit distant as he sits down.

"How are you?" he asks, after the waiter has brought us two teas and a few biscuits.

"I'm fine, and you?" I say, as if I have been sleeping and eating normally for the past week. If it is any consolation, he looks rather tired as well.

He nods. "I'm fine, too. Just busy and got a few things on—"

"Jimi, I—"

"I've got some news," he says abruptly. "I've had an offer of a big project overseas. It is everything I've worked for. A dream come true to take NuChance to the international stage."

My mouth is dry. "Overseas?"

"America." He goes on. "I have you to thank really. It came through a connection I made at the launch. They have seen what we're doing with young people here and want us to do the same in New York and work with inner-city kids there. They found a great facility in Brooklyn. It's a lovely brownstone and has three floors."

"So..." I am trying desperately not to cry. But this is a

sign, surely, a sign that we are not meant to be. "When are you leaving?"

"In a couple of weeks."

I swallow, my pride coming to the fore.

"It's an amazing opportunity, Jimi, I'm really happy for you."

He looks at me, right into my eyes, before he shakes his head.

"I'd better go, actually. So much to do before I go."

"Yes…" I get to my feet and put out my hand, as professional as they come. "Good luck, Jimi. You deserve this."

"Thank you." And I catch the mistiness in his eyes as he adds, "You deserve the best, too, you know. You're the most wonderful woman, Sade."

I blink.

But not quite wonderful enough, eh?

He walks away and then turns to look at me and for one minute it seems as if he wants to say something … but then he walks briskly towards the exit.

I wait until he's out of the door before I sink back into my chair and let the tears come.

―――――――――

As soon as I let myself into my house, I sit down on my sofa and stare ahead into the future.

At least I have cleared that up. It's over.

I unwrap my scarf from my neck and hang it up and my lips tremble. Yellow Blue Yellow. The first gift he had given me. The memory of a football match, a couple of months ago when everything had seemed so bright.

Chapter Forty

A few days later, the phone rings and I immediately pick up.

It's Vicky.

"Why aren't you answering your phone?" she asks.

"I just need some time alone. To be honest, I don't want to talk to anyone."

"When Bridget told me you had taken two days off work impromptu and you didn't answer my calls, I phoned your mum! Is this about Jimi? What's happened?"

"It's over, Vicky. He's moving to New York."

"Oh, Sade…"

"He obviously can't wait to get away from me. His behaviour speaks for itself. Let's just forget about it. I have to go into work tomorrow. Just stop sending me these ridiculous memes. I'm alive and well. I'm just sitting at home, eating chocolates and takeaways and binge-watching documentaries and legal dramas."

"And feeling sorry for yourself, I'd say."

"Don't start." My voice is tired. "Not any more. At fifty, I have decided that love is just an illusion. It's a scam."

"Whoa, hang on. It doesn't work with Jimi and you want to give up on love? Whether he is the right person or not, it does not mean you have to get cynical about life either. Look, I will come round after work and bring a bottle of something non-alcoholic and we can binge-watch a funny show."

"Whatever. Look, I am fine. I just need some time to get myself back together. I am used to the status quo. I just thought things might be different with him. I thought he really cared about me."

"He does. I know he does."

I reflect. "You know what? All I wanted to hear from him was that – although the opportunity in New York was a fantastic one – he was going to try some way to sort things out with us before he left. That he wasn't ready to give up on us and he wanted to get serious with his faith in God again because he loves me and wants to marry me."

"Maybe he wants that, but he isn't there right now with his relationship with God. It doesn't mean he doesn't care."

I laugh and it is dry and hard. "It doesn't look like he cares. Not a single text or message?"

Vicky sighs. "Like men are fantastic with communication? Look, Sis, I've got to go but I'll call you later. Stay strong. I know that guy really cares about you. I just feel it deep down inside. Trust me on this one. God has a plan in everything that happens. You must trust in Him."

December brings more heartbreak. This time for Sam. It turns out that Martin is a wasteman. Sam took the afternoon off work to surprise him because he'd mentioned he was off, too. Then she walked in on him in bed with another woman.

We meet up after work and have a chat.

"I let myself believe in him so much that I was prepared to do anything to hold onto the illusion," she tells me, sobbing. "I just wanted him to be 'the one' so bloody much."

"Oh, Sam." I hug her and smile. "It's soon going to be the new year. New hope. Maybe new love..."

She shakes her head. "I doubt that." She looks at me. "What about Jimi going to America? How are you dealing with that?"

My smile falters slightly. "It's life, ay, Sam." I put my arm around her. "Listen, why don't you stay here for the night, so you're not alone? I'll make up the spare room."

"Thanks, Sade." She leans in and hugs me. "Tell me everything's going to be all right?"

I hold her, and wish more than anything that it will be.

Maybe I really need to pray for myself and my friends more. Life can be so exhausting sometimes.

The next morning, after Sam has left to go back to her flat, I sit on my bed and stare out the window at the dull grey skies heralding another shower of rain. The weather matches my mood perfectly.

It doesn't help that Mum is still on the warpath. She rings me and spends half an hour telling me how she prayed I would marry a good man and how God would shame my enemies and her enemies, in fact everyone who said I would not marry a good man – or any man, period.

"I know my enemies have chased Jimi away," she says emphatically. "I hear them at church. Gossiping behind my back and smiling in my face. Oh, poor woman – not only did her husband leave her for another woman in Lagos, but her eldest daughter is fifty – and still unmarried. Her enemies have done this to her o!"

"Which enemies, Mum?" I snap. "Jimi left for New York because he wants to start a branch of his charity over there. That is all."

Mum huffs in disgust. "Hmmm. Could he not have put ring on your finger before he left?"

"Mum, please. Enough."

"What is difficult there? He says he has changed, but suddenly he says he is going to New York? It is not an ordinary something – I tell you. I will keep praying that he comes back."

I wince. Something about that night with Jimi when we nearly made love is bothering me. I feel as though it is me, not Jimi, who has ruined this. Me, with my head held high, always in the right.

"Sade. Are you still there?" Mum prompts, shaking me out of my reverie.

"Yes, Mum. Look, we have both moved on."

"Moved on to where? You this girl; you are a small girl in this world despite your big age."

308

I sigh. "Mum. Listen to me. A man who decides his life is in another country... Well, there's no future with me? You of all people should understand that."

I hold my breath, waiting for the outrage, but instead, true to form, Mum sticks to the story she wants to tell.

"As I said, you are a small girl. You don't understand a man's heart. I tell you that he will be back one day."

"Mum—"

"Anyway," she cuts in. "What are you doing on Sunday after service? Come round to my house and I will cook jollof rice and turkey for you and we can invite Kike and her family."

I sigh. "Okay, that sounds great. I look forward to it."

"Good." She softens.

I feel for her. She belongs to an era where women made marriage and motherhood the pivot of their existence. After encouraging their daughters to concentrate on their studies and their careers in their early twenties, they expect said daughters to be married and settled with children immediately after they graduate and cannot understand why that is not always the case. They just expect these fantastic men with wonderful jobs and husbandly attributes to pop out of the woodwork as soon as their daughters acquire all these degrees.

Sorry, Mum. It's tough out there in these streets nowadays. We are having to deal with the after-effects of the manosphere, sweet boys, cat fishers, red pill, fraudsters, misogynists, and men that don't really see the reason for getting married when they can get most of what they want without putting a ring on it.

Then there are others. They come packaged as tall dark-skinned men with grey beards, sexy voices, and devastating kisses. Men that are kind, generous, and seemingly have lots of emotional intelligence ... only to ghost you without explanation.

Chapter Forty-One

After church, I arrive at Mum's with a big bag of fruits, her favourite magazines, and a bunch of flowers. A bouquet of chrysanthemums, roses, carnations, lilies, and other winter hybrids.

I know she needs cheering up. This business with the Bishop has got her down a bit.

Mum is still wearing her church outfit. A pink skirt suit and a matching hat, complete with moderately heeled shoes.

"Good afternoon, Mum." I give her a hug and this time she does not stiffen.

"Afternoon, my daughter. What is all this?" She points at the bag of fruits and flowers.

"I just wanted to spoil you. Is that a problem?"

"Is okay. Bring it to the kitchen."

I follow her and watch as she switches on the oven and puts on the pot of stew.

"Will you eat Eba?"

My mum never offers an alternative, so we always knew that was what was available. "Yes, Mum. I will make the Eba."

She puts up a placatory hand. "Abeg. I don't want your Eba with bits inside. I don't know how you Oyibo people are making it. Let me make it myself. Just switch on the kettle for me."

I go to the sink to fill up the kettle and plug it in. "How was church today?"

"We thank God," she says, her voice even.

I frown. Usually, she is effusive about the Bishop's sermon.

"Did you see Aunty Remi?" I venture.

No answer.

"Mum. She has been calling you like for ever…"

The kettle clicks and I watch as she pours hot water into a bowl and adds Gari to it. She stirs vigorously until it becomes a smooth paste.

"Mum, you can't fall out over a man like this. Aunty Remi is going to marry Bishop Taylor and you have to be there. You guys have been friends for years."

"You do not have to be counting years we have been friends," she snaps. "My memory is still good. But *friends* do not keep secrets."

I sigh. "Aunty Remi didn't want to keep it a secret, but she didn't want to tell you about something that might just fizzle out. She told me that. And I don't blame her. Unfortunately, you found out anyway. But she never meant to deceive you, and she's so upset that you are upset."

Mum mutters something inaudible.

"What did you say?"

312

She looks up. "First, we do not waste time with this dating nonsense at our age. Second, friendship and loyalty always comes first. Especially a friend that I have known since we were girls. Since men used to chase after us."

I raise an eyebrow at her, but she focuses on dishing the Eba into two plates.

"Aunty Remi deserves to be happy, doesn't she?" I say.

"Of course I want her to be happy. It's just the way they went about things."

"They are adults, innit. It's their right to keep things to themselves for as long as they want to."

"I don't want to discuss this anymore. I wish them the best."

"Mum…"

"Please start dishing the stew before it gets cold."

We sit down, say grace, and start enjoying the delicious meal.

"Mum," I say. "You never told us about all these men that were chasing you guys."

Mum is eating with her fingers. It makes the food sweeter. So she says. "That's a story for another day. Don't look at me like that! I will have you know that we had men ready to die for us back then on the streets of Lagos. I was not serious about the things of God then, so I used to wear my little miniskirt and pack my hair up on my head like the Oyibo people in the magazines. Your dad and his sweet mouth convinced me to follow him and his dreams to this cold country in the seventies."

I laugh. I love it when my mum opens up like this. It is rare.

313

"What was Dad like back then?" I press, because she never talks about him.

"He was handsome. Full of ambition. This country sapped it out of him. The racism, going from job to job for peanuts, studying trying to make a better life for us in this country... I can understand why he left to go back to Nigeria. Things may not be perfect there but at least he felt at home. He felt he could make it and he did. That attracted the women and after that – chaos. He made it as a businessman, but as a husband to me and father to you and your sister, he was a failure. I don't pray for you to marry someone like him." She added with a tone of finality, "The minute you enter their house that is the end of romance."

I sigh and eat some of my meal.

"Jimi is like a bird," my mother reflects suddenly. "He is finding his wings. He wants to fly and conquer the world. He just needs time to figure out things."

"I never attempted to cut his wings." I stare at her. "And when did you become his ally – telling me how his mind works?"

My mother just looks at me. "Do you pray for him at all?"

"When it comes to the topic of prayer – that's not something I've been doing a lot of lately. Let alone praying for someone who says he doesn't believe in prayer, anyway." I shake my head.

"You need to remain in prayer," Mum reproves me. "It is because of prayer that I have been able to leave the whole issue with the Bishop at the altar with Jesus. I cannot allow any man to give me hypertension, or make me lose my friend."

"So you will call her?"

"I will," Mum confirms matter-of-factly. "I will call her and give her my congratulations. The Bishop never asked me to marry him, but we had certain conversations, which led me to believe that he was fond of me and ... that I should have hope that one day he would get over the loss of his wife. I will say no more. I am happy for them and know this is the will of God. They both deserve every happiness."

Relief floods through me. "Aw. Thanks, Mum. Aunty Remi will be pleased."

"Besides. If I am not there at her wedding – what kind of a day would it be?" Mum continues. "Very dull and undistinguished." She gets up from the table. "When we clear up and wash the dishes, we can have some cake that I made yesterday and watch a film. I like this – *The Devil Loves Prada*. The woman in it – I like her..."

"Anne Hathaway."

"No. Meryl Streep innit. She doesn't take nonsense and says it as it is, but she is wise. She knows people's true character and that makes her a good businesswoman."

"Mum, I kind of guessed you would say that."

"Let's watch a film and eat cake. We must not allow two men from the same household to steal our joy."

"Amen to that." I smile.

Chapter Forty-Two

Donny Hathaway is singing "This Christmas" again. The beauty of his voice has a warmth that stays with you, wrapping around your soul and filling it with warm, happy thoughts.

I love Christmas. I can never lose that joy and awe that I had as a child, anticipating gifts. Shiny wrapping paper, Christmas pud, jollof rice and chicken, Christmas gifts. Memories of Christmas past, of watching *Morecambe and Wise* on the TV as a kid, with memories of my father in the house.

Now, I like Christmas shopping in the West End. There is a certain ambiance in the stores. I love the perfume counters because of the sheer variety of the collections and the smartness and elegance of the stores. I love the smell of chestnuts roasting outside and the joy of the little children as they look at the toys in the shop window, reminding me of my childhood. Everything is shiny and new and it is a season even adults look forward to – a moment of magic out of the reality that is our lives. Sharing in that childhood innocence and joy and forgetting about adult stuff such as the mundane routine of work deadlines, bills, and health concerns … heartbreak.

I am ambling around Westfield when I run into Cyril and Chioma doing some Christmas shopping. She is smiling up at him and he has his arm around her. There is a glow about them; they look engrossed in each other.

I wave. "Hello."

Cyril breaks into a broad grin. "Hello, Sade. Nice to see you."

Chioma shyly fiddles with her beanie hat. "Hi, Sade. How are you doing?"

"I'm fine, I must dash," I say. "Still got some more gifts to buy."

"See you at church." Cyril grins as they walk off. But when I look back, I see his arm wrap around Chioma's shoulder as they go into another shop.

A few days before Christmas, Greg talks to me about becoming a senior project director. It's a great promotion, and I feel thankful for it. I need something to boost me after the year I've had.

Some good news at last. Vicky and Karl are planning a wedding!

I'm so happy for her, genuinely. She's been a good friend

to me these past weeks, along with Sam. And her news does give me more hope that maybe all is not lost on the romance front. Vicky has suggested internet dating, but I'd rather jump off London Bridge. I'm done with vain, flaky men. Besides, they all want a younger woman.

Instead, I focus on helping Vicky plan her wedding in the spring. Planning these things is my forte, and it's a welcome distraction. Along with the Mandarin lessons I've started doing. With all this, and the Inspired Network honouring me at church last Sunday for all I've been doing for singles, I feel maybe I am of some use to society, after all.

It's nearly Christmas Eve and I am on my way out, when I see that the postman has delivered a flat package. I bend to pick it up from the doormat.

It has a US postage stamp on it – somewhere in New York.

Jimi.

My heart is beating wildly as I open the package to find a CD titled *A Motown Christmas – 12 Best Hits from Motown's Finest* and a card.

> *Wishing you a Merry Christmas and all the best for the new year. Hope you are keeping well.*
>
> *Best wishes*
> *Jimi*

I bite my lip then place the CD in one of my kitchen cupboards along with odd keys, kitchen gloves, and other odd bits that I don't need anymore. I then put on my coat, gloves, and hat and slam my front door on my way out.

I remember my Bible reading from this morning. Oddly apt for this occasion.

> I charge you, O daughters of Jerusalem, that ye stir not up nor awake my love, until he please.
>
> Song of Solomon 8:7

Time to move on, methinks.

It is when I get to the station that I realise that the yellow and blue scarf Jimi gave me is tucked snugly around my neck under my big black winter coat – close to my heart.

Chapter Forty-Three

I decide to spend Christmas alone since Mum is going up to Manchester to be with Aunt Bunmi who has been a bit poorly. I don't tell her my plans, but she has some sort of sixth sense sometimes.

"You make sure you go to your sister's for Christmas," she orders me as I help her to the bus stop with her case.

"Will do," I say, having no intention of inflicting myself on Kike and Ayo for another year. They deserve to have a family Christmas without spinster me being there, especially as my moods have been wildly fluctuating since I received the Motown CD from Jimi. I don't want to be like Banquo's ghost at their banquet.

Vicky calls to check up on me, and I make the mistake of telling her about the gift.

"It means he still cares," she says, flatly. "Obviously."

"No, it means he feels sorry for me. The fifty-year-old virgin that cannot get a man."

"You do talk such nonsense sometimes," says Vicky. "Will it hurt you to send him a thank you for the gift?"

"Absolutely not. Please can we not talk about him ever again. Please." For the sake of my heart, my ego, and the dregs of my wounded pride.

On Christmas Day, I stay in and watch the Christmas service online, sing the carols, graze on snacks, and drink lots of fizzy drinks as I prepare my Christmas meal – which is some fried rice with yesterday's left-over chicken.

Immediately after Pastor says the grace, I get a phone call.

"Merry Christmas, Sade!" It is Aunty Remi bubbling with the effervescence of newfound love and seasonal joy to the world.

"Merry Christmas, Aunty."

"Are you not in church? It is so noisy where I am. You sound as if you are at home."

"I am at home."

Her voice rises. "Why? Are you sick or something?"

"No, Aunty, I just couldn't make it to church today."

"Folasade! You are not serious! How can you not come to church on Christmas Day! The day of our saviour's birth! I was thinking about you and was so happy that you would be in church, amongst friends, especially with your mum up in Manchester with Aunty Bunmi for Christmas. I am not happy with you at all!"

"Aunty—"

"Don't Aunty me." Aunt Remi sounds uncharacteristically stern. She is usually so bubbly and kind. And she never calls me by my full name, not even when I was a teenager.

"Pack a bag and get yourself in a taxi and come over to my house immediately. How can you be spending Christmas all alone in London when I am here?"

"Aunty, I don't mind—"

"Stop talking nonsense and come over now!" She terminates the phone call.

———

At Aunty Remi's, I help her with the turkey and the rice before her sons and their partners come over. One of the boys, the one who is married, is bringing his kids, too.

"They are nice, my boys' women," Remi says, "you will like them."

"Is the Bishop coming?"

She gives me a sharp look. "He is in Nigeria with his son."

I blink. "I thought Jimi was in the States."

"His son Femi lives in Lagos, you know."

"Oh, of course."

She points at the sink, where a basin of turkey legs marinate in some kind of brown savoury sauce. Smells like jerk. "Can you get those into the oven, my darling?"

I go over to the sink and wash my hands then start putting the turkey legs in the oven.

"You know," she says. "It is so odd to me."

"What's odd?"

"That you and Jimi are apart."

I say nothing. I focus on my task.

"I remember the Bishop telling me that he and Jimi had dinner in the summer and Jimi told him that he might just have found 'the one.'"

I turn to face her. "He said that."

"Yes. Bishop Taylor said he had never seen his son so carefree and happy."

"He never said that to me," I murmur.

Aunty Remi shakes her head. "No matter. All summer going up and down on dates and you people never really talked eh?"

I shrug. "I guess so."

"It is well, Sade. I will always tell you the truth."

"I know, Aunty Remi." I smile at her, tears stinging my eyes.

"I was married and it was to a good man," she goes on. "But we had our ups and downs. The good and the bad. Arguments, family issues... I had to deal with him being ill for years and with young children – it was God that helped me through – and your mum and the other church mothers. Sade, marriage is not the cure for the pain you feel deep down inside, because the best of men will fail us, they disappoint us, leave us alone in this world – sitting on a cold bed crying ourselves to sleep wondering what it might be like to have a man hold us in his arms again."

"Aunty, I never knew...You always seem so happy. So strong. You and Mum..."

She comes to me and touches my face. "Don't believe all this strong face Nigerian women wear for the world. We are tired of trying to be strong and dying inside. I will tell you what I would have told my daughter if I had one. Fifty without husband or children is not a death sentence, despite what our culture dictates. You are beautiful, intelligent, clever, you have your health, a good job, and one day the God that you love will bring a man your way that will appreciate all you are. It might be Jimi Taylor or someone else, but please don't spend another day putting your joy on hold for any man. I did that for the first ten years after I lost my husband, and I made a few mistakes with men that were not worthy to stand in my husband's shadow."

"Oh, Aunty..."

She looks me in the eye. "Promise me that you will be happy. I do not want to see you get to the point where you lock yourself away from friends, family, and even your future, because you thought something would happen with a particular chap and it did not. You only have one life."

I smile. "I get the picture, Aunty." I see her with new eyes now. I see the style, authenticity, class, wisdom, and the unapologetic way she lives her life. I want to be her when I grow up.

"I mean it. This is your new assignment. All this work, church, work thing you have been doing stops. As we go into this new year you are going to kick ass."

"Aunty!" I laugh.

"I heard it on the TV." She grins. "I like American soaps."

"Does the Bishop know what he is getting when he marries you, Aunty Remi? I mean all this 'kick ass' business."

She winks at me. "Of course he does. That is why he

loves me. Says I make him feel young again. He calls me every day from Lagos, you know."

I pull out a chair at the kitchen table, hoping for more tales from Aunty.

"Folasade. Are you sitting down? Do you know we still need to prepare the jollof rice?"

Chapter Forty-Four

New Year's Eve at church is a night of new resolve and fervent prayer that the next twelve months will be full of hope and joy and good things.

Along with prayers, there is a gospel concert followed by lots of hugs and greetings. It is a time when everyone gets a hug, even those that get on your last nerve.

Vicky is there, and I invite Sam, who didn't want to be rattling around in the house on New Year's Eve by herself.

"There's fireworks outside!" Vicky exclaims, and we link hands and join the gathering crowd outside at the back of the church.

"Happy New Year to us. No matter what the year holds," I say, and they both put an arm around me.

"Have hope in your heart," says Vicky. "That's all you can do."

January rolls in. As Sam says, the month is like one long hangover, and I hit upon the idea of having a girls' night out for Mum's birthday.

Me, Mum, and Kike.

All I need to do is to convince Mum.

I discuss it with Kike. "Femi Kuti is in town for a concert. He'll be singing all those old songs of his dad Fela's, and I know Mum still has a soft spot for Fela."

"Yeah, she has done since we were kids," my sister agrees.

"Remember when we were young and she would put on Jim Reeves on Sunday morning, having played Fela the night before," I reminisce.

Kike nods. "She would come back from a shift at the care home, put us to bed, lock herself in her room, and dance to Fela's 'Suffering and Smiling.' I didn't understand what she was on about. It was only when I got older that I listened to his music and it all made sense. Nigeria made sense."

I shook my head. "Do you remember the day she called Dad a zombie? It was when I was in Uni and had joined the African society on campus that I realised she was referring to one of Fela's records. You know, Dad being controlled by his family and all that?"

Mum has never gone anywhere in her life except church. Refuses to go on holidays. Doesn't go to restaurants – considers them a waste of money – but spends money she doesn't have on buying Aso Ebi for her friends' and relatives' naming or wedding ceremonies.

Kike reflects. "Okay, I'm in, but how do we get her to come out of the house to this concert?"

I decide to put on my project manager hat. "Let me think of something. I'll come up with a way."

"Sounds good. I'll go and check out tickets," Kike concludes.

———

In the end I tell Mum that Aunty Remi is having a small gathering – last minute, for Mum's birthday – and though Mum grumbles about the short notice, she gets into the spirit of it, and spends some time getting ready.

It's only when we get to the concert venue that she realises she's been duped. As soon as she sees Femi's name in lights outside the building, though, her own face lights up, and Kike and I exchange a smile.

"Bad girls," she scolds, but the sparkle in her eyes tells us she is delighted.

"Come on." Kike links arms with her. "Let's have some fun."

Inside, the stage is set for Femi – the afrobeat sensation – to take the spotlight.

As the lights dim, the crowd erupts in cheers. Mum, Kike, and I watch impatiently for him to emerge and then … he's here and his energy is contagious. Femi has his father's charisma and charm. His band play a pulsating rhythm that seems to reverberate through every heart in the room. We are glad that we got seats near the front, and fix our eyes on the stage.

The beat drops and ascends, and the crowd sways as one.

Then I see her. My mum, Ebunola, as she really is.

Effervescent. Beautiful. And free of all the societal constraints and cultural restrictions that have been put on her. She isn't just Sade and Kike's mum or Joseph Sodipo's widow.

Mum's dark skin shines and the lines of worry or bitterness of life have vanished. I look at her dancing to the beat and imagine her remembering the music of her youth when she had been young and carefree. A young woman, her hair in an afro, wearing a Jackson Five T-shirt and the flared jeans she'd bought from the second-hand boutique at Yaba, walking down the road with her best friend Remi Coker, the deputy head girl of the school – the one most likely, they said, to become a doctor because of her fantastic grades.

Probably neither of them had met their husbands then. She had met Joseph, a trainee accountant, later, and Remi had then fallen for Peter, who worked as an engineer in a nearby oil firm, before both men moved abroad.

I watch Ebun dance. As she dances, she closes her eyes, and I imagine her shutting out the thankless nights of caring for people who despised her because of her colour yet needed her care and support as they ventured into their last years. I imagine her closing her ears to the jeers of her husband's relatives because she was "unable" to have a boy and then later because her eldest daughter was unmarried at the big age of fifty. I can see her dancing in church with her hands raised in praise in front of the speculative glances of the friends and acquaintances who are staunch members of the Marriage Monitoring Aunties' Association.

After the concert, she turns to me and I see that her eyes are full of tears.

"Thank you. This is the best day of my life."

We hug her back. The day has still got a lot in store, as Kike whispers to her. I wonder what experiences didn't make the cut for the best day of my mum's life.

Backstage, we have arranged for Mum to meet Femi Kuti for a few minutes. He is gracious, his smile genuine. They talk about music, life, and the magic of connecting with people through art. He signs Mum's CD, and she promises that she will play it whenever she needs a reminder that life is still full of surprises. After listening to her praise and worship music, of course.

He smiles in this charismatic way his father had and bows his head slightly. "Welcome, Ma. Thanks for coming to my show." He touches his heart. "Hope you enjoy your birthday."

Then he gives her a hug and it feels so surreal and so heartwarming to see Mum and Femi, the oldest son of Afrobeat pioneer Fela Kuti, sharing their love for music. It is clear from her look of wonder that this is undoubtedly a special moment for her.

———————

The birthday surprises are not over. Kike and I have booked a room at an expensive hotel in the West End, so we can really top off the night. Kike goes ahead and leaves an envelope in Mum's room with a sizeable amount of money – something to show our appreciation. We hope she will spend it on a holiday abroad but know it will probably be spent on church offerings or Aso Ebi, or stored under her mattress where she keeps her "rainy day" money.

To Mum

> *We love you. We appreciate you. Thanks for all the sacrifices you've made for us and all the hard work you've done for this family. Wishing you a Happy Birthday!*

You are simply the Best
Sade & Kike xxx

"My daughters," Mum says, with tears in her eyes, "I am so proud of you both, and I love you. Even though you sometimes like to give me small trouble."

"Mum!" Kike is shaking her head but grinning and I feel a lump of emotion in my throat as I give my mother a hug.

I am glowing from the inside. Life is a symphony – a blend of melodies and silences, heartaches, and celebrations. Tonight is one of the good notes, and I realise that it is also one of the best days of my life.

Chapter Forty-Five

It's March, and there have been no more messages from Jimi since the CD at Christmas, which is fine. I have been busy with life.

Something about what Aunty Remi said that Christmas afternoon struck a chord. I had spent almost half of my life searching for a man to give me love. I had made the quest for love into an idol, a drug to make me feel better about myself after years of trying to live up to the ideal of the Nigerian Dream and win the approval of my mother and the members of the Marriage Monitoring Aunties' Association.

Now, I focus on taking each day as it comes and trying to find fulfilment in just being me.

This morning, I get an invite from Aunty Remi for her wedding in April. No Aso Ebi required. It's a small event – a sit-down dinner for friends and family – so it's likely Jimi will be back from the States. All I need to do is ensure it doesn't turn into a debacle, like when Sally and Harry had a go at each other at their best friends' wedding.

Jimi and I are both adults. Surely we can be civil and polite for a few hours. Besides that, the part of me that was full of passion and fight has kind of mellowed over the past few months. I do not want any man's stress in my well-organised life anymore.

Being in love is a high-octane dash full of exhilaration, but without structure, depth, or substance – it is like a Formula One car grounded due to dysfunction.

It looks great, but it is going nowhere fast.

There is a carpet of daffodils in the square and the evenings are getting lighter. It's a nice feeling when it doesn't get dark until later in the day.

Last week Dolapo gave birth to a cute baby boy, my second cousin. Dolapo has named her son Oluwaseun, meaning "Thank you, God."

At the naming ceremony today, I come face-to-face with Aunty Gbemi, who looks like the cat that got the cream.

"Folasade," she says with a sly smile. "You have not brought your husband with you."

I sigh. "As you well know, Aunty, I am not married."

"That nice man with the grey beard. Tall. The Bishop's son?"

"We never got married, Aunty. I would have invited you to the wedding."

Aunty Gbemi's eyes narrow under several layers of

foundation. "You are still acting like a small girl being choosy. And you will soon be collecting your pension."

"Aunty…" I am tempted to give her the unedited version of my current thoughts but thankfully, there is a greeting behind me, another church mummy hugging her and giving her congratulations on becoming a grandmother.

I take refuge in the ladies' loo, where I stand in front of the mirror and try and locate the new calm, cool, unfazed me, but I can't see her. Instead, I find myself dabbing away a few tears. Every time I come to these family gatherings, someone has to take a pot shot and it is always one of the usual suspects.

It has to stop.

When I emerge from the ladies, Aunty Gbemi is still there loudly boasting about her perfect daughter to another poor victim.

"Aunty." I tap her on the shoulder.

"Yes?" She looks surprised at my forthright tone.

"I might not be married. I might not have a child, but I am happy with who I am. I do not define myself by titles or a piece of metal on my left finger. Until it comes or if it comes, I will make something of my life and make it count. I would love it if you could celebrate me now and not when I have made it according to your definition."

Aunty Gbemi rears backwards, her hand on her chest as if she is having some kind of fit. "Is it me you are talking to like that? All I did was to give you advice about your life. *Otito koro*, as we say back home. Truth is bitter and it is time you started to face the reality of your life. You are in a fast car heading towards old age!"

I fix Aunty Gbemi with a determined glare. "As you remind me every single time you see me. I know my age. I don't need you to remind me how old I am, or that I've left it too long to have a child or that men only like girls with straightened hair and big bottoms – I don't bloody care."

"Don't you dare use such language on me! I will slap you into sense," Aunty Gbemi screams and my mother appears out of nowhere. A hush descends, as everyone who has been talking stops.

"It is enough, Gbemi," she says calmly.

Aunty Gbemi is standing there with her hands out as if to say, *What did I say to deserve this?* I know it must be difficult for her to bear the weight of my cumulative irritation, hurt, and resentment after all the shade she has heaped on me over the past two decades, but tough. She so had it coming.

"Are you siding with your daughter?" she accuses Mum.

My mother fixes her with a glare. "Sade, leave us. Me and your aunty have some things to discuss."

I stand there, still wanting to say my piece, when I realise it's a naming ceremony, for goodness' sake. Why do the women in this family always save drama for family gatherings?

I walk into the spacious sitting room and find Dolapo sitting there with the baby.

"My fave cousin. You look lovely as always! Love the plaits!"

I look at Dolapo and feel my heightened emotions subside.

"Thanks, Dolapo. You look so beautiful as well. He is

adorable." I bend to touch my new nephew's little hand. The baby smelt of talc, baby lotion, and absolute pure innocence and joy. Something catches in my throat and I wish I could change places with my cousin for one second.

Just one second to be a mum.

One solitary second of a lifetime of empty wishes.

"Hold him, Aunty Sade." Dolapo smiles and manoeuvres him into my arms.

"Are you sure?"

I look down at my nephew and he peers back up at me and holds onto my hand and I smile. I couldn't be a mum, but I will be a kick-ass aunty.

"You're a natural," says Dolapo.

I don't know what Mum said to Aunty Gbemi, but when we are leaving, she comes over and gives me a hug and tells me that God has told her I will be getting married soon and that she is sorry if she has caused me any upset.

I am shocked. Not just for the 180 she has done in her attitude to me, but also because she has never hugged me. Not even as a kid. Then again, neither did Mum up until recently.

"Thanks, Aunt Gbemi. I never meant to speak out of turn either. I just wanted to let you see where I was coming from."

She nods. "God will do it for you."

I smile vaguely at her usual platitude. As for the marriage thing – I am used to people praying for me over that.

On the way home I ask my mum what she said to her sister to make her so conciliatory.

Mum sighs. "Did I ever tell you that your dad first showed interest in your aunty? We all attended the same church back in the day," she says casually.

"Really?" My voice is incredulous. So this is why the woman has been behaving like a bear with a sore head.

"He felt she was too young and decided to ask my parents about me instead," she confides. "They gave their blessings. Then he went to England and sent for me. Gbemi has never forgiven me for that. I just thought I should tell you lest I fall dead one day and she paints another picture." Then she sighs. "I just told her that she would never have lasted a day with your father. They would have killed each other and she should be thankful that he turned her down. I advised her to live her life and stop blaming me that she didn't find man till she was thirty-two. She just calmed down and started to beg me."

Well done, Mum.

"Anyway," she went on, "another new member of the family has arrived. What a wonderful day."

She then begins to talk about another naming ceremony she is attending next week.

That's my mum for you.

Chapter Forty-Six

A couple of weeks later, I walk into the reception area at work and see immediately that people are behaving a bit strangely. They all have broad smiles on their faces.

It is Monday morning. People seldom smile and say hello. If you get a grunt and a shrug it's a big thing.

I stop in my tracks and look down at myself. Am I wearing my blouse inside out or do I have "Give Us a Smile" stuck to my back?

I shake my head and go past the open office area and to my office. My heart plummets. There are several gigantic bouquets placed around my desk. Then, from behind me, there is a large cheer and I turn to see a crowd gathered at my door.

What on earth is going on?

I am overcome by the strength of the fragrance from the different bouquets. Names I remember such as lilies, orchids, passion flowers, wild azaleas, magnolias, roses, tulips float through my senses. Then I spot the white card nestling in the gold gauze in which the first bouquet is wrapped.

I hear a cough behind me and it is Greg. He has a twinkle in his eye.

"Either that is a bouquet for all the hard work you put into the NuChance Foundation launch, or someone is smitten. I won't come in. There are enough flowers in here to activate my hayfever for months to come." He smirks and turns to the little crowd outside.

"Does anyone do any work around here?"

People start to go back to their desks chattering amongst themselves as they do so.

I close the door, speechless as I pick up the card.

Sade,

> *I do hope you are well.*
>
> *I'm fine. Not fine fine but kinda ok.*
>
> *I'm sorry I haven't stayed in contact. It's long overdue, but these flowers are just to say that I'm so sorry.*
>
> *I will say that until you believe me. I really am sorry.*
>
> *You were honest with me, but I wasn't honest with you. When I last saw you I felt overwhelmed. I realised that this was it. That this woman is "the one." That to be with you I needed to do the work on myself and seal the deal, but it freaked me out and I did what our gender is good at doing. I ran.*
>
> *I love you. I have for a long time – it just took time with myself, and with a very wise man, to process all the feelings chasing themselves round my head.*

*Could we catch up some time and have a proper chat? I'd
like to talk about the future. That is – if you still think we
have one. I believe we do. I believe God thinks that too. Hey,
me talking about God – I must be in love ay. My dad told me
to write to you, to be honest. I've lost time, loved ones, and a
lot of things in my life but I don't intend to lose you.*

Love,
Jimi xxx

My lips tighten as I feel the heat drowning me and
wonder whether it is menopause or the fact that I am angry
or a mixture of the two. I feel a bit dizzy and hold onto my
desk to get my balance back.

Vertigo. Not the Hitchcock type. Just menopause
reminding me it isn't going anywhere yet.

*I can't do this again with you, Jimi Taylor. I just can't. God
give me the strength to get past my emotions on this one.*

I look at the flowers, wondering how I am going to
divide them up around the girls in the office. I do not want
them in here activating hayfever or any foolish inclination
to believe Jimi wants something permanent and can love
me the way I need to be loved.

Over the next few days, Jimi's name flashes up on my
phone several times, and each time I ignore it. The fifth
time, I am sorely tempted to pick up, but I tell myself I am
doing the right thing and I leave it.

On Friday morning, Mum rings and says it is very

important that I come and see her after work. She says it's something urgent.

I go straight to her house after work only to find her looking – thankfully – well, as usual, and the house full of the smell of cooking.

"Mum, what's going on?"

"Come in. Come in. Put your bag down and come and get some food," she orders.

I put my laptop down and follow her into the kitchen wondering what all this is about.

She points to a chair next to the kitchen table.

"Sit down. We need to talk."

Fear grips me.

"Mum, what is going on, are you ill?"

She shakes her head. "Jimi said he has been trying to call you?"

I sigh, annoyed. "Mum, I've had a long day. You can't believe what the transport is like out there and you want to start this conversation. I do not want to talk about Jimi Taylor again."

Now he has Mum on his side!

"The problem with you women nowadays is that you have PhD in book and primary school wisdom when it comes to man," Mum retorts.

I close my eyes.

"Is your eye paining you?" Mum inquires.

"No."

She pulls up a chair and faces me. "If you like, close your eyes. Just open your heart so you can hear what I am going to download into your head."

I know it is going to be a long evening.

Chapter Forty-Seven

Saturday mornings are my lie-in days. I dream of what could be. I plan fresh work and life priorities. Nowadays I think about new initiatives for Inspired Network at church and the challenges of my new position.

Senior Project Director ay.

So, while I'm lying in bed enjoying the sweetness of sleep, suddenly the doorbell goes, so I rush to pull on a T-shirt and throw on my bathrobe and head downstairs ready to say something to the person who has dared to interrupt my Saturday. I can see it is a man and as I peer closer through the glass partition, his silhouette looks very familiar. The way he holds his head. The way he puts his hands in his pockets as he waits on the other side of the door.

Oh God. It's Jimi.

Jimi. Here. Now. I look an absolute mess. I had imagined looking all sophisticated and superior when I set eyes on him again probably at his Dad's wedding. My silk bonnet and comfortable M&S dressing gown are not going to cut it.

Another knock, so I wrench open the door and glare at him.

"Hi, Jimi."

He stands there looking sheepish. The grey in his beard seems to have caught up with the hair on his head. In just six months he has aged a little, though his eyes hold a hint of hope – of what I can't exactly define.

"I thought you were in New York?"

"I've concluded my business there," he says. "Got a good manager in charge of things, so I'm back here now. Permanently," he adds, looking at my face.

"Welcome back." I fold my arms across my chest.

There is a long silence while we stand there observing each other.

He coughs. "Yeah. Can I come in? For a chat?"

"Why?"

"Hey. A few words and that's it? I thought we were friends."

Friends. That word again.

I look up at him trying to read his expression but can't. "Friends ay…"

"Look, Sade. I've been a bit silly. Hopefully not irredeemably?"

I sigh. "*What* do you want, Jimi?"

"You," he says. "I want you, Sade."

I stare at him. "Just like that. You want me and what am I supposed to do? Jump for joy because you just decided to waltz back into my life? If you could see the hair under my silk bonnet – the grey isn't painted on. Life has done that to me. Just so you know I'm no small girl whose intelligence you can insult!"

He scratches his head. "I deserve that. I know I owe you an explanation."

I raise an eyebrow.

"Can we go inside?" he suggests and he looks a bit self-conscious. "I want to have a private conversation."

I turn round and meet the speculative glance of one of my elderly neighbours, who is lurking at his door, reading a newspaper. "You all right, Sade?" he asks, eyeing Jimi and then glancing at me to see if I am in any distress.

"I'm good, thank you." I smile at him and he disappears into his home.

"This is the second or third time in all the years I've been living here that my neighbour has spoken to me," I whisper to Jimi. "You might as well come in."

He comes in and we stand in the passageway.

He doesn't say anything. Just stands there drinking me up; my face, my eyes, the M&S dressing gown that has seen better days, that I promised myself I would change when Bae arrived.

"All I want is for you to hear me out," Jimi continues. "After you've done that, if you don't want to have anything else to do with me, I will leave you alone. Did you get the flowers?"

I ignore him and walk into my sitting room, where I sit down. Jimi follows me.

"Sade, I do know what I want. I have always known what I want – I just got sidetracked by myself."

"Go on."

"That evening when we nearly slept together, you were

right in a way, my hesitation wasn't because I didn't want you but because I felt that heap of responsibility and concern rush through me. It was a big deal. For you and for me. Mostly, I wanted to be sure you were okay, but a tiny part of me was freaked out."

"Thank you for your honesty," I tell him.

"When the job offer in New York came in, I made up my mind that it was the best thing. That I could never measure up to you. I knew I had to reach you not only on the physical level but emotionally and spiritually as well, and I was not at that place. I wanted you but I knew you were vulnerable and I did not want to take advantage. So I ran," he admitted.

"Yeah, you did. All the way to Brooklyn," I retorted.

"I had to take time out and it's been good to look at myself and my own mistakes in life. I needed time to build myself up into the kind of man that would stay. The kind of man that would commit 100 per cent. The kind of man that would not start something he couldn't finish without his ring on your finger... I know you are the kind of woman with whom it has to be more than just the physical."

"I just didn't know where I stood with you," I confess.

He sighs. "I know and I'm sorry about that. New York was a fantastic chance for me to grow. To grow myself and grow the business. I needed time to get my head right and I knew I had to do it by myself. You see, I knew that if I included you as part of the package, I would just get distracted... Especially in that M&S contraption you got on, bareface and ..."

I can't help the laugh that escapes my mouth.

"Jimi. That day at the café, you were so cold..."

"I was protecting myself. There was a voice in my head saying, 'Well done, boy, you dodged that one.' I feared committing myself to something that I used to think would choke the life out of me. I ran away but I ran away from what I needed, what I wanted, what I craved – you. You saw through my I-don't-care attitude and the pain I couldn't articulate; saw through all that and still cared about me. You with your crazy hopes and optimism, your commonsense advice, you and the inner beauty that radiates out of you whether you are happy or sad, you and the fact that you care so deeply for everyone around you – your sister, your mum, and even the singles in your church. I missed everything about you, from your corny jokes and sarky tongue to our discussions on music and theatre and politics..." His voice lowers. "I missed the sparkle in your eyes, and the grey flecks in your hair, and the way you catch your breath when I kiss you, and the way your heart beats closer when I hold you in my arms."

I am trying to ignore the delicious things he is saying about me and concentrate on the most important thing. "That doesn't change the fact that you still don't share my faith."

He sighs. "Look I didn't tell you at the time but that day when I met with Pastor Keith we prayed together and I knew something changed in me. Pastor Keith made me realise that I couldn't blame the God I didn't believe in for my life choices." He gives a small smile. "He was kind of right. Look, Cyril has told me I've been a fool, Pastor Keith and Pastor Sandra have said I've been a fool, and so has your mum."

"My mum was singing your praises a few days ago.

That is a miracle. What did you do to her? Must be the Taylor charm."

"She suggested the flowers in the first place. Your sister Kike also helped, along with your Aunty Remi."

"And coming here – whose idea was that?"

"All mine," he says. "With some help from my son. He is in the car waiting outside." Jimi looks a bit embarrassed. "He decided to come to London for uni. Today he was in Westfields – not too far from you – and I thought to offer him a ride home."

"Go bring him in."

"Er… Not quite yet."

"Why not?"

Jimi's eyes reach out to me. "Because I want to make it clear to you that I'm not the same Jimi that left. The one who believed that he could conquer the world all by himself. In New York I sat down and asked God to take me back to the days where I had faith in Him. I wanted that peace in my life again, and in those first lonely weeks in New York I found Him again and I found myself. I'm sorry I didn't call, but every time I prepared myself to say something, I chickened out…"

"Oh!" I remember a certain Christmas gift.

He adds, "I sent a CD at Christmas as a kind of a peace offering to see how things stood."

I nod. "And I ignored it."

"So I thought, *Leave it. She's over you, man*, I told myself. But I wasn't over you, and I kept praying for an opportunity, so I sent the flowers and the letter."

"I ignored that too."

"So I left it. Then my dad rang and told me that I was

the biggest loser ever if I didn't fight for you. So I've been calling and you still didn't pick up. So I called your mum and still you didn't budge. So here I am. Telling you that I'm sorry and that I want you back in my life … if you'll please, please give me a chance?"

I look at him for a long time and then nod silently and he pulls me up from the sofa until I am looking up at him and then our lips lock in a long kiss. By the time he lifts his head I am full of happiness and bubbly thoughts of the future.

"I love you," he whispers.

"I love you, too. Never stopped," I admit.

He sighs as he holds me close, his eyes twinkling. "Do you understand what that really means to a bloke who feels as if he is about to combust here?"

I blink, realisation dawning that I can make him feel that way and feel attractive and desirable with my soon to be fifty-one-year-old self. Despite the grey hair! Bwoy.

His eyes fill with such tenderness. "I had better go and get my son."

I look at him and realise that I don't ever want to be anywhere else but with him. For life. I am not ready to unpack myself for anyone else. He is the only person I can be my true authentic self with.

He releases me, goes towards the door, turns back, rummages around in his pocket, and kneels down again.

"I forgot something important." He pulls out this little dark blue velvet box and opens it.

I peer inside and there is the most exquisite diamond engagement ring I've ever seen.

"I got it in the States."

"How did you get my ring size?" I ask unnecessarily.

He looks puzzled and adorable at the same time. "How do I know? Did you ever fall asleep on the sofa in front of the TV while watching a film with your mum? That was probably when – I don't know. I mean we have been planning this for some time. I mean we have a crew of supporters."

"Really?" I wonder exactly who's been in on this.

He winces. "Really. Look, my back can't take this kneeling thing too long, you know. Despite my vigorous keep-fit routine, I'm forty-six. I want you to be my wife."

I feel a tremble of joy run through me, and we lock eyes.

He grins and slips the ring on my finger, and it fits perfectly.

"Folasade Iretiola Sodipo. Will you marry me?"

I nod slowly. "Yes, Jimi Taylor. Yes, I will."

Acknowledgments

Writing *The Marriage Monitoring Aunties' Association* has been an extraordinary journey, and it would not have been possible without the support and encouragement of so many wonderful people.

First and foremost, my deepest gratitude goes to my mentor Pastor Ade D'Almeida.

Secondly, to all the vibrant vivacious aunties of the world whose wisdom, humour, and spirited personalities inspired the essence of this story. You bring colour to the canvas of our lives and even when we don't always want your advice – sometimes we need it! Also to all the single women out there living life and excelling, despite the valleys of life, and not letting anyone dim their shine.

Thirdly, to my sister Kemi Oloyede and my brother-in-law Yinka Oloyede who have supported and prayed me along this journey. Also thanks to my brother Ife Awonubi and his lovely wife Aneka for all your love and support. Thanks to you all for being my cheerleaders, my sounding boards, and my pillars of strength throughout this process. Your belief in me kept me motivated on the days when words seemed out of reach.

Thanks to all my close friends, mentors and former colleagues that put up with me while I worked during the day and wrote at night.

A special thanks to my editors, Charlotte Ledger and Ajebowale Roberts, for being so passionate about wanting Sade's story to get out there. Thanks so much for your expert guidance and patience, and to the entire publishing team at One More Chapter for bringing this vision to life. Your brilliance turned my dream into reality. Also to Hana Rowlands for her advice on the manuscript in making it into something I'm proud of.

Lastly, thank you to every reader who picks up this book. You are the heart of this story, and it is my hope that you find joy, laughter, great memories and love within its pages.

With gratitude and love,
Ola Awonubi

ONE MORE CHAPTER

The author and One More Chapter would like to thank everyone who contributed to the publication of this story...

Analytics
James Brackin
Abigail Fryer

Audio
Fionnuala Barrett
Ciara Briggs

Contracts
Laura Amos
Laura Evans

Design
Lucy Bennett
Fiona Greenway
Liane Payne
Dean Russell

Digital Sales
Laura Daley
Lydia Grainge
Hannah Lismore

eCommerce
Laura Carpenter
Madeline ODonovan
Charlotte Stevens
Christina Storey
Jo Surman
Rachel Ward

Editorial
Kara Daniel
Simon Fox
Charlotte Ledger
Ajebowale Roberts
Jennie Rothwell
Tony Russell
Sofia Salazar Studer
Emily Thomas
Helen Williams

Harper360
Jennifer Dee
Emily Gerbner
Ariana Juarez
Jean Marie Kelly
emma sullivan
Sophia Wilhelm

International Sales
Peter Borcsok
Ruth Burrow
Colleen Simpson
Ben Wright

Inventory
Sarah Callaghan
Kirsty Norman

Marketing & Publicity
Chloe Cummings
Grace Edwards

Operations
Melissa Okusanya
Hannah Stamp

Production
Denis Manson
Simon Moore
Francesca Tuzzeo

Rights
Helena Font Brillas
Ashton Mucha
Zoe Shine
Aisling Smyth
Lucy Vanderbilt

Trade Marketing
Ben Hurd
Eleanor Slater

**The HarperCollins
Distribution Team**

**The HarperCollins
Finance & Royalties
Team**

**The HarperCollins
Legal Team**

**The HarperCollins
Technology Team**

UK Sales
Isabel Coburn
Jay Cochrane
Sabina Lewis
Holly Martin
Harriet Williams
Leah Woods

**And every other
essential link in the
chain from delivery
drivers to booksellers
to librarians and
beyond!**

ONE MORE CHAPTER

One More Chapter is an
award-winning global
division of HarperCollins.

Subscribe to our newsletter to get our
latest eBook deals and stay up to date
with all our new releases!

signup.harpercollins.co.uk/
join/signup-omc

Meet the team at
www.onemorechapter.com

Follow us!

 @OneMoreChapter_

 @onemorechapterhc

 @onemorechapterhc

 @onemorechapterhc

Do you write unputdownable fiction?
We love to hear from new voices.
Find out how to submit your novel at
www.onemorechapter.com/submissions